Ace Books by Thomas A. Easton

SPARROWHAWK
GREENHOUSE
WOODSMAN
TOWER OF THE GODS

TOWER OF THE GODS

THOMAS A. EASTON

ACE BOOKS, NEW YORK

This book is an Ace original edition,
and has never been previously published.

TOWER OF THE GODS

An Ace Book / published by arrangement with
the author

PRINTING HISTORY
Ace edition/May 1993

ISBN: 0-441-81930-3

Ace Books are published by The Berkley Publishing Group,
200 Madison Avenue, New York, NY 10016.
The name "ACE" and the "A" logo
are trademarks belonging to Charter Communications, Inc.

PRINTED IN THE UNITED STATES OF AMERICA

10 9 8 7 6 5 4 3 2 1

Dedicated to:
My mother

TOWER OF THE GODS

Chapter
One

PEARL ANGELICA STOPPED at the foot of the bluff and patted the leather carrybag that swung from her shoulder. She sighed and absorbed the scents of soil, mossflowers, forest trees, and distant frost, herald of the changing season.

When she peered across the valley spread before her, she caught her breath. Who were those three figures who trod the yellow dirt trail that cut the moss two kilometers away? *What* were they? They were bipeds much like humans, and they walked erect. But something about them seemed strange, misshapen, yet not quite truly alien.

They were moving slowly toward her, weren't they? Then she would wait right where she was, she thought, and be glad for the chance to stand still. Her calves hurt from the steep descent.

The strangers must have entered the valley along the stream that drained the lake. The path they were on skirted the center of the valley, where the tree, the Tower, her people had grown stood a solitary pillar. From time to time they paused and turned to stare toward that wonder, or toward the few orange pumpkins that served as scattered quarters and work spaces, the Macks and Roachsters on the yellow tracks that cut the moss. There, near the lake, was the pumpkin where her father, Frederick Suida, waited for death, only rarely summoning enough awareness to speak sensibly or stare out the window at the Tower he had proposed and planned. To the north of the Tower, a dozen dozen slabs of grey stone marked the small graveyard that held those bots and humans who had died on the planet.

She touched her bag again. There was very little in it besides the papers that had wrapped her lunch. This region, so close to the base, had long since been picked quite clean of novelties, and there were field workers whose job it was to sample more distant regions. What she really sought were the panoramas of this world, for her heart yearned for whatever their equivalents might be on the homeworld she had never known. That those equivalents existed, she had no doubt. The pictures her people had brought with them could not lie.

Nor did they look much like what lay before her. Not even the autumn pictures, for here the trees went only from green to grey. And instead of grass, First-Stop—Tau Ceti IV—had thick mats of a plant that resembled moss, if moss could have purple leaves and myriads of tiny white flowers and plump white berries. This ground cover softened the floor of the valley right up to the edges of the small lake off-centered to the west, where it was replaced by reeds and other water-loving plants. At the landing field a little to the east, the yellow soil was darkened by the scorchmarks of plasma flames. Where the encircling bluffs plunged to meet the valley, the moss rose up, thinned, grew patchy, gave way to shrubs and other plants. Above, the nearly cloudless sky was an inverted bowl, its rim scalloped by the bluff-tops and bordered by the now dimming green of the forest that thrived on higher ground.

She looked upward, past valley, Tower, clouds, and sky. If it were night, she might be able to see the orbiting *Gypsy,* the starship her people had carved from an asteroid and fitted with Q-drives.

Pearl Angelica shook her head in frustration. She and many of her colleagues sought creatures whose genes might give the gengineers new tools or which might fit whole into the *Gypsy*'s contained ecology. The great ship held people, their creatures, the plants that produced both food and oxygen. But they had left Earth without being able to gather all the organisms and genes they needed. For one thing, they had no bees to pollinate the plants. They had to fertilize all their flowers by hand.

The Gypsies of the *Gypsy* were wanderers just like their namesakes of old Earth. But the latter had only had to carry their homes with them. Wherever they went, they were surrounded by a living environment that met all their needs. Yet . . . Those ancient gypsies had long forgotten their land of origin. Their roots were a matter of guesswork for story-tellers and scholars. Would that happen to her own people?

Would they move on through the starfields of the galaxy? Would they lose even what little contact they still maintained with Earth and the Orbitals and gengineers who had chosen to remain in its solar system? Would they forget Earth, reduce it to the status of myth or less? Would she never get the chance she craved to see once more the world of her ancestors, the world of her roots?

That dream was hopeless. She was a bot herself, and the Engineers would never let her taste the soil of Earth. Morosely, she let her roots uncoil from the bushy ruffs that covered her calves and grope for the dirt beneath her feet. Her mood began to lift at the first comforting rush of root-ease. Her posture relaxed. A hint of a smile appeared on her lips.

But then she sniffed, her shoulders tensed, her roots retreated from the soil. There was in the air an animal muskiness that had not been there a moment before. It was not the strangers. They were still far off, and the wind was toward them.

There was sound, the lightest of scratchings, the crunch of one pebble against another on the ground.

She turned toward the trail that descended the bluff at her back. It was flanked by moss and shrubbery, shadowed by saplings, paved by dirt that shaded from the valley's yellow to a rich brown, almost black, where the forest's trees overhung the top of the steep slope. Weathered slabs of stone jutted from the surface as if to form an irregular staircase.

At the base of the trail stood three round-bellied Racs, quietly staring over the valley and grooming each other's thick fur as they waited for her to notice them. Each wore a belt and shoulder strap that supported several small pouches; Pearl Angelica knew they held stone blades, herbs the Racs found satisfying to sniff or eat, polished bits of wood and bone, of Gypsy glass and metal debris.

The largest of the three Racs was a black-eared male whose light yellow fur bore a single black stripe from the top of his head to the base of his spine. A stone-tipped spear leaned into the crook of one elbow. Pearl Angelica recognized him as one of those Racs who wandered in and out of her people's buildings in the valley, studying the visitors to their world.

Most of his tribe were content to keep their distance. Other tribes . . .

The male pointed. She turned, and now the strangers were close enough for her to realize why they had seemed both alien and familiar. They too were furred and dressed in straps and belts, but thick tails hung to their knees.

An early model, she thought. The Racs' ancestors had been raccoonlike forest animals, nearly the size of a German shepherd but with larger brains. Not long after the gengineers had reached and named Tau Ceti IV, they had blunted the muzzles and enlarged the brains even further. But they had done it in several steps, only the last of which had removed the tail. The earlier versions had then been settled elsewhere on the globe. Most people thought they must have forgotten by now that the Gypsies existed.

Yet here they were.

She faced once more the three beside her. They had the polite dignity of creatures who felt inferior to no one, not even the technologically advanced Gypsies. The male stared self-assuredly back at her with the rich, brown eyes of his kind. His eyebrows were shelves of bristling hairs. "I am Blacktop," he said, and he raised one blunt-clawed hand to scratch at the side of his flattened, chinless muzzle.

Pearl Angelica nodded at him and scratched at her cheek with her fingertips. The greeting gesture was recognizably the same in both the Racs and their wild ancestors, as if it were as wired into the Rac nervous system as the smile was in humans.

The two females repeated the gesture. The smaller held only a basket, suggesting that she intended to gather mossberries in the valley. The other held a shorter, lighter version of Blacktop's spear; she, like he, would hunt the animals that also sought the berries. Both females had more common pelt markings, stripes and swirls of olive on grey, though the olive of the smaller was a little greener than that of most Racs.

"Leaf," said Blacktop, shifting one hand to the shaft of his spear and using the other to indicate his smaller companion. "And Cloudscurry." Then he pointed toward the approaching strangers. His voice rose in pitch and grew smoother, almost melodic. "Who are they?"

Pearl Angelica recognized the vocal change. When a Rac was feeling peaceful, even happy, its tone scraped against the ear as if a snarl must lie not far beneath the surface.

"I have no idea."

The strangers had noticed them now. They no longer paused to study the valley's marvels. They walked faster, almost jogging, yet it was clear that it would be several minutes yet before they arrived.

"Winter comes," said Blacktop to Pearl Angelica. His voice said he was still feeling anxious or aggressive. "Will you still be here when snow covers the moss?"

"Of course," she said. She scowled, knowing as they knew that it was only a matter of time before the Gypsies did indeed leave this world. "We are not ready to go yet." The gengineers had chosen the Racs for their attention because they seemed on the evolutionary verge of sentience already. Soon enough, they would leave the new species to its own devices.

Now Leaf said, "They can't leave." A row of swollen nipples was visible down each side of her chest, embedded in her fur. Somewhere, in the Rac village in the forest atop the bluff, she had a litter of unweaned children. Her voice grew smoother, angry. "We still have too much to learn."

The strangers were now within hearing range, but they said nothing. Neither the Racs nor the bot spoke to them, though all four carefully studied them and the things they carried. Their markings were much the same, olive stripes on grey backs and sides, creamy bellies, black rings around their tails. They were clearly males. Their pouches bulged as if with supplies for long travel. Stone-bladed knives were thrust through slits in their belts. Stone-tipped spears filled their hands.

"Why do you think we call this world First-Stop?" asked Pearl Angelica. "We have to leave, as soon as . . ." She turned back toward the valley and pointed at the tree that rose a kilometer away. It was almost two hundred meters tall. "We're almost done with the Tower."

The tallest of the strangers leaned his spear against one shoulder, barked, scratched his muzzle—a trifle longer and sharper than Blacktop's—and spoke in tones that were rough enough for politeness's sake but were also touched with the gloss of caution. "I am Wanderer."

His companions repeated the greeting gesture. "Stone-rapper."

"Shorttail." His tail indeed was shorter than those of his companions.

Blacktop, Leaf, Cloudscurry, and the bot answered appropriately. Then Wanderer said, "I did not expect to find the Valley of Creation."

Blacktop grunted inquiringly.

"We have tales of a valley where we were raised from beasts, taught to speak and make things like these." The stranger indicated his spear and belt and pouches.

"The tales are true," said Pearl Angelica.

"I did not believe them."

Blacktop said, "Then why are you here?"

"To see the world tree," said Wanderer. "My mother saw it once from a distance, poking above the edge of the world. She told other stories, and people laughed. They did not believe her. I did."

"It is no longer a tree," said Leaf in a voice that almost purred. The fur on her shoulders was stiffening and rising, giving the impression that her arms and claws were powered by immense muscles.

"We see." Wanderer was pointing toward it. His fur twitched in response to Leaf's, but he managed to suppress the bristling. His companions were less successful. Their fur bristled too, and their tails swelled and jerked from side to side. Cloudscurry joined Leaf in her challenge to the interlopers, leaning forward, ready to kill or die.

Blacktop and Wanderer had more presence of mind. Both males kept their fur flat, roughened their voices, and smacked the shafts of their spears across the challengers' bellies. Leaf and Cloudscurry, Stonerapper and Shorttail blinked and settled back on their heels, though their fur did not go down.

"You called it Tower," said Wanderer at last. "But it *was* the tree. My mother said it held up the sky. When it fell, the world would end."

"It will not fall," said Blacktop.

"It still has bark and branches."

"Not for long."

"It is already dead."

The slender pinnacle that dominated the valley gleamed yellow-white where it had already been stripped of limbs and bark. Bioblimps hung in the air about it, some suspending workers on long lines while they wielded chainsaws and other tools. Others wrapped their tentacles around massive limbs that had just been cut from the Tower's shaft, slowing their fall toward a pile of severed branches to the south.

The Bioblimps were descended from jellyfish scaled up and freed from the sea. They had been designed on Earth for hauling cargo and passengers through the skies of a resource-poor world, not for holding workers precisely still in mid-air or for following the same short paths over and over again. They were straining to do jobs for which they had never been intended, their gasbags swelling as they generated more hydrogen for added lift. The hum of the propellers on the small control cabins slung beneath their gasbags was clearly audible despite the distance.

Leaf laughed deliberately, insultingly. Cloudscurry joined her, tentatively at first and then more vigorously.

Stonerapper and Shorttail stiffened and began to sing in their throats.

Blacktop and Wanderer once more used their spears as staves. For a moment it seemed that the junior Racs would pay no attention, but then they settled back on their heels.

Pearl Angelica's mouth was dry. She was sweating. Struggling to smile and deflect their attention, she indicated the workers on the ground. They were bent over the buttresslike roots that heaved out of the soil, boring holes, inserting hoses, activating pumps. The distance was too great to tell whether they were humans or bots except by the flashes of color that were their clothes or leaves.

"They're flooding the wood now," she said. The pumps would force thousands of gallons of water thick with silica and other minerals into the wood. "In a year or two, every pore will be filled with rock. It will last for millennia."

"Tell us again," said Leaf, her voice still ominously smooth. She meant, "Tell them." "The tip swells. It does not taper into thinness like on a real tree."

"We will hollow it out," said Pearl Angelica. Workers were in fact already standing on the flange that surrounded the bulbous tip of the Tower. "We will make a chamber at the very top. In it we will leave records of who we are, where we came from, why we came, even how we came."

"You will tell us how to do everything that you can do," said Blacktop.

"Even how we made you," Pearl Angelica agreed, nodding.

"But it is too high," said Cloudscurry. She was watching the strangers from the corners of her eyes. "We cannot reach it."

"You must learn some things by yourselves," said Pearl Angelica. This was policy, but she thought it made sense. "When you have learned enough to reach the top of the Tower, then you will be ready to use what you will find there."

"It is for us," said Leaf. She was glaring now. "Just us. No one else. Not savages with tails."

"We made you all," said the bot. "It's for all of you."

But Leaf insisted: "For *us!*"

"It is our world too," said Wanderer in a voice as smooth as hers.

"It is our valley!"

"We were here before you!"

"You heard her say it," put in Stonerapper while Shorttail lifted his spear above his head.

"You were expelled, discarded like broken pots."

"For whoever climbs the Tower," said Pearl Angelica. Suddenly she felt far less certain of what she and her people were doing. By making successive "editions" of the Racs, they had created races. The last made, the one that dwelt nearest the valley when the Tower was completed and the Gypsies left, would all too naturally think itself the Gypsies' heirs, the Tower's owners, the god-blessed best of all Rac kinds. Other kinds or tribes or races would surely never agree to such superiority unless it was forced down their throats by force of arms.

Or was she seeing them as more human than they really were?

No. She could see it in their postures and gestures, hear it in their voices, smell it in their scents, suddenly more pungently animallike than ever. Leaf and Cloudscurry and all their tribe would do their best to keep the Tower theirs alone.

Blacktop made a placating gesture and with obvious effort roughened his tone. "God helps those who help themselves." Then he turned back to the bot. "Are you gods?"

The comment and the question startled her. She had just thought the word, hadn't she? She had not said it aloud. As far as she knew, no one had taught the Racs anything about religion. Speech, yes, and the making of huts and fire and tools, of pottery and baskets. But never religion.

Her father had once told her the reason why: Humans were all too prone to letting others take the responsibility for their lives, and the Racs' intelligence, like their genes, was much like the humans'. They must therefore be protected against the human error, or else all the Gypsies' efforts at creating an intelligent species that might someday join them in space might be wasted.

"Why do you even ask?" she said.

"I can read," said the Rac. When the females beside him eyed him admiringly—Were they his mates? His kin?—he took a deep breath and swelled his chest. "Most of us cannot. I learned when I was young."

"Who taught you?" She knew that she would have to pass on word of this unexpected skill. No one had thought reading was something that would do the Racs any good at this stage in their development. But the Racs were capable of numerous surprises.

"My playmates. Human children." He paused, and then he repeated his question: "Are you gods?"

"No!" Pearl Angelica's denial exploded from her lips. "You've been in the library, haven't you?" There was a small one in the pumpkin nearest the base of the Tower.

When he nodded, she sighed. "No," she said. "We're not gods. We're just makers. When we came here twenty-five years ago, we found a world without intelligence, though it had animals—your ancestors—that seemed promising."

"You were fleeing," said Blacktop. It was no secret, why the Gypsies had built the *Gypsy* and left Earth. "But here you have no enemies. You could stay if you wished."

"What are gods?" asked Wanderer. He was watching them intently, his eyes darting from speaker to speaker.

"You made us," said Leaf, thrusting her chinless face forward. "From the wild ones. And Blacktop has told us, makers are gods. That is what gods do."

"No," said Pearl Angelica again. "People made you. *We* made you. And not without mistakes." She paused as Leaf showed the strangers her teeth, revealing her thought that *they* were mistakes, still tailed, less smart, less favored by the gods. She thought of the Gypsies who said they should have waited until they had perfected the Racs' new model and feared that, by releasing the early batches, they had only guaranteed a future of racism and war. They had taught neither, just as they had not taught religion; now conflict seemed inevitable.

"*We* made you," she repeated. "The way we . . ." She gestured toward herself. "Look at me." She wore only a belt and an apron of many pockets. From her thighs to her shoulders, she was covered with scalelike green leaves. Her legs and arms, her neck and face, were covered with pale green skin, her head with red-bronze petals. She unfurled her roots from their ruffs and lifted a leg to draw their attention to them. "I'm a bot," she said. "My ancestors were plants. The humans, the gengineers, they changed them into . . ."

Stonerapper interrupted. "You're not like the others."

He had seen the other bots as he had walked across the valley. They had lawns of small blossoms, not just petals, on their scalps. Their leaves were long fronds that curled around their torsos. Small bulbs between their thighs held extra brain tissue.

"One like them was my mother," said Pearl Angelica. "They changed her seed. They moved my bulb inside me. They gave me a longer life." That last was her greatest difference. Few other bots lived more than ten years. She was already in her fourth decade. "But they only changed. They didn't make. Changed the way they changed the wild Racs into you. Changed the way they changed a tree into . . ." She pointed toward the Tower in the distance. It had begun as a sequoia; the gengineers had shaped it a little and hastened its growth tremendously. "Not made, not really, but remade." She thought of her Uncle Renny Schafer, who once had been a sentient, talking dog but had chosen to become human in order to have the woman he loved. "Remade," she repeated. "We are not gods."

There was a long pause while Leaf hefted her empty basket and eyed the vast expanse of moss and mossberries and mossblossoms. These blossoms would be wasted, for the first killing frosts were not far off, but the moss cared nothing for that. It was programmed in its genes to try endlessly to reproduce, to generate berries and seeds enough to survive harvesting by the wildlife of this world, and now by something it had never faced, something it might one day prove unable to survive, sentience, Racs eager to cache supplies against not only winter but also drought and flood and every other catastrophe they might someday imagine or create.

Finally, Pearl Angelica spoke again. "You're better off than we are. Than I am."

The Racs blinked and looked startled. They were far more used to thinking of the Gypsies as holding all the advantages. But they said nothing.

"You're here," said the bot wistfully. "You're home. We are a long, long way from home, and most of us will never see the world we came from. Most of us do not even care. But I do. I want to see Earth. I want to sink my roots into its soil and taste my root-home." Her voice died wistfully into a silence disturbed only by the sound of rustling leaves on the slope of the bluff.

Finally, Cloudscurry asked quietly, "Were you ever there?"

Pearl Angelica shook her head. "I was born and raised in space. But I remember the look of Earth. I could see it from the station, and later from the *Gypsy,* before we left. I was only a sprout, but I remember. I remember."

All six Racs stirred uncomfortably, but the bot paid them no further attention for a long moment. Finally, she said, "It's a long way off now. When we leave—and we must—it will be longer still."

"When will you leave?" The way Leaf shifted her basket on her arm suggested that she was now less interested in the answer than in getting on with her gathering. Cloudscurry touched her furry arm in silent enforcement of her attentiveness, and she stilled.

"When the Tower is done. When I have found . . ." Her tone turned thoughtful. "We need bees. Small animals that visit flowers and carry the yellow dust that makes them set their seeds."

Blacktop puffed his cheeks in a grimace of resignation to the inevitability of the Gypsies' departure. Then he nodded. He knew what she meant by bees.

But so did the strangers. "We will catch some for you," said Wanderer.

"No!" said Cloudscurry. Her shoulder fur was once more bristling. "This is our valley. Our task. *We* do things for the gods."

"You are visitors," said Blacktop. "Guests." He did not seem quite comfortable with the concept, as if it were something else he had encountered in the Gypsies' books. Certainly these strangers were the first visitors or guests the Racs had ever seen. "You will sit and tell stories of your home. We will do the work."

"I've caught some myself," Pearl Angelica cautioned them all. "But they cannot live aboard our ship."

"Remake them, then," said Cloudscurry. The miracles of gengineering seemed quite routine to her and all the other Racs, even though they were centuries from a similar capability themselves.

The bot sighed. "The gengineers say they're too busy already."

Suddenly stiffening, Blacktop lifted his spear and pointed toward the Tower. The other Racs spun with him. Pearl Angelica turned and saw a Bioblimp straining at a tree limb that had just been cut from the Tower's shaft. The limb, as large as many a forest tree, was a little too heavy for the Bioblimp to lift; the best the genimal and its small propeller could do was slow the fall of its load, guiding it toward the slash pile to the south. But . . .

Hard by the base of the Tower were the pumpkin shells that served the project's supervisors and workers. A little further off, set by itself with a view of both the Tower and the valley's small lake, was the pumpkin that housed Pearl Angelica's father and his nurses.

"Wrong direction," said Wanderer. He swung his own spear toward the lake. "It will land . . . there."

Pearl Angelica gasped. He was pointing toward the isolated pumpkin in which Frederick Suida's life guttered like an exhausted candle flame. "My father! Dad!"

Cries of alarm rose in the distance as others realized what was happening.

"Your father? But you're a bot," said Leaf. She sounded perplexed, for bots, though they had breasts and in form resembled human females, were like the plants that had supplied half their genes. They were dioecious, both male and female, makers of both pollen and eggs. They were also considered "she" by both humans and themselves.

"My mother was his wife." And Donna Rose had been as short-lived as every bot except Pearl Angelica. She had died years before. Frederick, half human, half pig, not plant at all, had lived longer. But his time too had come. He had been ill now for months, bedridden, attended by physicians and nurses. The pumpkin had been his choice at the beginning, that he could be near his daughter, that he could watch the Tower grow and be finished. Now he too rarely knew where he was or what he had done. And he was a target.

A figure, brilliant yellow in the coverall most humans wore, not the leaf-green of the bots, appeared in the doorway of Frederick's shelter. It faced briefly toward the shouts, looked upward, and turned to rush inside once more, leaving the door wide open behind it.

People were running toward the pumpkin. Others flagged down a Mack, its descent from a bulldog plain in its squashed face and bowed legs, opened the cargo pod strapped to its back, and crowded aboard. Two insectile Roachsters, long and low and spiky in their profiles, their passenger compartments embedded in the shell of their backs, left their dirt tracks and rolled across the mossflowers.

"Too late," moaned Pearl Angelica. "They can't stop it. Oh, Dad!"

Air currents lifted the Bioblimp, dropped it, pushed it first to one side, then the other. But the straining engine and propeller defeated the breezes and kept the gengineered jellyfish and its burden slanting through the air toward a spot somewhat beyond the pumpkin.

"It will drop the limb," said Blacktop. "Soon."

Even as he spoke, the yellow coverall appeared once more in the pumpkin's doorway. Others, clad in other colors and in the green of bot leaves, followed. They were carrying a stretcher, on it a single body covered with white sheets. They ran, and in that moment the Bioblimp uncurled its tentacles and released its load just as the Rac had foretold.

The Bioblimp, still fifty meters above the ground, leaped upward as the weight of its burden fell away. The tree limb, propelled by the momentum its carrier had given it, slanted steeply downward. Air resistance swept its leafy branches upward as if they were the vanes of a dart. Its thick butt hung down, swaying, plunging.

"He's out!" breathed Pearl Angelica exultantly. "He's safe!"

The massive limb struck the domed top of the pumpkin, smashing through, small branches lashing in elastic reaction, breaking, showering leaves and twigs and larger pieces over the ruined structure below. A moment later, the crash of the impact rolled across the valley to the bot's ears.

The limb now jutted from a jagged hole in the pumpkin's dome. The building's windows were shattered. The walls were cracked. The pumpkin itself was knocked askew on its stone foundation cradle.

The small cluster of refugees had turned to view the disaster by the time the Mack, the Roachsters, and the running Gypsies reached them. People milled and gestured, and Pearl Angelica could hear that their voices were rising in frenzied chaos.

Overhead, the rogue Bioblimp hovered above the scene as if to savor the havoc it had wrought.

"It has to be an accident," said Pearl Angelica. She was aware of an extra fillip of relief as she thought, accidents don't happen to gods. We have escaped divinity.

All six of the Racs shook their heads. "It was too exact," said Cloudscurry. She spun her spear in one hand and jabbed its point emphatically into the dirt between her feet. "Right to the heart."

"But why would anyone want to kill my father?"

All seven stared at the Bioblimp as if it might speak to them in answer to her question. As they watched, the door in the side of the vehicle's control cabin opened. For just a moment, someone stood in the opening, and then he—or was it she?—jumped. When the sunlight caught the spinning body, it revealed only that it was wearing blue.

"A human!" breathed Blacktop in a smooth, tight tone that even to Pearl Angelica's alien ear suggested awe and dismay.

"But why?" cried the bot once more.

"Your ancient enemies remain."

"It was an accident," said Pearl Angelica. "It had to be."

"No," said Blacktop. His voice was smooth with anger, yet it was also patient, definite. "They could not have followed you. You, your people, have told us they do not have the means. But they hide among you."

Leaf glared at the stranger Racs. "Or they come upon us. They sneak through the valley and plant seeds of hate."

Pearl Angelica stared at Wanderer, Stonerapper, and Shorttail. "They couldn't have," she said. "You can't make evil happen just by wishing it. And I don't think you stopped to talk to anyone. You were heading for the village up there, weren't you?" She pointed to the top of the bluff, where the Racs made their home and the smoke of their fires was visible from afar. When the strangers nodded, she blinked. Tears filled her eyes. She bowed her head and clenched her fists. "But how could the Engineers have done it?"

"You are gods," said Blacktop. He sounded more convinced than ever. Then, to forestall the protest promised by her suddenly raised head and open mouth, he added, "Or makers. And I have read. All gods have enemies who seek to undo their works. The battle is ancient and eternal, and it has come to us."

"You brought it," Leaf virtually sang at Wanderer, her hand tight on the handle of her basket, her voice as smooth as Blacktop's.

"It followed them," said Blacktop chidingly. "They could not escape it. Nor could we." He paused while Pearl Angelica turned back to the view of disaster across the valley. Other Bioblimps had the rogue in tow. Bots and humans were gathered around the body of the would-be assassin. Frederick Suida's nurses still clustered around his stretcher. Others were already climbing over the damaged pumpkin, removing whatever furniture and other items had survived the bludgeon that had fallen from the air, estimating the damage, already planning the necessary repairs.

Finally, thoughtfully, Blacktop said, "Even if the humans had never come, all we lacked was awareness, and they have told us that that was only a matter of time."

"A million years or so." When Pearl Angelica began to shake with shrill hiccups, prelude to the hysterical laughter of relief, Cloudscurry dropped her spear and wrapped a furry arm around her shoulder. She quieted, though the tears flowed more freely than ever.

Eventually, she was able to speak again. "How could killing Dad undo anything? The Tower was his idea, but . . . All he can do now is watch."

"The Tower is too big to harm," said Cloudscurry. "But without your father, perhaps your people would lose interest. You would not finish it. You would not fill the chamber at the top."

"And you would leave immediately." Leaf gestured anxiously. "You would abandon us."

"Your ancient enemies remain, and they are ours as well," said Blacktop. "We will hold this in our minds and in our histories. You will leave, and in your absence they may try to destroy . . ." He shook his spear toward the Tower. "But it is ours. You are giving it to us. And we will keep careful watch until we are able to climb it. Be sure of this, we will keep it safe."

Wanderer began to nod as he spoke. When Blacktop fell silent at last, he said, "The Tower is new and strange. But my people know of the humans. They made us too, and we have tales of the days when we lived here as you do now. We will help you protect the Tower."

"No!" cried Leaf. "It is ours! You will never touch it or see it again or know . . . !"

"Leaf!" Blacktop's bark was stern, and the female Rac stopped talking and seemed to wilt.

"They *are* the enemy!"

Pearl Angelica was suddenly thankful that the Racs had a leader like Blacktop. Perhaps there would be no war after all. But still . . . "Knowledge." She leaned against Cloudscurry's furry side as she spoke. "It's the only sort of treasure you can give away to others and never give it up. The hardest thing about it is getting it in the first place."

"Climbing the Tower," said Wanderer. He was staring at the immense spike with a speculative twist to his mouth.

Blacktop wore the same twist when he eyed the leader of the visitors. Finally, he said, "We need no berries today. Come. We will take you to the village." He gestured, Cloudscurry removed her arm from the bot, and the six Racs began to climb the bluff.

Pearl Angelica stared after them for a long moment. The village was set not far from the edge of the bluff, just past the border of the forest. As they walked up the path, Leaf bent to the scattered patches of mossberries within her reach, gathering a taste of what she must have planned to feed her children. Blacktop strode with his head bowed, thoughtful, surely planning how to tell his fellows about other races of Racs with tails and subtly different faces, about gods and ancient enemies and the Racs' mission as a species, or perhaps only as a tribe, to guard the Tower against all harm. Mission, she thought. That might be all it took to lead to conflict. Not races, not racism. Certainly Earth's history suggested that a sense of mission could do as much damage as any sense of difference.

But then she put all thought of the Racs from her mind and looked toward the valley once more. The distant crowd seemed less frantic now. Another Mack had arrived, and people were carrying the body of the terrorist toward its cargo pod. Others stood quietly about her father's stretcher, their postures suggesting that despite the excitement and the jostling he must have received he had come to no harm. Still more were walking back toward the Tower and their tasks.

Hoping fervently that Frederick truly had suffered no harm to worsen his condition, she began the hike back to her father.

Chapter
Two

PEARL ANGELICA'S LAB was a narrow room that smelled of dried leaves, tissue preservatives, and disinfectant. One of its long walls was dominated by a table that held a microscope and a computer, a mouse-glove resting beside the keyboard, auxiliary screens on the wall behind it. To the left of the table was a wall of shelving, storage for specimens, nets, traps, and reports. The end of the room to the right was occupied by a small sink, a coffeemaker, a rack of mugs and other glassware. Above the sink, set in the pumpkin's curved wall, a window showed the nearby Tower's base looming against a backdrop of pillowy grey clouds. Veils of distant rain seemed to sweep the tops of the bluffs beyond the lake.

The computer screens showed the resource inventory maps she had helped prepare for the Tower cache. She was supposed to be looking for errors before they were impressed on the ceramic tablets the Gypsies hoped would outlast metal or glass. Here were the minerals, fossil fuels, fertile soils, and forests that the Racs, if they followed the human pattern, might well have despoiled long before they scaled the Tower, with line drawings to demonstrate the heights and breadths of majesty that would once have existed. Other workers had enumerated birds, with drawings of skies opaque with migrating flocks; fish, with pictures of rivers so thick with spawners one could walk dryshod from bank to bank; grazing animals, with herds to fill every view past all horizons; sea beasts spouting, swarming, mating. A world of bounty, and every time she looked at any of the maps, her own or others', she wondered how much of that bounty would be left by the time the Racs had learned how to climb the Tower. Earth, she knew, had once been just as rich.

On the microscope's stage was a small clear-sided box containing a many-legged creature she had found burrowed into a scrap of bone. Its head was fixed to the interior surface of the box's lid, and a computer screen showed its oscillating mouthparts grinding away at the box's plastic.

But at the moment the bot was paying no attention to the inventory maps or her specimen and its potential as a biological drill or, enlarged, as a tunneler. She was leaning her buttocks against the edge of her worktable, facing the doorway in the room's fourth wall. "Uncle Renny," she was saying to the man who had just knocked on the door's frame.

"I came down as soon as I heard." Renny Schafer was of medium height, lean, the bridge of his nose a straight slope from his forehead, his silver hair cut short and stiff. Prominent canines gleamed whenever he opened his mouth. He was one of those who piloted the *Gypsy*'s Q-ships. "Is Freddy all right?"

Tears gleamed in her eyes. "He wasn't hurt, but . . ." She shrugged. "It did shake him up. He's not making much sense."

A look of pain crossed the man's face. "Less than usual, you mean." His old friend's illness had left him able to do little more than breathe and twitch an occasional muscle. Sometimes he could talk, but his mind was only rarely lucid. "I had hoped to say hello."

"He probably won't recognize you. Though maybe he'll improve a little when they get his place repaired and he's back in familiar surroundings."

"Have they got any better idea of what's wrong with him?"

She shook her head. When Frederick Suida had fallen ill, his physicians had said the gengineering technology that had made him a sentient pig in the first place had been too primitive. So had been the gene-replacement techniques that had later made him human. Now his chromosomes were disintegrating, apparently at random, scrambling the operating instructions in each of his many trillion cells, and each cell was going awry in its own way. Some cells turned cancerous and could not be repaired by tailored viruses. The physicians removed the resulting tumors as rapidly as they

made themselves apparent, but they could do little when the
masses of rogue tissue were deep within the brain. Some cells
stopped working; the physicians cloned replacement organs,
but again they could do little when the cells were brain cells
and other neurons. Some cells began to act like other types,
skin cells secreting stomach acid or hormones; these were the
easiest to repair, often simply by reprogramming their errant
genes.

"There are just too many things wrong," she said. And they
went wrong far too rapidly for any lasting help.

Renny was not really her uncle. But he had been a friend
of her father's for so many years, and the two men had had
so much in common, that he felt like kin. She had called
him "uncle," and his wife "aunt," as long as she had known
how to speak. She tightened her lips as she hoped that the
gene manipulations that had made him a sentient dog, and
later given him his human body, had been more polished,
less clumsy. Otherwise, he too might . . .

She stared at the wall beside the man. It held another rack
of shelving and a freezer cabinet whose shallow drawers
held several thousand preserved tissue samples. It also bore
a poster-sized photo of the display case in which one of
her biologist predecessors had mounted the few insects and
spiders that had inadvertently accompanied the Gypsies into
space. The insects included a dozen flies, several fleas, a few
cockroaches and lice, and a number of beetles and moths.
There were also three bedraggled bees which had died and
been preserved before anyone had thought to try to multiply
them. Pearl Angelica did not even know whether they were
male or female, but she thought that did not matter. If the
gengineers had gotten to them while they were still alive,
before their own internal enzymes, and then bacteria and
molds, had destroyed their DNA, they could have cloned
as many as they wished. They might even have been able
to make a queen, and then . . .

Following her gaze, Renny tried to help her change the
painful subject. "Where's the original?"

"Up there. On the *Gypsy.*" But then her mind jerked back
to her father and his illness. "The bots . . ."

Uncle or not, he understood. "It doesn't happen to the
Macks and Roachsters and Bioblimps. And anyway, bots

don't live long enough to worry about genetic collapse."

Ten years. Twelve at most, with few exceptions. "But me . . . ?"

He sighed and reached out to clasp her shoulder with a large and comforting hand. "Yes. But the technology was better developed when Hannoken worked on your seed. You'll live longer, as long as me. You'll have time enough to deteriorate quite naturally. But it may never happen. I hope it won't. You have so much potential."

"Potential!" She said the word as if it were a curse, though she knew what he meant. The people around her had been telling her the same thing—"You have so much potential!"— for as long as she could remember. Humans said it to any child who could tie her own shoelaces.

Bots said it more selectively and more accurately. They could link their roots within the soil, directly or through the honeysuckle that had once served them on Earth, and still did in parts of the *Gypsy,* as a sort of extended nervous system. They could thereby gauge each other's intelligence more precisely than any human test. They could also pass information directly from brain to brain, which was in fact how bots learned enough in their brief childhoods to function as adults. Pearl Angelica had been learning in that way, as well as others, for far longer than any bot had ever managed. When her longevity had become clear, her bot kin had begun to watch her carefully and to say those words of promise— "You have so much potential!"—more often than ever.

Potential! As if all that mattered was what she might become! As if what she was already—a biologist laboring to prepare a species' legacy and to sort through a whole world's fauna and flora for future usefulness—meant nothing! As if her value, her contribution to the bots, the Gypsies, and the future, depended on . . . Not on her intelligence; intelligence was ability to learn or capacity for knowledge, efficiency and speed of information processing, ability to solve problems, all those brain functions essential to survival. But on how much she knew.

"Yes, potential," said her uncle. "Even at your age, that has to count for something. The good you might do . . ."

She cut him off with a curt flap of her hand and indicated the corridor at his back. Light, reflecting off the walls outside the lab's entrance, was vanishing as the door to the outside of the pumpkin sighed closed once more. They could hear the soft sounds of unshod feet approaching down the hall. Renny stepped backward half a pace and turned his head. "A pair of Racs," he said. "I wonder what they want."

When they stopped outside the lab, Renny moved aside to let them enter. "Wetweed," said the one in the lead, introducing herself as Racs almost always did when they met a bot or human. Her pelt was marked with swirls of a green so dark that it was almost black. In one hand she held a small wicker cage containing a two-legged animal that looked like a cross between a hummingbird and a bat. It was the size of the former and it had feathered wings striped with yellow, but its body was covered with dense, brown fur; neither feathers nor fur were quite like their Earthly equivalents. Its head bore large semicircular ears and a long, bristly snout from which protruded a coil of tongue like a butterfly's.

"Cloudscurry," said the second, eying Renny as both Racs touched their muzzles. "Blacktop sent us."

Wetweed held up her cage. "You wanted . . ."

The man and the bot returned the greeting gestures. "A dumbo," said Pearl Angelica. "Thank you." Dumbos were one of First-Stop's principal pollinators. There were many species, differing in size and markings, in the flowers they serviced, in the time of day when they preferred to be most active. This one was one of the smallest she had ever seen.

As she took the cage and set it on a shelf beside the window above the sink, Cloudscurry asked, "Is your father all right?"

"He seems no worse," said Pearl Angelica.

"No worse?"

The spoon banged against the side of the small beaker in which she was mixing sugar and water with which to feed the dumbo. Didn't they know? But most Racs, all except the very few like Blacktop who wandered through the Gypsy settlement and learned to read of gods and other matters, mingled very little. They were not hostile, and they could pass the time of day quite pleasantly when they crossed a Gypsy's path, but they preferred to live their own lives in their own way.

"He has been ill for a long time," said Renny.

"If that assassin, that terrorist, had succeeded," said Pearl Angelica, "he would have lost only a few weeks or months." The words suggested that she thought her father's death would not matter much. Perhaps it wouldn't to Frederick, to the Gypsies, to the universe as a whole, but her posture, hunched stiffly, rigidly, over the beaker of sugar water, said that it would matter enormously to her. He was rarely even resident in the home of his flesh; soon he would not be there at all to feel the pain of his body's dissolution. He had made his contribution to his people. And the universe never even knew he was alive. But she knew. She would miss him. She would feel the pain. She would grieve.

She wept quietly.

"The terrorist was human," said Renny to the Racs.

"The enemy within," Cloudscurry said smoothly.

Renny nodded. "An Engineer. At least a sympathizer. He must have been among the refugees we took from Earth, and he must have stayed quiet until he felt he *had* to act. Then he knocked out the Bioblimp's pilot and tied her up. I wish we knew why."

Pearl Angelica choked words past her tears: "Maybe it was the first time he thought it would work."

Renny shrugged. "It almost did. I'm glad he won't get another chance."

"Surely he was not alone," said Wetweed. "Did he have helpers? Did someone tell him what to do?"

"If he did," said Pearl Angelica, "we won't find them. They've had over thirty years of practice at keeping their mouths shut." Then, as if declaring the topic done, she poured the sugar water she had mixed from its beaker into a large test tube and busied herself with attaching a rubber stopper pierced by a bent glass tube.

"True," said Renny. "But we'll try anyway." He faced the Rac. "We have security people, specialists in such matters. They'll talk to his friends and neighbors, his workmates and supervisors. If there's anything to find, they'll find it."

Pearl Angelica attached the feeder she had prepared to the side of the dumbo's cage. She stood still then, staring intently as the creature approached the glass tube that projected into its space, sniffed, extended its hollow tongue, and began to drink. Her silence spoke loudly enough to make the others fall silent too, to bring them to stand beside her and watch the dumbo's throat and abdomen pulsing as it drew in the fuel it needed to remain alive a little longer.

It was several minutes before the creature stepped back from the feeder and fanned its wings. By then its abdomen was visibly distended and there was a sizable bubble of air in the feeder bottle. "Tell me, Wetweed," said Pearl Angelica, "what do you know about these things? Where do they lay their eggs?"

"In water," said the Rac.

"She watches them," said Cloudscurry. She laughed in the Racs' way, snorting and showing teeth. "Like her name, she hangs over the edges of streams. And that Stonerapper should be called Stoneturner. That's all he does all day, turning over stones and studying what lives under them. Just like her."

"I like him," said Wetweed. "I study what I see, and so does he."

"Bah!" snorted her companion.

"But what has he seen? I have seen the dumbos coupling in the air above the water. I have seen them lay their eggs, and the eggs hatch into tiny wiggling tasty-tails . . ."

She fell silent as Cloudscurry opened her mouth, revealing numerous pointed teeth and arcing ropes of glistening saliva, and closed it again. "Yes," said Wetweed. "They devour each other, small fish, whatever they can find. They grow . . ." She held her hands before her, half a meter apart, to indicate how big the tasty-tail larvae of the largest dumbos could get. "And we eat them, don't we? They're delicious! If they escape our hands and traps, they become the dumbos that fly from flower to flower."

"I wish they would do," said Pearl Angelica. "They're pretty. But we don't have open water on the *Gypsy*. Not in any form that would let them reproduce. Can you keep looking? For one that nests in trees or underground?"

Wetweed shook her head dubiously. "I have never seen such things. But I will look."

When the Racs had gone, Pearl Angelica told her Uncle Renny, "I didn't want to hurt their feelings. But I looked at the dumbos years ago."

He glanced toward the cage, where the captive dumbo was once more drinking sugar water. "Did you actually try them out?"

She nodded. "I took a few up to the ship, just males to keep them from accidentally moving in for good. And yes, they liked some of our plants just fine. But not all of them, and not enough to solve the problem. And besides, they spent much of their time searching for open water, running water."

"Maybe they were looking for females?"

Now he was looking at her face, his expression sympathetic. She knew her eyes were swollen, her cheeks tear-streaked. "I found them by a park fountain."

"Wouldn't the fountains do for . . . ?"

"We drain them when we're maneuvering." She found a tissue and scrubbed at her face. "The larvae look like giant earwigs, with pincers like so." She gestured with both arms and smiled wanly when he shuddered.

"A little tinkering?" he asked.

"Maybe, later, when the gengineers have the time. I have some samples on ice." She indicated the cage by the sink. "That's where this fellow will go. But what we really need is bees, from Earth."

"They would add a homey touch."

She nodded. "It's too bad no one brought any. We'll have to ask for some, the next time a courier goes back."

"Your Aunt Lois is the next one scheduled. Should I speak to her?"

Pearl Angelica shook her head. "I'll do it myself." After a moment's hesitation, she added, "Maybe I'll even beg a ride."

Later, when he had left her alone once more, Pearl Angelica asked herself, Why *shouldn't* she go herself? The *Gypsy's* couriers only made the trip once a year, taking turns between their journeys to other stars in search of more worlds worth visiting. The trips home maintained contact with the Orbitals and gengineers and bots who had remained in Earth's solar system, in the habitats and stations, on Mars, and elsewhere. They kept intact the thread of common culture, common history, and passed back and forth whatever new ideas had occurred to each group's scientists, gengineers, and Engineers.

If only she could be sure that Frederick would live until she returned! The trip wouldn't really take very long. The smaller drives of the Q-ships were much more efficient than the behemoths that moved the *Gypsy*. They bit off larger chunks of distance as they tunnel-skipped through space, and they cycled faster. The *Gypsy* had taken years. A Q-ship needed only weeks.

And the trip would give her the chance she craved. She would be able to see Earth again. Perhaps she could even visit the world that had given birth to her ancestors, both plant and human. Perhaps she could stand in a field or forest beneath blue sky and white clouds and gaze upon lakes and streams, rivers and oceans, mountains and plains . . .

First-Stop had them all. They looked much the same as the pictures the Gypsies had preserved in books and on veedo-tapes. But they weren't the same. First-Stop was an alien world. The colors were different. And while it nurtured life so much like that of Earth in its chemistry that the two could eat each other with impunity—only the outer forms differed to any significant degree, and nothing Earthly with fur or feathers, much less both, metamorphosed from larvae the way the dumbos did—while its landscapes and ecosystems were instantly recognizable to anyone who had seen or read of those of Earth, while the DNA and proteins were so much the same that the gengineers had only needed to map the genes and isolate the protein tools, the enzymes, used by First-Stop's living things before they could redesign the Racs' animal ancestors for sentience, First-Stop was not Earth.

Despite all the similarities, she craved the planet of her origins. She yearned to sink her roots into its soil, to taste its deepest flesh. She dreamed of *knowing* Mother Earth and all her secrets, and even of living out her life within the embrace of her gravity. She did not entirely agree with what most other Gypsies accepted without a qualm, that exploring the cosmos, seeking other sentients and creating them where they were lacking, was the best of all possible destinies.

She knew the dream was futile. Earth was ruled by those who would not tolerate bots and gengineers and all the rest of what they had once rejected as blasphemous, obscene. At very best, the most that she could hope to have was a distant view of the homeworld, root-home, through a viewport or on a veedo screen, before she must return to her present place. But even that, that moment of even distant contact and then the fading memory, would be better than what she had now.

Yet maybe—she dreamed, she hoped—maybe the Engineers had eased their dogmas. Maybe they had come to their senses, found it possible to accept the technological novelties they had once rejected, given up the worst of their murderous bigotry. Maybe they had even embraced the novelty she represented and with it change and prosperity.

Indeed, the couriers had brought the news years before that the Engineers had bought Macks and a few other genetically engineered creatures from their exiled neighbors. The mechanical technology they had wished to build had simply not been up to the demands of necessity. They had lacked the metals to build trucks and other vehicles and the energy to run them. They had had to compromise their principles if they were to build even a partially mechanical civilization.

They must have mellowed, she told herself. They had to stop thinking of us and our products as anathema. They had to grow more tolerant.

There had to be a real chance that she could at least, for a moment or a day, touch the Earth of her dreams.

Chapter
Three

THE CONSTRUCTION OF the *Gypsy* had begun in the asteroid belt of Earth's distant solar system and been completed in orbit around the Earth. It had been crewed by Orbitals, those people who had lived in stations and habitats and on the Moon at the time, by gengineers fleeing the pogroms of Earth's reactionary Engineers, and by a few rescued bots. They had had in common only their tolerance for novelty, their lack of the Engineers' neophobia, their fear of persecution and extermination. Since then, they had forged a group identity, found a sense of mission, and adopted the name of their ship. They were Gypsies. "Orbitals" were those who remained in Earth's solar system.

Now the great ship turned about its long axis, a misshapen cylinder whose surface still bore many of the knobs and fissures that had marked it for untold eons. The cracks had been filled and sealed. The largest protrusions had been carved away. Its tail had been hollowed to house its massive drives. Its tapered nose ended in a round of polished metal. Forests of antennae and other instruments adorned its skin. But it was still, despite all that had been done to its surface and despite all the paraphernalia that clung to its hide, quite visibly what it had always been, a rock from the depths of space.

A minnow seeking to kiss a whale, the Q-ship that had lifted Pearl Angelica from First-Stop approached the smooth surface of the *Gypsy*'s nose and the bay that lay behind it. The bay's door irised open, revealing a hollow drum whose walls turned with the rotation that gave the great ship its centrifugal substitute for gravity. The Q-ship drifted in, past the two other ships berthed on the turning wall, toward the still center of the cavity's opposite face. Magnets pulled it into position as the iris closed, a docking tunnel eeled toward the Q-ship's hatch from a niche near the bay's outer rim, a buzzer sounded, and Pearl Angelica was free to debark with the other passengers.

As she undid the restraints that held her safely in her webbing and let the webbing itself snap back onto its ceiling-mounted roller, the bot wondered: Was she doing the right thing by coming here? By even thinking of leaving her lab and her work for the weeks that would be necessary? But Uncle Renny had not discouraged her, had he? Perhaps he understood.

She hefted the small bag that was all she carried and stepped from the docking lounge into the long corridor that, one among many, twisted through the *Gypsy*'s depths. All the ship's internal tracks followed such convoluted paths, limiting vistas, letting each curve reveal small surprises, carrying their users from heavier to lighter, coreward gravity, sometimes—but only briefly!—so light that wheels and feet no longer held the pavement and hands must grab for lines or rails, and then back uphill again; the planners had thought to avoid the straight path of boredom. When her turn came, she chose a bicycle from the rack to one side. She would leave it at her destination, as this one had been left for her by someone else.

The bicycle carried her silently into broader corridors where other Gypsies strolled and pedaled and drove Macks and Roachsters, smaller models of the same gengineered vehicles that served the workers down on First-Stop. There were armadillo-based Armadons as well, only recently re-created from tissue samples and the original specifications, and litterbugs, scoop-jawed descendants of pigs, that patrolled the pavements and retrieved whatever wastes the other genimals left behind them.

The animal pungency of the genimals was compensated by abundant plant life, smelling of flowers, refreshing with moisture and oxygen. Every twenty to thirty meters, rock and metal planters interrupted the centers of the corridors with flowering shrubs, snackbushes, and small fruit trees. Similar sprays of foliage softened the rock walls, framed the doorways, and formed islands at corridor intersections.

The *Gypsy* was far too large for pedestrians. It held three cubic kilometers of volume, only half of which was the native nickel-iron of the asteroid the great ship once had been. The rest was tunnels, chambers, caverns, enough to give each of its 25,000 residents 60,000 cubic meters of space.

Less than a hundredth of that space was devoted to living quarters. The rest was storerooms, engine rooms, bays for the Q-ships, broad corridors, farms, and parks. And still there were whole sectors of the ship that, though they had been bored and excavated like the rest, were dark, unventilated, untenanted, held in reserve for future need.

In the generation since the *Gypsy* had left Earth's orbit, its population had already increased some forty percent. Growth had slowed in recent years, but it seemed inevitable that eventually all the empty portions of the ship would be filled. Later still, it might be necessary to build a second *Gypsy* to absorb surplus population.

Pearl Angelica's route took her through the broad entrance to one of the *Gypsy*'s parks. Just within the entrance, a row of three transparent cylinders represented the cross-ship elevators and a holographic map revealed the *Gypsy*'s pattern of interwoven wormholes; on the map, a glowing bar showed which of the ship's many corridors happened to overlie each other, comprising nominal levels, at this point; elsewhere the same corridors might meet at ordinary intersections. Nearby, water ran over a pile of mossy boulders to collect in a broad pool. A child sat on the pool's stone curb, using a stick to push a small boat under a spray of droplets.

To either side of the fountain, the path split to wind past lawns, flower beds, bamboo clusters that might have provided the child's stick, and groves of trees entwined with honeysuckle vines. The vines were thick with creamy blossoms. The bot shook her head when she saw an unkempt woman holding one of the blossoms like a wineglass in her hand; a dozen others, emptied of their euphoric wine, littered the grass around her folding chair. Even here, she thought, there were honey bums. The addiction had not been left behind on Earth.

There was also, rooted in a lawn beside another grove, a class of young bots surrounding a teacher and a bioform computer. The computer would be passing recorded lessons through its roots to the honeysuckle, which would in turn pass them to the bots. The teacher was there to operate the computer, select the lessons, and comfort those for whom the sudden inrush of data proved too painful.

She nodded to a friend with many-colored scalp blossoms, one of those who monitored the Racs in their daily lives when she was down on First-Stop. Then she looked up at the canopy that bent above her head like thick green gauze. It belonged to a weeping willow whose leaves— thanks to a playful gengineer—now resembled feathers. Most of the *Gypsy*'s vegetation had grown from seeds brought aloft by refugees. A few plants—she bent to pick a cluster of mossberries, pulpy, sweet, and tart, from a stone-rimmed bed—were native to First-Stop. Future worlds would add still more diversity, but . . . Not far away, young bots and humans perched on ladders that leaned against flowering trees, using artists' paintbrushes to ensure the formation of fruits and seeds. Others, ladderless, flicked their brushes over smaller plants.

The park's ceiling arched above, raw rock visible behind the constellations of lamps that simulated the sun for the plants and the Gypsies who wandered and played among them, their patterned coveralls rivalling the flowers in their colors. No one wore the solid blue of the man who had leaped from the Bioblimp down below. Blue was the color of the Earth they had fled, of the Engineers, their enemies, as well as of the homeworld's skies and seas.

She sighed and turned her head to watch a small terrier chase a ball, catch it, tumble, growl, and race back to its young master. There were few animals aboard the ship, only dogs and cats and the descendants of mice and rats that had stowed away or escaped from labs. Seeds had been more portable.

The ship, she thought as she pedaled onward, really did need bees or other pollinators. They could not be had from First-Stop, but on Earth . . . She passed through the park's other entrance arch into a second corridor. She found a rack and clamped the bike into place for some other to use. She walked past a small tavern, redolent of beer, sausage, fish, and hot oil; a shop that—so said the hologram that seemed to bulge from the wall beside her—offered coveralls and other garments, the finest in utility or fashion; a food market whose bins overflowed with vegetables and fruits from the *Gypsy*'s garden chambers. She reached a row of residences, showing only numbered doors to the corridor and its passersby. When she found the one she wanted, she needed no key to enter; the scanner in the frame knew her well and swung the door wide for her.

"Aunt Lois?"

"In here, dear."

The entry's white-painted walls supported several small paintings and photos of Earthly scenes—a snow-capped mountain, a forest glade, a city street clogged with traffic thicker than the *Gypsy*'s corridors could ever know, window-waffled buildings rising high above. Pearl Angelica gave them each, even the city, a wistful stare before she followed the pale green carpet into the apartment's living room. Here the walls and ceiling were pale blue, the furniture brown wood, leather, and fabric, the effect one of landscape, of earth and growth and sky. Near the door to another room Lois McAlois was seated at a small desk beneath a wallscreen full of columns and graphs. Her hands were poised above a keyboard, but her face was turned toward the bot.

Lois McAlois's face showed the weathering effects of over fifty years of living; the deepest lines were those left by laughter and good humor. Silver streaks in her auburn hair suggested that in another twenty years she would be a striking elder.

"I'm going over the status reports for the *Quebec*," she said. The *Quebec* was her Q-ship, the one she would fly on this year's courier mission to Earth, or to that space around the homeworld that held the Gypsies' allies. Of the eight other Q-ships, half were away at any time, searching nearby systems for worlds the Gypsies might visit next. The other half served as shuttles to and from First-Stop; they were also used to train new pilots.

"You'll be leaving soon."

Lois nodded. "A few days. The cargo's already aboard. We're taking mossberries, fish, a few baby Armadons." "We" meant the pilot and her ship; there was rarely any other crew. "And we have a year's worth of what our people have done, all on floppy cards." Novels, short stories, monographs, music, and art. She would exchange it for what the Orbitals near Earth had produced.

"I'd like to go too."

Her aunt's eyebrows rose. "Whatever for?"

Pearl Angelica explained the lack of suitable pollinators on First-Stop. "And we need them here," she said. "We need bees to pollinate the flowers on this ship, not people and ladders and brushes. And Earth has them."

Aunt Lois gave her a shrewdly skeptical look. "It *is* a waste of labor," she agreed. "But you could just have put a request for bees through channels. You don't have to go yourself."

The bot shrugged uncomfortably. "There's nothing pressing here, and I should talk to a bee expert."

"I'm sure we have one or two among us."

"And I knew you were almost ready to leave. I was afraid going through channels would take too long."

"All you had to do was call me."

"But it's been a while since . . ."

"You still didn't have to pitch your case in person, though you know you're welcome." Lois McAlois paused a moment, smiling gently, before adding, "What do you really want?"

Pearl Angelica hadn't thought she was still as transparent as she had been as a child, when Aunt Lois had always been able to tell that her offers to do the dishes or dust the furniture meant that she wanted a favor. But . . .

"You want to see Earth, don't you? Visit it, even."

The bot grinned and nodded. "But we do need bees."

"They won't let you land. You're not the right kind of human for them."

"She can still get a lot closer than she is here." Renny Schafer stepped out of the apartment's next room. Beyond that were kitchen, bathroom, bedroom, storage space. She hadn't known her uncle was there. "At least she can see it from orbit."

"I thought they were growing more tolerant," said Pearl Angelica.

"Not that much," said her uncle.

"It's been a year since the last we heard. It's possible."

"Barely," he replied with a shake of his head.

"I think the odds are lousy, but . . ." Lois McAlois's look turned thoughtful. "I suppose I could use some help with those Armadons."

Renny snorted. "You don't know what you're in for. The rest of us left Earth very happily, and we don't want to go back."

"Not even if things are better there now?"

"They've made some progress, but not enough." Renny's voice was sad, as if he wished he were wrong. "Not in their attitudes, and not in their technology. When we left, they had a lot more than thirty years of work ahead of them to rebuild a functioning civilization."

"A lot can be done in even twenty years," Pearl Angelica said. "Think of the difference between the end of World War II and the first landing of men on the Moon."

"They hadn't managed it last year."

"How much of their progress can you see from space?"

"The Orbitals there have spysats. They don't miss much."

"But . . ."

"What do the other bots say?" interrupted Lois McAlois.

"I haven't asked them," said Pearl Angelica. "I don't plan to."

"You know they won't be happy. They'll think you're putting far too much at risk."

"My 'potential'?"

When Lois nodded, Pearl Angelica gave an exasperated sigh and crossed her arms over her chest. "It's *my* potential, and I'll risk it if I wish. Besides, they have tissue samples." She stared at her aunt. "Can I go?"

Lois glanced at her husband, and both shook their heads, smiling ruefully. "Of course, though . . ."

"Thank you." She turned toward the apartment's entry, unwilling to give her aunt another word. "I'll feed your Armadons and shovel their litter. I'll work my passage."

"That's not . . ." But their niece was gone.

The Tower soared above the valley, limbless now, almost all its bark stripped away to reveal the creamy wood that would in time weather to a faded, silvery grey. The pile of branches, some thicker than a human torso, was visible to the south, jumbled, jagged, needles already browning. When they were dry enough, they would be burned and the air would fill with smoke. The ashes would fertilize the valley's soil.

Pumps throbbed, pushing the minerals of pseudo-petrification into the wood. The sound of chainsaws, muted by height and angle to a snarling mutter, fell from what would become the records chamber at the Tower's tip. Wood chips rained to the ground at the Tower's base, their scatter marking the shadow of the prevailing breezes, pointing toward the blackened landing field and the Q-ship that had brought Pearl Angelica back to First-Stop. Its bulbous nose rose on a fat stem from a bundle of cylindrical tanks that could be filled with powdered rock, water, anything that could be turned to plasma and thrust.

She began to walk toward the pumpkin where her father lay abed. The marks of its repairs—sheet metal covering the hole in the roof, newly painted window frames, grey patching compound filling the cracks in the orange walls— were visible even from a distance. Other marks, she thought, were less obvious but just as real and harder to patch up. The pumpkin in which tools were stored now had a lock on its door, and the people she saw seemed to go about their tasks more quietly, with less banter, every Gypsy on the planet keeping a distrustful eye on every other and being watched in turn.

Next to the pumpkin's door hung an antique brass bell the size of two fists. A cord beside it supported a small wooden mallet. There was also the glass eye of the scanner unit that recognized her as an approved visitor and clicked the lock. When the door did not open as it should, she used the mallet and bell to announce her presence. As footsteps sounded within the building, she tugged on the door's brass handle, but her efforts were futile until someone lunged against the other side.

A human in a grey coverall patterned with yellow leaves, panting slightly, faced her. He peered suspiciously beyond her, to each side, and toward the Bioblimps above the Tower before he said, "The frame's warped."

"Then you should get that fixed too," she said, but the nurse only shrugged and turned away. Perhaps, she thought, they felt the pumpkin would not be needed much longer. She hoped the need for it would not end before she returned from her journey.

"He's in here."

She stood in the entrance to her father's room. Its open window was graced by light curtains that moved in the breeze. The walls were the lightest of greens, the carpet thick, the furniture a desk, a potted bioform computer whose screen and keyboard leaves were thick with dust, two padded chairs, and a small table that she recognized from when Frederick Suida had been a healthy, active man. There was also a bookcase full of books and boxes of floppy cards that she knew he had been unable to use for months. A veedo screen, silent and pictureless, hung from the crack-webbed ceiling.

The room's centerpiece was far less homey: a high bed from whose foot projected cranks, along whose sides rose steel rails. Beside it were a rack for intravenous bottles, empty now, cardiac and brain activity monitors, their screens tracing the spastic rhythms of a life too near its end. On it, his hands still upon the light cover, lay her father, his only motions an uneven rise and fall of his chest, a quivering of an emaciated thigh muscle. His eyes were open, their pupils hazy with cataracts.

"Hi, Dad." He was not truly her father but her mother's husband. But he had raised her, loved her, supported her, as only a father could do. And he was the closest link she still had to her mother. Her voice shook. She did not feel like a bot three times as old as any other, like an ancient who had outlived all her generation. Nor did she feel like a grown human woman, old enough to have had children of her own. Her father's mottled skin, lumpy with myriad tiny tumors, his grey hair, shaggy with bristly tufts, his weakness, his inevitable death, all affected her as if she were a child— a frightened child—all over again.

His eyes blinked. His flattened nose, the only remnant of the pig he once had been, twitched. His lips parted. "Angie." His whisper was hoarse and strained.

He recognized her! Her heart leaped, and she grinned. Then she covered his hand with her own as she struggled for more words. "I'm . . . I'm going back to Earth, Dad. Just for a visit. With Aunt Lois."

He blinked again. "Porculata?" he managed. "Where . . .? The shoats! Tommy! Muffy."

Names from his past, names that reminded her of stories he had told. His first wife, a pig like him but gengineered to be a living, talking bagpipe. Their children. Friends. All gone, long gone, long dead, victims of the Earth she wanted so badly to see. Her eyes filled with tears and she squeezed his hand, hoping he could feel it.

"We used to sing," he whispered. " 'With his bloody big dingle . . .' " His voice cracked and broke and faded. " 'Shakin' my anther for you.' "

His eyes blinked closed. There was a soft beep from one of the monitors, though she could see no change in the tracing of his heartbeat. The brain waves, then.

Someone touched her shoulder. She glanced aside, saw that the nurse was not the one who had met her at the door—his coverall was predominantly yellow, not grey—and said nothing. She looked back at her father. His eyes were open once more, but now he did not seem to see her.

The nurse said gently, "He's not . . ."

"I know." She stood up and stared down at her father. After a long moment, she asked the nurse, "How long does he have?"

The man shrugged. "His heart could still be beating a year from now. His mind . . ."

She closed her eyes. "Then he won't die in the next few weeks."

"We don't expect him to."

"Then I can go." She sighed. "On the Earth run. I should be back in . . ."

"Plenty of time," the nurse said gently.

"If you get a chance, tell him . . ."

She stood on the step outside the pumpkin's door, staring toward the Tower where its peeled sides gleamed in the afternoon sun. Her eyes felt grainy. Dried tears drew the skin above her cheekbones tight. Her throat hurt.

Tell him I love him, she thought. I've said it before, but never enough. Never enough.

When she had landed earlier, all her attention had been for this pumpkin. Now, looking back the way she had come, she could see the slope past the Tower, rising gently, almost imperceptibly, toward the bases of the valley's encircling bluffs. There was something new there, stones set in lines, Racs carrying more stones from the bluffs, setting them beside the others. To one side stood the trio of visitors who thought the Tower held up the sky, their tails twitching back and forth.

She walked away from the pumpkin, away from her dying father, toward the Tower and beyond it. When she was close enough, she could see that the Racs were arranging their stones in a broad arc open toward the Tower. The bottom of the arc was ornamented with a triangular stem, and in a moment she realized that the arc itself would be nearly parabolic when it was done. The Racs were laying out a rude sketch of a dish antenna.

One Rac, distinctive in his dark ears and back, seemed to be in charge, telling the others where to place their stones. "Blacktop," she called. When he turned toward her, she touched the side of her nose and gestured inquiringly. "What is this?"

"A watching place," he said. "I said that we will not let the Makers' Enemies harm our Tower. Here we will stand sentinel. We will guard the treasures that you leave us until we can make them ours."

"But . . ." She hesitated, nonplussed. The shape before her made her think not only of communications and radar antennae, but also of the Earthly churches she had seen illustrated in the Gypsies' books. Blacktop must have seen the same pictures, and if his people could not yet build walls and buttresses and steeple spires, they could at least mark out a foundation and a floor plan. "I told you, we are not gods."

The Rac waved one hand dismissively. "You still have Enemies."

This time she heard the capital on the word. As he turned back toward his fellows, she made a resigned face. No, they were not gods. But the Racs did not see them as ordinary mortals. Let the Gypsies leave, and they would soon be a pantheon to shame the Greeks and Romans, complete with enemies that echoed the dreams of Christians and Zoroastrians.

What position, she wondered, would her father occupy in that pantheon? What position would be her own?

And would it be for good or ill? When Frederick had told her why the Gypsies had not taught religion to their creations, he had also said that when primitive humans on Earth had met representatives of more advanced cultures, or even people of other skin colors, they had sometimes called them gods. They had offered sacrifices, abased themselves, surrendered control over their own lives, and then stagnated. They had never fulfilled the potential that was within them.

She hoped the Racs would never let themselves be so handicapped.

She had said good-bye to her father and her Uncle Renny. She had found her friends and told them where she was going. When Caledonia Emerald, that bot with the variegated blossoms, met her at the *Gypsy*'s dock with a wish of luck, they had embraced.

"I'll watch the Racs as usual," said her friend. "You find what you want."

"Bees," Pearl Angelica had said.

"And root-home." They had embraced again and blinked away the tears that came to their eyes. And now . . .

The *Quebec*'s cargo bay was a long cylinder. The passenger nets were furled. The rear half of the bay, closed off by an insulated partition, held those few tons of goods—crates of frozen mossberries and fish from the oceans of First-Stop—that Lois McAlois was delivering to the Orbitals of Earth's solar system. The front half was empty except for a large pen covered with netting. Its walls and floor were thickly padded, and in it eight young Armadons, two litters of quadruplets, one of males, one of females, bounced endlessly, restlessly back and forth. If there were anything resembling gravity to hold them to the floor, they would be rolling just as restlessly; their tessellated shells swelled out in wheels atop which ran their legs, reversed at the hips.

At the moment, the Armadons were the size of cocker spaniels. When they matured, they would be much larger. They would also have sizable cavities in their backs; with the installation of windshields, doors, seats, and control computers, they would become vehicles. Their feed was stored in metal drums strapped to the wall to one side of their pen.

Forward of the cargo bay were two small sleeping cabins. The nose of the Q-ship held the bank of screens, indicators, and controls that let the pilot guide the ship from place to place. Lois reclined in a padded couch, working the ship out of the *Gypsy*'s bay. Beside her, Pearl Angelica occupied a similar acceleration couch and stared through the viewport above the controls as metal walls gave way to fields of stars and First-Stop rolled into view, as blue and white and brown as ever any photo of old Earth.

The planet disappeared from sight. The *Gypsy* appeared to the left. The pilot's hands moved decisively. Thrust pressed them both into their couches, and their mother ship slid back, fell out of the port and the view, fell behind. They were on their way.

"The Q-drive," said Lois McAlois. Their acceleration was barely enough to make them feel half again as heavy as on the surface of First-Stop, but the gee-forces still dragged at her voice. "It depends on quantum fluctuations, the spontaneous appearance of matter-antimatter particle pairs. We warp the probabilities, make the pairs appear in floods, and when they annihilate each other, we use the energy they release to turn our reaction mass into plasma. That's what propels us."

Pearl Angelica barely registered her aunt's patter, a speech memorized long ago and meant to comfort whatever passengers she might carry. It was not ignorance or uncertainty about the Q-drive that made her fingers twitch and the scale-like leaves of her torso quiver. It was the thought of her father, Frederick, Freddy, Dad, so ill, so far beyond the reach of cure. Would he still be there when she returned? Would he be alive? Or . . . ?

With an effort, she stilled her fingers. She took a deep breath, and another, but her leaves still trembled. She could have waited, couldn't she? But the next trip to Earth would not be for another year, and Frederick might still be living then. So she would put it off once more, and then the *Gypsy* would leave First-Stop for its next destination. She would never see Earth if she did not go now. Nor would she get its bees, though that might not be a problem once the *Gypsy* reached its next stop.

She tried to set her worries aside by finding the words that would prompt her aunt to continue. "And then we begin to skip . . ."

The pilot nodded. "Yes. We've long known that electrons and other particles could jump from place to place, even across an energy barrier. They don't seem to be entirely material, and they have a finite probability of being almost anywhere, though they are more likely to jump shorter distances. The same thing, of course, is true for anything made of these particles."

"Such as the *Quebec*," said Pearl Angelica.

The gees could not go too high, or the Armadons would die, but they were still enough to slow her aunt's nod. "Even that. Even us."

"But for larger objects, the probabilities are . . ."

"Infinitesimal. Nothing ever moves. But before we left Earth, we learned that the probability warp device could make macroscopic tunneling happen. Ordinary velocity sets the vector. Only tiny fractions of a meter at first. Then larger fractions, a meter, two. We learned to cycle the device in nanoseconds. By the time we left the system, we were traveling well over the speed of light. Einstein be damned."

"But it took us years to get here."

"The *Gypsy*'s big. The *Quebec*'s smaller. It moves faster, a lot faster. Three weeks to Earth. Not five years."

"How long will we be there?"

"A week. Maybe two. We won't be gone two whole months. Now watch. We're far enough from the ship." Her hands moved, the thrust of the drive died to just enough to give them a sense of weight, and something in the bowels of the ship began to hum. The hum quickly rose in pitch until it disappeared in the ultrasonic range. An Armadon squealed in response. The nearer stars began to flow backward in the viewport.

Pearl Angelica did not hear her aunt say that they could see the stars so clearly, their hues unshifted by their speed, because when the light reached them they were not going faster than light. They gained their vast speed only as the net effect of many timeless leaps from point to point. In the vanishingly short intervals between the leaps, they were virtually motionless, the speed their acceleration gave them negligible by cosmic standards.

The bot was thinking: two months. And her father should still be alive when she returned. Though the odds were not good. And then she realized . . . "Aunt Lois, could the probability warp help Dad?"

"Improve his chances? Throw the dice and make his cells return to normal?"

Pearl Angelica nodded abruptly, urgently.

Lois McAlois shook her head. "I don't believe it." Her voice was sad, resigned. Frederick Suida had been her friend for many years. "There are just too many cells to fix. Trillions of them, right? And every one of them needing fixing in a different way. You'd have to roll the dice afresh for every one of them, and there are so many that would take forever."

Chapter
Four

"ARE THOSE BEASTS secured?"

"I'd like to secure them, all right. In a box, with a heavy weight, at sea." Pearl Angelica yawned at her aunt, who blinked owlishly to prevent her own gaping reply. Both women were exhausted, for they had spent much of the trip cleaning up after and chasing the eight Armadons in the cargo hold.

The initial period of zero-gee, even though it was followed by constant acceleration, had not agreed with the beasts. Shortly after the *Quebec* left the Tau Ceti system, all eight got sick. Pearl Angelica strove valiantly, but the genimals added to the mess—from both ends—much faster than she could remove it. Lois McAlois had to help.

Of course, they had to remove the netting that covered the pen's top. In addition, in the struggle to mop the floor, clean goo out of the Armadons' wheel hubs, and calm the creatures' whines and moans, one of them—they never decided who—left the pen open. Shortly after that, all eight Armadons were loose in the *Quebec,* racing back and forth and round and round the available floor space, their legs pumping and their wheels spinning madly. Nor did they slow their catastrophic eruptions until sometime after aunt and niece loaded an injector gun with sedatives.

Unfortunately, they didn't dare keep the Armadons unconscious for the entire trip. They got all eight back in their pen, with the netting top back in place and the pen's gate shut tight. When the genimals woke up again, they were safely confined.

They also got sick once more, and that started the whole procedure over again. The women *had* to open the pen to get in, and as soon as the gate began to move, the beasts charged it. Fortunately, they never got into the ship's control room or the small cabins in which the women slept.

The journey was four days old before Pearl Angelica asked, "Why don't we tranquilize them *first?*"

That worked, but every time the Armadons awakened from their drugged sleep, they got sick again. As a result, both Pearl Angelica and Lois McAlois could barely stand the sight, smell, sound, or even thought of Armadons.

"But they're tranked," Pearl Angelica added now. "The pen is shut, and the net is on, tight." She yawned again and tried futilely not to let the ship's animal stink enter her nose.

"We're coming into the system now. I should have told you more about what to expect, but . . . Mechin' beasts." The pilot fell silent as she cut the drives. Pearl Angelica felt her weight leave her seat. Her semicircular canals protested as the *Quebec* swung about, and she swallowed hard until the thrust returned. "We're decelerating now," said her aunt.

The stars were always there, and the light that reached them between the flickers of the tunnel-drive was enough to maintain an illusion of constancy. The ship existed so briefly at any one spot, however, that messages were chopped into unintelligibility. When the ship's com burped a phrase of staticky noise, Lois therefore switched off the tunnel-drive. Pearl Angelica immediately heard: "Hallo, Gypsies! What's the news?"

"*Quebec* here." Muting her microphone, the pilot summoned a diagram onto a screen and told her niece, "That's Saturn Base. A habitat outside the rings. Our course brings us near them first, but we don't stop. Actually, we're already past them."

"How near did we get?" asked the bot.

"It's a relative term. If we'd been much closer, they'd never have spotted us in time to hail us. You might be able to see the rings, but not much more." Not waiting out the time delay demanded by the millions of kilometers between the ship and Saturn Base, she began to talk. "The Tower's nearly done. An Engineer terrorist dropped a branch on a pumpkin and almost killed Frederick Suida. We still haven't found a good target for our second leg. And I've got eight littering, puke-brained Armadons for the folks on Mars. They can have a barbecue. You'll hear everything later on."

The com speaker interrupted her. "*Quebec?* Is that you, Lois? Of course it is. Sam Hendricks here. This is the first time I've been on the com when you came by. We met when you were regrowing your legs. You hauled me out to the Belt as part of the *Gypsy*'s construction crew . . ." He paused as her earlier message reached his ears. "Armadons, you say?" His laughter was unconscious and genuine. "On a spaceship? In zero-gee? I haven't seen one of those since . . . you know. Glad Freddy's okay. I heard him sing once, on an old veedo tape. But don't hang around out here. They're waiting for you!"

"Hi, Sam. He's not okay. Real sick, though it's not the litterhead's fault. Hasn't got long. I'll talk to you again on the way home." She activated the drive once more, but it was less than an hour before they heard again: "Hallo, Gypsies! What's the news?"

"That's one of the Belt stations," she explained before she repeated her brief summary of the news she brought.

And again: "Hallo, Gypsies! What's the news?"

"That's Mars."

When she finished her spiel once more, Pearl Angelica said, "There's a lot of us here."

"Everybody didn't sign on the *Gypsy*. About a third of them stayed here. Orbitals, gengineers, even bots who didn't want to go a-wandering. They've bred since then, especially the bots, and now there's more here than with the *Gypsy*. Almost all the Mars colonists are bots."

"Do you think any Engineers are . . . ?"

"Hiding among them? Of course there are. A lot of the refugees came from prison camps, and some of the prisoners had to be Engineers who had gotten someone mad at them. They weren't about to stick their heads up, and we didn't have any way to identify them, so . . ."

"Haven't they done anything?"

"How could they? *We* couldn't, though we always knew there had to be a few on the *Gypsy*. We just didn't know who they were. And it's the same story here. But here they've got a pretty strong security force. If someone starts acting funny, they jump on them, fast. Not that they always catch . . ."

Earth and its Moon were now visible in the viewport as a pair of silvery dots, one larger than the other. Lois fell silent while she fine-tuned their course.

"Where do we stop?"

"Munin." Munin and Hugin were the two LaGrangian habitats that shared the Moon's orbit around Earth, sixty degrees ahead of and behind the Moon. They were named for the pair of ravens the Norse god Odin supposedly had carried on his shoulders; each day they would circle the Earth, gathering news for their master. The habitats took a month to make the same journey.

When Lois finally resumed her explanation of the Orbitals' security problems, she said, "There's spying, of course. A few years ago, someone gave the Engineers the designs for the Q-drive. Now they're on the Moon, and I've heard they're trying to get a Q-ship working."

"I hope they don't get the tunnel-drive," said Pearl Angelica.

The pilot shook her head. "They'll have to invent that on their own. They can't steal it. Not even the Orbitals here have it, though everyone knows *we* do." She pointed to a blinking dot on one of the screens before her. "There's another ship out there." Her fingers moved over a keyboard, and lines of text appeared on the bottom of the screen. "It's heading for the Moon. From the Belt."

"An Engineer ship?"

"No. Probably just a metals shipment."

"You mean there's trade?"

"Of course. In fact, there's quite a lot of contact. You'll see."

"There's Earth." Pearl Angelica's voice was awed. The larger silver dot had become a distant marble, small and blue, marked with traceries of cloud. It looked much like First-Stop, but it was Earth, the world from which all her ancestors had come. The homeworld. Root-home.

"And the habitat." The ship rolled, and their destination was visible in the viewport. Munin was a double ziggurat or wedding cake, a broad disk from whose two faces rose two stacks of progressively smaller tiers. From each tier sprouted a forest of antennae and heat radiators. Here and there were silver-gleaming bubbles, plastic balloons attached to airlocks and inflated to provide extra room for storage, work, and living. Docking facilities were on the smallest of the tiers, around which all the rest turned to give the habitat's residents a sense of weight.

The *Quebec* cut its decelerating thrust while still two hundred meters away from the dock and its waiting clamps. As weight vanished, Pearl Angelica heard the Armadons in their pen, thrashing, banging, squealing. Their tranquilizer shots had worn off, but she only smiled and leaned toward the viewport. The genimals and their messes would soon be gone, no more concern of hers. Meanwhile, Earth swelled in the distance.

They drifted closer to the habitat. Pearl Angelica sighed her disappointment as a lampreylike docking tube blocked the view of Earth and fastened itself over the hatch. She shifted her gaze to one side, where the dock's clamps held the nose of another ship, a large, barrel-bodied craft with a single wide, triangular wing and, painted on its fuselage, a red cross surrounded by a golden cogwheel. "Is *that* an Engineer ship?" she asked.

Lois McAlois ignored her. The com was saying, "How's your reaction mass? Supplies? Crack your hatch now. We'll have unloaders in there right away. Quarters are ready. Folks are waiting. And that's a medship."

"They have a hospital here," said Lois finally. "The top Engineers come up when they need a cancer cured or a piece regrown."

"Nothing like a genefix," said the com. "Sounds like you've brought us a tourist. We'll show her around while you're busy."

"What will you be busy with?" asked the bot.

"I have to talk to their techs," said her aunt. "They'll have some new stuff we may be able to use, and I'll have to show them what we brought."

When they emerged from the docking tube, they found a broad, brightly painted chamber in which a number of humans and bots clung to taut lines that ran from wall to wall and from dock openings to the mouths of corridors leading deeper into the habitat. A bot with orange scalp blossoms and an elastic belt that kept her fronds from spreading propelled herself toward them with a smile, her hands shifting smoothly from line to line. "I'm Mary Thyme. Move over here." She made a face. "Your ship stinks."

"Those Armadons," said Pearl Angelica. She yawned. The habitat's air tasted of machine oil and human sweat and—less prominent, suggesting distance and transport on ventilator breezes—flowers, gardens, growing things. A hint of musk seemed to come from a cluster of brown animals that clung to several parallel rods mounted on the wall well away from any of the room's entrances or exits.

Lois grabbed a line and pulled herself toward the habitat's representative. Her niece tried to do the same but fumbled her grip and began to tumble in the air; Mary Thyme grabbed her ankle as she went past and drew her in. When Pearl Angelica had grabbed the line, the local bot patted at the scalelike leaves that covered her torso and said, "You're different."

"New model," said Lois. "One of a kind."

"Ah." A gesture sent several coveralled workers toward the ship. The bots among them were barefoot; the humans wore snug socks with thin, rubbery soles. A moment later, the first of the Armadons came sailing into the air of the chamber, its legs flailing, complaints issuing from its elongated snout, animal stench accompanying it. When a clot of dung flew from one wheel-rim, Pearl Angelica ducked. One of the creatures on the wall rack unfurled membranous wings, opened a wide mouth, swooped, and returned to its perch. "They're new," said Mary Thyme, pointing. "Flying litterbugs. Flitterbugs."

"I hope you can spare a few for me to take home," said Lois.

"Of course."

Near the far wall, four men with unforgiving faces scowled at the scene, and Pearl Angelica felt a twinge of apprehension. They were flanked by a man and a woman in white Orbital coveralls. They themselves wore loose, dark blue pants tight at waist and ankle, light blue shirts printed in black and gold with large cogwheels and springs and other mechanical imagery, and short lapelless jackets whose collars were curls of padded fabric. The jackets were green, lemon yellow, pink, grey, any color but blue. Two wore ankle boots; two wore sandals.

Mary Thyme noticed the direction of the bot's stare. "Engineers," she said. "We sell them Macks and bioform seawater filters, but they still don't like gengineering or genimals. It's not mechanical enough, even when they need it."

All the Armadons were now floundering in the air of the chamber and bouncing off the lines. One was drifting toward the Engineers, one of whom reached toward a pocket of his jacket. A scrawny dock worker promptly headed off the errant genimal and shoved it toward a corridor. Others pushed it further on.

"They'll have weight soon enough," said Mary Thyme. She was laughing silently. "And then . . . Maybe you'd take them out to Mars?"

Lois McAlois and Pearl Angelica simultaneously and violently shook their heads, and the habitat bot chuckled. "We can handle it. And here's the rest of your cargo." The smallest box of all came first. "The floppies. I hope Vosima has done something new." As the rest quickly followed, she peered at frosty labels. "Mossberries. First-Stop fish. What a treat! They'll go straight to the galleys."

"I'm sorry we can't bring more," said Lois. "But . . ."

"'S all right," said Mary Thyme. "You folks always say that, but we grow most of what we really need and get the rest from Earth." She looked at Pearl Angelica as if she knew that she were the one who needed information. Lois, after all, had been there before. "Though they won't give us anything with genes we don't already have, at least in a gene bank. They say they won't surrender their 'birthright,' as if it wasn't ours as well." Her eyes darted now toward the Engineers by the wall. "We pay with powersat energy, circuit chips, raw materials, medicine. They ask a lot."

"But you could grow everything you needed," said Pearl Angelica. Even the *Gypsy* could be self-sufficient, she knew. It had been so for the full five years of the voyage to Tau Ceti.

Mary Thyme looked toward the Engineers once more as she nodded. Her orange blossoms quivered to her motion. "We don't want to break the ties. Earth's a mudball and they can have it, but it's still the homeworld."

"Do they let you visit yet?" asked Lois McAlois.

"Uh-uh. We're banned. Humans too. They'll take the Macks, but we're worse than garbage in their eyes."

"But they need you more than you need them," said Pearl
Angelica. "Can't you insist on landing rights?"

Mary Thyme shook her head. "What do we have for an 'Or
else'? Turn off the powersats? Lock them out of the hospital?
We couldn't do that—or we wouldn't—and they know it."

Lois barked a laugh. "So the treaty favors them all the
way."

"Some of us think there must have been a sympathizer or
two on the negotiation team, but . . ." The other shrugged,
and when Pearl Angelica yawned once more, said, "You're
tired. Shall we go?"

"We get enough tourists from Earth," Mary Thyme was
saying the next day. "While the Chief Engineers are in our
treatment tanks, their aides and gofers want to see everything,
and we oblige. Their traders are the same way between deals.
And we get patients and traders from the rest of the system
too. Though we don't have to hold their hands."

"Have to?" asked Lois McAlois. Munin's corridors were
narrower and their lines were straighter than on the *Gypsy*.
They held little nonsentient greenery, which was concentrated in the habitat's agricultural levels. But they too held
doorways, in this area opening into apartments set aside
for visitors and the small restaurants and other businesses
that catered to the needs of transients. Lois, Pearl Angelica, and their guide were sitting at a small table in one of
the restaurants now, drinking coffee that had come from
the habitat's own gengineered plants, just as on the *Gypsy*.
Models of the first spacecraft to explore the solar system—
Sputnik, Viking, Voyager, Galileo, Magellan—hung from
the restaurant's ceiling, while the walls were covered with
the photos their cameras had sent back to Earth. "You just
don't trust the ones from Earth. I'll bet you work for Security."

Mary Thyme just grinned. "Would I admit such a thing?
Especially since here I am, sticking close to a couple of our
Gypsy friends from the interstellar depths. Why shouldn't we
trust *you?*"

"Is this the first time one of us has brought a passenger?
Maybe you're afraid we've been taken over by hidden Engineers, and . . ."

"They wouldn't send a bot," said Mary Thyme. "But I'm sure she isn't along just for the ride." She looked at Pearl Angelica, her eyebrows lifted inquiringly.

"I did need help with those Armadons."

"If I had known . . ." said Pearl Angelica.

"You'd have managed." Their guide's eyes were still on the Gypsy bot, patiently waiting for her to explain her presence.

"Bees," said Pearl Angelica. When the other's face turned puzzled, she added, "We don't have any, so we have to pollinate all our plants by hand." She mimed daubing with a brush. "And there aren't any suitable animals on First-Stop. I wanted to get some from Earth."

Mary Thyme looked doubtful. "We reproduce our plants by cloning."

"We do that too, but we need to pollinate the flowers if we want the fruits."

"Aren't you afraid of being stung?"

Pearl Angelica shrugged. "If that becomes a problem, I expect the gengineers will find time to make them stingless."

"Why not seedless fruits?"

"We have some."

"She wants to visit Earth too," said Lois, and her niece nodded.

Mary Thyme shook her head. "That's not possible. They never give permission for us to go down there. They come here."

"Can't we land anyway?"

"Their weapons are much better than when the *Gypsy* left," said Lois. "I wouldn't even want to try to land."

"Then we should ask." Pearl Angelica's voice held a slightly plaintive note. She had been warned of the ban, but still she hoped.

"It won't do any good. But . . ." Mary Thyme inspected the bottom of her empty cup. "If you're done, we can call them now."

The answer did not come for two more days. By then Mary Thyme and Pearl Angelica had confirmed that neither Munin nor Hugin nor any of the Earth-orbiting stations had bees. There were none on Mars, in the Belt, or at Saturn Base.

Nor did there happen to be a copy of the honeybee genome in any of the available gene banks, though there were hints that the bee's genes had been on file before the Engineers had seized Earth and destroyed so much biological technology.

They had seen the hospital and the tanks in which tailored viruses corrected the defects that turned cells cancerous and induced damaged hearts to heal and lost limbs to grow again. They had seen Munin's farms, its labs, its shops and theaters. And Lois McAlois had had several of her necessary meetings.

"It's like being inside an eyeball," said Pearl Angelica quietly. All three were standing on the inner surface of Munin's observation bubble, the largest of the plastic spheroids that bulged from the habitat's stepped hull, held there by the centrifugal force that substituted for gravity. Behind them a metal stairway rose toward the open door of an airlock that would automatically close if anything broke the bubble's thick skin. Around them was foggy translucency, a bowl quite large enough to hold a hundred people. Ahead of them the bubble's skin was clear, dimmed by the external silvering they had noticed from the *Quebec* but still offering a broad view of blackness and stars and, when Munin's rotation brought the gigantic pupil into position, the Earth itself, three-quarters full. Sharing the view with them were perhaps a dozen Orbitals, both coveralled humans and bots, as silent and as awestruck as they. A young boy, perhaps eight years old, stepped daringly onto apparent nothingness, spreading his arms as if he would fly to Earth or heaven. Half a dozen men stood near the stairs. They varied in the colors of their skins and in their heights, but all were slim, muscular, and hard-faced. They wore the pants and jackets of Engineers, and they watched not the view but the Gypsies. White-coveralled Security agents were not far away from them.

The sound of footsteps on the stairs drew Pearl Angelica's attention from the sight of an Earth that seemed to roll across the star-dusted sky. She saw a young woman in a pink coverall marked with black diagonals. She was carrying a small envelope, offering it to Mary Thyme, saying softly, "From their Division of Trade," and turning to go.

The ripping of the envelope was loud in the bubble's hush. Mary Thyme withdrew a single sheet of paper, read it quickly, and held it toward Pearl Angelica. Its few lines of print were stark against the white paper, and no less stark in their import:

"We regret that we cannot fill your request for a colony of honeybees. Policy insists that this portion of the human birthright belongs to Earth alone.

"We also regret that we cannot permit synthetic biological intelligences to visit Earth. Policy insists that Earth remain uncontaminated by unnatural beings."

"Litter!" said Pearl Angelica.

"But how did they know you were a bot?" asked Lois McAlois.

"They may have assumed it," said Mary Thyme. "Or maybe they think we're all unnatural. Certainly they never have given permission for one of us to go down there."

"Or someone told them," said Pearl Angelica. "There are enough Engineers up here." She scowled meaningfully toward the stairs.

"That's possible," said their guide. After a moment, she added, "I'd like to see it too. We have the spysat photos, but it's not the same."

"It's changed a lot since we left," said Lois. "There used to be twelve billion people on that planet. Now there's . . . what?"

"Maybe two."

"What happened?" asked Pearl Angelica.

"They destroyed the only technology that could feed so many."

"Now the forests are coming back," said Mary Thyme. "The fallout's gone from the air and water."

"It must have done some damage while it was there," said Lois.

Their guide pursed her lips and turned toward the observation bubble's pupil. As she spoke, several of the bubble's other visitors drifted closer. "DNA damage. We see it in the hospital. More cancer. Birth defects. And we know it's affected plants and animals too, especially those that breed rapidly and have had many generations to sort out the lethals. We actually see a few new features in the food they ship us, though nothing major. There must be so much more down there . . ." She shook her head ruefully. "The gengineers would love to be able to study them."

"It wouldn't take long to get the bees," said Pearl Angelica. "Or to taste—"

"No," said Lois with an abrupt shake of her head. "I can't risk the ship, or you."

"My 'potential,' you mean."

"That's what would bother the bots. Losing *you* would bother me and Renny." Lois didn't mention Frederick, Pearl Angelica's father, but she did sigh deeply before she added, "I'll be done in a few more days. We can go home then."

"But we have to try . . . !"

"Excuse me." Pearl Angelica turned and saw that the speaker was one of the Engineers who had been standing near the stairs. His companions were pushing forward beside him, edging the Orbital listeners aside. Their complexions, it suddenly struck her, were not merely rough but pocked and scarred by past infections. The marks spoke eloquently of an environment far less sheltered than the Orbitals' habitats or the *Gypsy*.

"I couldn't help but hear," the Engineer went on. "You want to visit Earth?"

Pearl Angelica nodded eagerly. "Yes! But . . ." She held up the message that had barred her from the world below.

The Engineer did not even try to read what was written on the paper before he snorted contemptuously. "We might be able to help."

"Really?" The Gypsy bot took a step toward him.

"No!" said Lois McAlois and Mary Thyme together. "You can't—"

"Of course she can," said the Engineer. He grasped her wrist and tugged. "Just come with us."

"Remember!" cried Mary Thyme. "They hate bots!"

"But I want—"

Lois seized Pearl Angelica's other arm, and for a moment the bot was stretched between the two opposing forces. But then one of the other Engineers drew a cylindrical object from a pocket and pressed a button. A parsley-scented mist engulfed both women.

Pearl Angelica gasped as she saw Mary Thyme recoil and her aunt collapse upon the floor. In the edges of her vision she glimpsed white coveralls falling too. Then her own muscles weakened and her world grew dim, faded out, went black. She knew nothing of Orbitals being hurled aside, of a child's arm snapping, of screams and shouts, of herself being seized, thrown over a shoulder, and carried at a run from the bubble.

Chapter
Five

THE FOREST'S EDGES, like those of forests everywhere, on Earth as it was on First-Stop, were crowded so thickly with small bushes and saplings that anyone who approached from open ground might be pardoned for believing the forest choked with underbrush, pathless and impenetrable. But if one pushed through the vines and stems and brambles just a little past the border zone, one found a surface deep with half-decayed organic matter, darkened by the dense canopy held high overhead by massive trunks, bare of all undergrowth except for the most shade-tolerant of small plants. Here there were paths indeed, the widest of them trodden by the local sentients, the Racs.

Many of these footpaths converged where the ground sloped gently toward the steep dropoff at the edge of the bluff. Here the underbrush had been cleared away to provide a vantage point, a vista of moss-covered valley floor, of that tree the visitors to their world, the Gypsies, had grown to dwarf the largest in any forest any Rac now living would ever see and now were carving, petrifying, and polishing into a Tower that would last for ages, of the orange dwellings they had grown for themselves, of the paths the feet of their giant animals had worn through the valley's carpet of moss, of the blackened ground upon which landed the vessels in which they journeyed to and from the sky.

In the center of the clearing, a ring of stones surrounded a bed of ashes from which a wisp of smoke arose. Back a bit, among the trees, was the scatter of small domes, framed with bent saplings and covered with slabs of bark, leaf thatch, and hides, in which the Racs lived.

One of the huts was new, the leaves upon its roof still green. Before it sat the three visitors to the village, each one wearing across his rotund abdomen the belt and shoulder strap that supported tools and pouches. The one named Wanderer occupied a rounded boulder and was still and watchful. The other two sat cross-legged on bare dirt beside him, their tails twitching restlessly behind them. Shorttail was scraping a piece of rock the length of a straight stick as long as he was tall. Stonerapper was turning a small rock over and over in his hands, perhaps thinking of how best to chip a point for the spearshaft being shaped beside him.

The local, tailless Racs squatted on the bare ground between their huts and their communal firepit, facing the edge of the bluff and the one who stood there, arms stretched to either side, silhouetted against the dimming evening sky. From their angle, they could see both the long-shadowed Tower and the arc of stone that opened toward it, the watching place whose building Blacktop had urged upon them.

No one was speaking. All were listening, to the sough of breeze in the canopy overhead, to the creak of branches, to the scuffles and squeals and chatters of their wild kin in the forest, to the clangs and rumbles of tools in the valley below. They were waiting, waiting for what would someday be recorded as the first sermon to be delivered on this world.

Blacktop slowly bent both his arms, bringing his hands toward his face. With sweeping, exaggerated movements, he scratched his muzzle, first on one side, then on the other. Each member of his tribe returned the gesture. A moment later, the visitors did likewise.

In one of the Rac huts, a pot toppled and shattered. The sound turned heads, and all saw the creature that scampered, striped tail defiantly erect, into the deeper shadows. Stonerapper stood and hurled his rock. There was a yelp of pain. Someone made a sound of complaint and exasperation. Someone else produced the teeth-baring snort that was Rac laughter.

When the tribe turned back toward Blacktop, he was pointing over their heads, toward the trees that now concealed the mischief-maker. He spoke in a voice as coarse as gravel, as roughly rasping, as reassuring as a sandbar beneath a swimmer's feet: "I hear the voices of our grandmothers and grandfathers. They are as they have always been, small and handless, speechless, often hungry. We are different."

After a moment of silence, he repeated himself: "We are different. We have been changed by our world's visitors from the sky." He turned to indicate the Tower and those who had made it. "They gave us speech and hands and minds with which to use them. They gave us destiny.

"They gave us knowledge too. First they taught us the secrets of shelter and fire, spear and basket, knife and pot."

His voice rose in pitch and volume and grew smoother, almost melodic, in emphasis. He held a clenched fist aloft. "What is second?"

No one answered, though they stirred before him.

He answered his own question, speaking more quietly. "The Tower. They give us the Tower, and they tell us that there is so much more to learn, an endless forest of secrets."

One member of his audience stood erect, a stone-tipped spear in one hand. His fur was pale, almost white, and the dark lines that patterned the pelts of so many others were in him broken into trails of dots. "I am Pathways," he said, and his voice quickly lost its initial roughness as anger crept into his words. "It is no secret that they know more secrets than we do. Look!" He held his spear above his head and shook it. "This is the strongest weapon that we have. But to them it is weak, a mere pointed stick, little better than a rock to hurl. What do *they* have? Why do they not teach us how to make greater weapons?" He spat, and his voice was suddenly smooth again. "They fear us. They know that if they make us equal to them, we will destroy them. We will expel them from our world. We will even surpass them as we have surpassed our wild cousins."

Blacktop's sigh was a gust of wind, a theatrical gesture of body and arm designed to reach every Rac gathered in the shadows before him. "I, for one," he said. "I have no wish to destroy them or expel them or shame them. They have done us nothing but good. They have made us. They have raised us above those cousins. They have taught us . . ."

"But they have not taught us everything!" The voice was desperately silky.

"No more than we teach our cubs everything. Some things they must learn for themselves."

"Are we then cubs?" cried Pathways.

"Of course we are. We are a new people. We have existed for only a few years, and already we have secrets it took our Gypsy friends thousands upon thousands of years to learn."

"But we need more if we—"

Leaf's voice rose above the others: "We must defend the Tower, keep it ours." She was looking not toward Blacktop but toward the shadows under the trees, where the strangers sat. "Sticks and stones are not enough."

Blacktop shook his head. "They are right," he said. "They are right when they say we are not yet ready for all those secrets that will let us be like them. We must earn them."

"How?" said a rough voice from the shadows.

"We must find secrets of our own. By ourselves, without the help of others, we must learn how to find secrets, and how to use them." Blacktop's voice was now as roughly calm as the other's. "Then we must find those secrets that will let us climb the Tower and reach the treasures, the secrets of our Makers, at its tip."

Voices murmured from his audience: "How can we do that?" "Only flying beasts and wind can go that high." "Will they leave us their Bioblimps?" "It cannot be climbed."

"Surely they will take their flying beasts away with them," said Blacktop. "This task, they say, is ours. We must learn to fly, or to build a tower of our own that we can climb."

"But how?" "We cannot!"

"They can," said Blacktop. "And they had no teachers, no Tower to draw them on. They learned their own ways, and they say that we can do the same.

"And I believe them. The day will come when we will reach the treasure they have left us. We will gain their secrets. We will learn how they made us and how they travel in the sky. We will be able to make Bioblimps of our own, and more."

"How long?" Pathways slumped where he stood. "How long will it take us? How long will it be before we too can visit the stars?"

"Many years, many generations, more time than we can yet imagine. But the day *will* come, and then we too will be gods."

"Gods?" said someone, voice smooth with anxiety. Blacktop, whom they would soon call their priest, had mentioned gods before, but the concept was still new and strange. "What are gods?"

Blacktop turned away to stare out over the valley. The sky was darker now. Shadows were merging into dusk, the sounds of labor falling quiet. In a moment, he drew a stone knife from the belt around his waist and stepped toward the border of the clearing. In silence, he chose a sapling as thick as two of his fingers, cut it near the ground, trimmed away its branches and its top to leave a stick somewhat less than two meters long, and carried the result back to his position before the tribe.

"Gods," he said then. "They know what they are. Their library, there . . ." He pointed with the stick toward the Tower's base. "It is full of knowledge of many things, even of gods. And I have been there. I have read. I have learned, and they have made no attempt to stop me."

"Then they believe in sharing all they know." That smooth voice was Wanderer's.

"No!" Leaf was leaping to her feet. "The Tower is ours!"

"Sit down." Blacktop thumped his stick on the ground. "Yes. They freely share. Yet they do not fetch it to us as we fetch food for infants. What they have is ours, but only if we exert ourselves to reach it." He pointed with the stick once more. "To climb the Tower. To learn to read. To search through that library."

His knife was still in his hand. Now he lowered his stick and began to remove its bark. "Gods. Even when they dwell on a mountaintop, in a sea, or in the sky, they know everything, all secrets, all that happens everywhere. They live forever, and they can make bushes burn and never be consumed. They can make water flow from rock and food fall from the sky. They can pile up stones to make a mountain, or rain stones and fire upon those who defy the rules they set. They make worlds and fill them with trees, beasts, and people."

A sigh swept through the Racs who squatted before him. "Ahh," they said.

One added, "And how must we treat such beings?"

"We must obey the laws these Makers give us," said Blacktop. "We must hold them high and worship them and find ways to glorify them." He paused in his peeling of his stick, staring down at the curls of bark that were accumulating at his feet, hesitating as if he had seen or thought of something he did not like.

"The Gypsies have many gods themselves," he finally said. "Some of them demand blood, the deaths of children and young females and captives from other tribes." When a smooth and angry tone rose from his audience, he added, "Others ask only that fruits and flowers be piled at their feet. We will have to learn what offerings please our gods best.

"If we succeed," he went on. "If we succeed, if we glorify our gods in the ways they wish, then when we die we will journey into the sky. We will be with our gods forevermore among the stars."

"One lifetime until we join our Makers in the sky, then," said a voice. "Not many lifetimes."

"And if we do not?" Pathways sounded angry, skeptical.

"If we do not, then when we die, we will be punished." Blacktop removed the last bit of bark from his stick and set his knife aside. Quite unceremoniously, he then gathered up the shreds and curls of bark and tossed them onto the coals in the firepit. Smoke thickened and billowed. Small flames appeared, and then the mass of bark was crackling. "An age of agony," he said quietly. "An age of fire and torment will be ours. And only if our gods are kind and merciful will they ever lift us from that punishment. Then, perhaps, they will return us to life and give us another chance to obey their laws."

The silence that followed was broken only when Wanderer asked, "But what are their laws?"

Blacktop looked as if the question made him uncomfortable, but he answered without delay: "They have given us only one law, to learn, to climb the Tower."

"Will we all be punished then, if we cannot climb the Tower?"

He shook his head. "Surely we will be in obedience to the gods as long as we pursue the goal they have set us. We know them now . . ." He turned toward the valley, set one end of his stick on a patch of earth, and leaned upon it. It sank into the soil, and when he let go it stood alone, its tip oscillating back and forth. "They are not cruel, not so cruel as to punish all the many generations that must pass before the Tower's treasure is finally within our reach."

"Are there truly no other laws?"

"They have given us no others. But I have learned . . ." It was now too dark to see anything in the valley except the shaft of the Tower, but that was enough. He pointed toward the library near the Tower's base. "Their gods have given many more to them, and some seem suitable for us."

No one said a word as a young Rac stirred the ashes in the firepit, heaped glowing coals together, and added small branches. Flames licked at the air and lighted the faces that looked toward Blacktop. Red-orange glints danced in unblinking eyes, and lips seemed to flicker.

His back remained toward them, but he still seemed to hear their silent demand that he continue. "Do not kill," he said musingly. "They eat meat, though, so that must mean do not kill other sentients. Do not lie or steal or envy what others have. Honor your forebears. Worship no other gods. Treat others as you wish them to treat you."

"And which," asked Pathways. "Which is the most important? The last, that says it all?"

"None of those," said Blacktop. "For *our* gods have urged none of them upon us."

"What then?"

"Just this: learning. The pursuit of secrets. The pursuit of the Tower. We will have proved our virtue when we have climbed it and made all its knowledge ours."

After a moment's pause, he asked, "Does someone have a gourd?"

"A melon?" A hand held one above the heads before him.

"That will do nicely." He accepted the offering and retrieved his stone knife from the ground where he had set it. As soon as he had scooped two holes through the melon's warty rind, one on either side, he impaled its base on the tip of the stick he had planted in the soil.

"There," he said.

"What is it?" asked Pathways impatiently.

"The Tower," said Blacktop, indicating the shaft of the stick. "The treasure house atop it, its doors standing wide and waiting only for our perseverance and success in finding secrets that will lead us to them. And within . . ." He reached through one of the openings he had carved, groped, and withdrew a fistful of melon flesh. He held it before the tribe, melon juice dripping from his hand and soaking the fur of his arm.

Then he put the sticky mass in his mouth. He chewed and worked his lips, and in a moment he spat into the palm of his hand.

"Within it," he said at last. "The seeds of greatness, of godhood, that we must gain."

The brilliant variegations of Caledonia Emerald's scalp blossoms were invisible in the gloom of the chamber where she leaned intently over a veedo monitor. It showed the view from one of the many tiny low-light cameras hidden in the trees around the clearing: Blacktop, his seed-covered palm held out, open, inviting, welcoming, promising. "Fascinating," she said. "He has the actor's gift, doesn't he? But not everyone there's as open-minded as he is. That Leaf . . ."

"We're on our way," said Lucas Ribbentrop, whose shock of white hair was the most visible nonelectronic item in the room. It was even more visible in better lighting, which also revealed just how young its owner really was. "We're gonna be gods." One dark hand flipped a selector switch, and the screen before him showed the stone watching place in the valley. "The church." He flipped the switch again and zoomed in upon the stick and melon. "The central icon, the idol." He pointed at his partner's monitor. "The high priest." When the bot indicated Leaf, he added, "And the crusader."

"I wish Pearl Angelica was here to see this," said Caledonia Emerald. "And I wonder what the higher-ups'll say when they find out."

"They'll be surprised."

"Not at being gods. Religion is just too easy to invent. But the doctrine?"

Chapter
Six

THE FIRST THING to enter Pearl Angelica's awareness was pain: It screamed behind her forehead, ululating in time with her pulse, rising, falling. It whined from her wrists, where something thin and tight held her hands together. It lurked at her ankles, where cold metal ringed her flesh. It cramped her calves.

The second was sound: A roar that reminded her of a Q-ship lifting into space, trembling the air but without the sense of thrust, the pressure against a seatback. She was lying on her side, and the pressure against her skin felt like normal weight. Engines, then, vibrating some metal shell around her, pushing her through air or water.

"Think they'll buy it?" said a rough male voice.

"They'd better," said a second. "Or we'll . . ."

The first voice laughed. "Just give her to me."

"She's coming to," said a woman.

Am I? Pearl Angelica asked herself painfully. Her awareness *was* returning. She could hear. Whatever pressed against her cheek, she now could tell, was smooth, cool, soft. There were odors, soap and sweat, floral perfume, stale food, hydrocarbon fuel.

She supposed she was coming to, or she wouldn't hurt so much. The headache was the worst. She grunted as she recalled being seized and tugged and finally the spray of aerosol that had ended all resistance. She was awake. Lois would be too, and any others the gas had overcome. She winced at the thought that Lois must be sharing her pain. She hoped her aunt had suffered nothing worse.

A hand rocked her shoulder and tipped her face into a flood of light. She grimaced. "Pull the shade there, 'Livrance," said the woman. There was the rasp of plastic against plastic, the light dimmed, and then she said to their prisoner: "You can open your eyes now."

Pearl Angelica obeyed. She was sprawled on a leather-covered sofa in a cylinder less than half the size of the *Quebec*'s cargo hold. To each side the walls were pierced by oval windows in a pattern that she recognized from old veedos: She was in an airplane. The nearest window was covered by a sliding shutter; beside it half-crouched a non-descript man of middle height and roundish face. His skin was dark, his hair was a pelt of tight curls, and he might have been in his thirties. The pattern on his shirt was one of keys and open padlocks. 'Livrance. Deliverance? She wished it were true.

The other two stood beside the sofa, their heads bent beneath the low ceiling. The woman's skin was lighter, sal-low, tight across her cheekbones and around her mouth. Her hair was straight and black, and her eyelids folded orientally. The other man had light brown skin, heavy bars for eyebrows and mustache, a prominent nose. He was looking at her as if she were already his to do with as he wished. She did not think she would enjoy his wishes. She closed her eyes again.

A hand smashed her cheek and rocked her head. "Look at us!"

"Take it easy, Hamid," said the woman. "She's still groggy."

The bot moaned and blinked and stared. Hamid and the woman were younger than she, in their late twenties. They had not yet been born when the Engineers had seized Earth. All three of her captors wore the pants and shirts and jackets she had seen on the Munin habitat. Their eyes were dark, brown or black, fixed on her as if she were less even than vermin, an object to be exploited, a mess to be wiped away as soon as they could find a rag.

She struggled to sit up. Brusque hands swept her legs off the sofa's cushions. Metal rattled almost musically and drew her eyes to her feet. A chain linked the cuffs on her ankles to each other and . . . Cloth tightly wrapped her lower legs, hiding her roots. She would not be able to run, even if she got the chance. Nor would she be able to taste whatever soil they let her near. Earth's? Was that the sky through which they flew? She glanced at her wrists, where thin cords were buried in her flesh. She worked her mouth, which was dry and tasted foul. "Engineers," she said.

"That's right," said the woman. A metal chain ran around her neck and inside the front of her shirt. "I'm Prudence."

"What . . . ?"

'Livrance snorted contemptuously. "That depends on your friends."

Pearl Angelica did not ask why they had kidnapped her. As groggy as she still was, as much in pain, she thought it clear that they wanted something. They were holding her for ransom, and if the Orbitals and Gypsies refused to pay, she would never return to First-Stop, her friends, her father, the Racs. She moaned.

"We've changed, you know," said Prudence. "It's been more than thirty years since we got rid of your sort."

"And we don't want you now, genny," said 'Livrance.

"We use Macks now," said Hamid. He was staring at her breasts, and her leaves suddenly seemed much less than an adequate covering. She wished she had the long fronds of her kin, a coverall, even a blanket.

"Only because we don't have enough fuel for trucks," said the other man.

"And we have Sponges to get metals from seawater," Hamid glared at his fellow. He seemed to be trying to convince her that the Engineers had changed so much that they were no longer any threat at all.

"We use what we must of the old technology," said Prudence. She made a face. "As long as we must."

"But not for long," said 'Livrance.

"I could use *her*," said Hamid.

Pearl Angelica wished she dared to shake her head, but her headache was still throbbing. The airplane tipped, banking onto a new course, and through the windows on one side she could see roads and buildings, fields and forests and small lakes, far below them. A vaster body of water—but still a lake and not a sea; a far side was visible, and on it the distinctive outlines of many buildings—was visible to one side. When she tried to move her feet much more than the distance between the sofa cushion and the floor, she found that her hobble was chained to a leg of the sofa.

The attachment seemed so solid that she was sure the sofa was bolted to the floor.

She bent to touch the wrappings that concealed her roots. Even though her fingers were numb from loss of circulation, the fabric felt rubbery, as if it were that of ordinary elastic bandages. "Why . . . ?"

"They're obscene," said Hamid. "So we cover them."

"Too tight," she said, and her fingers moved awkwardly, sought an edge, began to pluck.

"Leave them alone," said 'Livrance.

She grunted and leaned back. They had changed, had they? Perhaps they didn't slaughter bots anymore, but then they didn't have them to slaughter, except for her. And when their demand for ransom was refused . . . They used genimals because they had to, not because they were really any more tolerant than they had been. And they looked forward to needing the genimals not at all. Through the haze of pain, she wondered how they would manage that.

The plane leveled out of its bank and began to tilt its nose down. The floor tipped away from her, and she felt as if she were perched precariously at the edge of a cliff, or perhaps on one of the bluffs that ringed the valley on First-Stop. A voice issued from a grille in the ceiling overhead: "Take your seats, please. We will be landing shortly."

Grinning, Hamid leaned over Pearl Angelica to pull the ends of a seatbelt from among the sofa's cushions. He buckled it around her waist and drew it tight, but then his hands did not leave her. They pinched and poked and bent her scalelike leaves aside to expose her skin. She tried to block his hands with her arms, but he only seized her biceps with one hand, squeezing cruelly while the other kept on with its insults. He stopped only when Prudence said, "That's enough, Hamid. Sit down and fasten your own seatbelt."

She rubbed at the lines still embedded in the skin of her wrists, at the bruise on her upper arm. She paced restlessly, enjoying as much as she could the freedom of being able to use feet that were not chained and hobbled. She scowled at the grey and greasy soup that filled the bowl on the narrow shelf built into the concrete wall at chest height. It had come to her over an hour before, and it had been tepid then. Now it was cold, the grease congealed into floating plaques.

She stared at the door of her cell. It was a massive sheet of rusty steel. Beneath a grilled window was the narrow hatch that had admitted the soup and a slice of stale, dark bread. Around its edges was a gap barely wide enough for a fingernail. A heavy metal plate covered what she thought must be the lock.

She sat on the thin mattress of her bed, spread upon a broader, lower concrete shelf, wondering if she would be here long enough for cold, greasy soup to seem appetizing. There was no window to the outside, not this far underground. The only light came from a small fluorescent fixture in the ceiling, covered by a heavy screen. What came through the grille in the door was too dim to count.

She stared at the filthy porcelain of the lidless toilet and the tiny sink with its single dripping tap, at the walls, marked with water stains, graffiti both faded and fresh, and splotches of . . . what? Soup that other prisoners had rejected? Or . . . ? She bit her lip and looked at the floor, where the long elastic bandages that had wrapped her lower limbs lay tangled. Elastic, she thought. No wonder they had hurt. But now her roots, at least, were free.

As if in response to her thought, they writhed in the air, as prehensile as fingers or tentacles. Would they ever touch Earth's soil? Would they even taste the dirt of Munin again, or the *Gypsy,* or First-Stop?

She wished she knew how far below the surface the Engineers had hidden her. There was a hint of salt in the air, as if her tiny cell were hidden in the bowels of some abandoned salt-mine cavern. Perhaps, she thought, that accounted for the rustiness of her door.

She wished there were some soil within her reach, just a little, just enough to fill her soupbowl, if only it were soil of Earth. She would eat the soup then, even that foul stuff, just as she had eaten the dry bread, and fill the bowl with the dirt. Then she would set the dish on the floor, and . . .

The plane had bounced twice when it touched the ground, and then its wheels had settled into a chattering report on the runway's ruts and potholes and general lack of both pavement and maintenance. A glass and concrete terminal had come into view as they slowed, but the plane had turned away from it and toward a hangar some distance to one side. Beside the hangar had waited a squad of men of a sort the bot recognized from old veedos she had seen. They carried short-snouted automatic weapons. With them were a long-bedded truck with a rack of ground-to-air missiles elevated to launching position and an armored personnel carrier with a heavy machine gun mounted in a turret on its roof. The men wore blue coveralls decorated with golden cogwheel patches. The trucks were painted olive drab. Nearby stood a boxy black automobile whose windows were tinted so dark that the interior was invisible.

"Detroit," Prudence had said. "It's the capital now."

Of course, thought Pearl Angelica. Just as it had been the capital of the twentieth century's Machine Age, though government had then been centered elsewhere.

She sat still when Hamid, one hand on her thigh, unfastened the chain and seatbelt that held her to the sofa. Her headache was beginning to fade at last, and she felt as if she might be able to struggle. But there was no point, she knew. She could not escape, and if she did, she had no way to leave the planet, to return to Munin or to First-Stop. She could not even be rescued; that was what the soldiers and their weapons were there to prevent. Her aunt would have to leave without her, and her father . . . Tears filled her eyes as she thought that he might finally die before she could see him again.

"Let's go." 'Livrance's hand on her shoulder pulled her to her feet and pushed her toward the plane's exit.

Moments later, she was in the back seat of the car, pressed between the two men, cringing at the insistent probes of Hamid's fingers, sighing with relief when 'Livrance said, "Hamid!" Prudence was in front, beside a uniformed driver who spoke no word to any of them as he started the nearly silent engine, pushed buttons that locked the doors with audible clicks, and rolled his vehicle past the soldiers, through a gate, and onto a patchily paved roadway.

At first the road was flanked by broad strips of empty ground. Trees and brush had been removed for a hundred meters to either side as if the Engineers feared that enemies might hide within it and leap out in ambush. But Earth's soil was there, visible wherever grass and weeds did not grow, and she yearned. If only . . . But she was a prisoner, her roots

as bound as her hands, and not even the odors of Earth's soil
could reach her within the sealed car.

As they neared the city, the cleared strip filled in, first with
the honeysuckle-cloaked rubble of one-time homes and shops
and offices, charred beams jutting into the air as remind-
ers of . . . She wondered how much had been ruined by the
Engineers themselves when they seized power so many years
before, how much was the result of the pounding the Engineers had taken from space as the bots and gengineers had
fled the planet. The Orbitals had used chunks of lunar rock
to smash missiles and launchpads, airports and factories.

Then the rubble was cleared away in patches to reveal bare
ground planted with crops. She recognized the brilliant green
and tall stems of corn, the bluish green of cabbage. A field of
what looked at first like tomato plants puzzled her, however.
These plants bore clusters of yellow oblongs she had never
seen before. Were they some leftover from the time of the
gengineers? Or were they some strange mutation?

Newer buildings came into view, two and three stories tall,
built of masonry, much of it bearing the smokestains and
fragments of ancient mortar that said it had been reclaimed
from the rubble piles. And then there was a tall framework
of what looked like steel tubes over which crawled what must
have been several hundred small machines. Each one trailed a
flexible strand; some of the openings in the framework were
already filled with translucent webbing.

The car pulled to the side of the road, and Hamid said, "See
those Spiders? We're not so backward, you know. We've
made a lot of progress with artificial intelligence. Before
long, we'll even be able to make von Neumann machines."

"An old idea," said 'Livrance. "Machines that make copies
of themselves. Tell them what to do, turn them loose, and
wait. They'll build anything you like."

"We don't have the people," said Prudence. "But those
things are already rebuilding the cities for us."

Pearl Angelica let her gaze descend to street level, where
a dozen sweaty, dirty humans shoveled rubble into the maw
of a machine that apparently generated the substance of the
web. Other workers emptied plastic drums from the open
cargo pod of a Mack truck. In the street itself, she could
see several massive wads of Mack waste, and she realized

that she had not yet seen a litterbug.

"We've got all the energy we need," said Hamid. "Hydro, wind, even nuclear."

"And powersats," said 'Livrance.

Hamid grunted as if he hated to admit how much the Engineers depended on the Orbitals. "They're lucky we buy their power," he said. "They'd starve if—"

"We just need better batteries," interrupted the woman. "Or fuel cells. Something compact and portable." She gestured, and the car resumed its journey.

"That's where we're going," said 'Livrance. He was pointing to the right, toward a multistoried edifice whose sides reflected the sky wherever the glass its long-gone builders had used to sheathe it was intact. Large areas, long vertical triangles the shape of shards, were filled in with the flat sheen of the Spiders' weavings.

When they reached the building, however, Pearl Angelica learned that the building itself was not their goal. It was surrounded by a broad plaza dotted with shrubs and small trees in concrete planters, benches, and fountains. Flowers surrounded a sign that said "Government Center" in large, ornate letters. But the building's broad doors were blocked by stone curbs and metal railings.

The plaza's traffic was a mix of human and machine, of men—women were hardly to be seen at all—and knee-high robots that scurried among the swinging legs. Everyone and everything flowed purposefully toward and away from a single cavernous stairwell that led deep beneath the surface. It seemed clear to the prisoner that the Engineers feared another war with space and had gone underground in search of safety.

The people in the plaza showed their pained awareness of the small procession—a bot in chains, her three captors leading her toward the lip of the stairwell, the men's hands on her elbows propelling her onward whenever her hobbled legs could not match the pace they set—in the way they elaborately ignored it. They fell quiet. They turned their eyes toward the empty building that dominated the plaza. They bent their paths away as if afraid to get too close.

By the time Pearl Angelica and her captors reached the staircase, they had it almost entirely to themselves except for

the machines which, caring nothing for who or what they
were, concentrated on the tricky task of clambering from
step to step. Half carrying the bot, Hamid and 'Livrance
rushed her down the stairs, Prudence following close upon
their heels. Three flights of steps below the surface, the bot
noted heavy doors poised to swing closed upon command,
hydraulic cylinders as thick as her torso visible in the shadows behind them. One more flight, and a low-ceilinged foyer,
its concrete bare of signs or graffiti, held the doors of several
elevators.

When the elevator had finally stopped, Pearl Angelica had
been only seconds from the cell she now occupied.

"You've heard that we were doomed," said Prudence. "That
the resources we needed for a new Machine Age simply were
no longer there. No metals. No fuels."

Pearl Angelica nodded. The cuffs that had bound her
ankles were now on her wrists, with lengths of chain,
leashes, linking her to 'Livrance and Hamid. But they were
outdoors now, standing on the plaza beneath racing clouds,
and even this much freedom from her prison was enough to
lift her spirits.

Yet her roots were bound once more, and her legs ached.
When her captors had finally come for her, they had scowled
to see the wrappings on the floor. 'Livrance had held her
while Hamid had wound them back in place. Only when
the man's hands had begun to wander further up her legs
than necessary had the darker man released her. She had
tried to kick Hamid then, but he had only stepped aside and
laughed.

"But the metals were still there," said Prudence. "We just
had to dig them out of the dumps. And the fuels . . ." She
shrugged fatalistically. "There were a lot of deaths . . ."

"Eighty-five percent," said the bot. Before the Engineers'
revolution the world population had been over twelve billion
people. Afterward, the total had been less than two billion.

"It cut the need," said 'Livrance. "It made success possible."

The men tugged at her chains and led her to one side of
the empty building, that monument to another age, to the
edge of the plaza, where a raised walkway and a stone wall,

waist-high, waited for them. Here and there, honeysuckle leaves and blossoms peeked above the wall's edge, signs that the vines climbed the wall from whatever lay beyond.

From any distance, nothing seemed to lie past the plaza's border. The air was empty, no buildings, no trees, nothing. But by the time the men stopped her beside the wall, Pearl Angelica could see a drop of five meters or so, a broad river, its waters stained with oily sheens and floating rubbish, and a bank which, though it was choked with honeysuckle, still showed signs of streets and fallen buildings. One wider avenue, kept bare of the vines, stretched toward a single wharf from that part of the city south of the plaza. The green-draped, blossom-speckled ruins and the river they bordered stretched out of sight to right and left. Occasionally, the vines trembled as if something moved beneath them. Animals? she wondered. Or honey bums?

She blinked away the wetness that the honeysuckle, unex-pected reminder of the *Gypsy,* brought to her eyes. The soil of Earth was there too, just beyond her reach as long as her captors kept her on the rocky surfaces of plaza pavements and tunnel floors. So was the honeysuckle, the honeysuckle net that no one here on Earth could possibly use. She imagined tapping into it with her roots and finding it empty, echoing, a nervous system without tenant except for herself, without thoughts except her own, inquiring, yearning.

She shuddered wordlessly.

"That used to be slums," said Prudence. "Warehouses, docks, factories. The Greenhouse Effect meant more rain, greater flow in the river, more frequent floods. With fewer people, we could afford to abandon the land and let nature take its course."

"Can we go down there?" the bot asked. "I need . . . Dirt. Earth. My roots . . ."

Prudence shook her head. 'Livrance jerked the chain to her left wrist. When she cried out at the sudden pain, he said, "No. It took us too long to scrub your kind from our world. We kept finding small groups of bots for years."

Hamid laughed. "Unnatural monsters," he said, though the look he gave her did not say he thought her monstrous. "We had to destroy them. And they were saboteurs and spies too. They poisoned farms, attacked labor camps."

She had known that only a few had managed to escape the planet. She had thought that all the rest had died before and during the final upheaval. Yet, she told herself, she should not be surprised that a few had survived for a while. A planet was a large place.

She felt a sudden rush of pride: Her kin, fighting back despite all loss of hope. Doing what damage they could even as they died. Never surrendering, knowing that if they did they would only be slaughtered. One with all the resistance fighters of human history. Indeed, human themselves, as human in spirit if not in body as any Engineer.

"We're being nice to you," said Prudence. "But we can't take any chance that you might drop some seeds. You'll stay on pavement."

"Then why did you kidnap me?" she finally asked. She did not try to tell him that she was too human to reproduce by seeds like other bots. "If you don't want bots on Earth, why did you bring me here?"

"You came to us," answered 'Livrance. "You asked for bees." He laughed briefly, his tone condescending. "That's not much, but it's the first thing your kind has wanted of us."

She was puzzled, and she let it show. "You trade with the Orbitals."

"Only those in the habitats," said Prudence. "Your group went to the stars."

"And if you're asking us for anything at all," said Hamid, "even if it's only bees, that's a sign that you've made a mistake."

"We'll exhibit you," said Prudence. "We'll show you to our people as a sign . . ."

"A sign that *we* made no mistake when we got rid of you," said 'Livrance. "That the future is ours, not yours."

"Then you won't ask for any ransom?"

"Of course we will," said Prudence. "We've got your Q-drive already. But you've got a star-drive, a way to travel faster than light. We want that too."

That had been the end of the buoyancy that had come to Pearl Angelica when she had left her cell and seen the sky once more. It had also been the end of her freedom, for 'Livrance and Hamid had almost immediately tightened their grip on her chains and pulled her from the plaza's edge, from the view of river and trees and honeysuckle, back to the stairwell, back to the depths of the Engineers' underground fortress, back to her cell.

Now she sat on her sleeping shelf, staring at the elastic bandages that had compressed her roots against her skin. They twisted in her hands, just as her roots writhed in the air, stretching as if they sought the soil that was nowhere near.

She had just barely managed to hold onto the moment of pride she had felt when she learned that bots once, while there were still a few left on Earth, had fought back against their oppressors. But it was a struggle to keep her spirits from dropping as low as they had been when she had first seen her cell.

Her ransom was the very secret that made the Gypsies safe. Even if the Engineers moved off Earth and into the solar system, even if they destroyed the Orbitals in the habitats, on Mars, and elsewhere, the Gypsies were out of reach.

Surely they would not pay the price her captors were demanding for her.

And when the Engineers realized that their demand was futile, she would die.

It was no consolation that she would die on the Earth which she had yearned so much to see.

Chapter
Seven

PEARL ANGELICA LOOKED up from the edge of her sleeping platform as footsteps echoed in the corridor outside her cell. A familiar voice said, "I'll take it in," and a key scraped in the lock. The rusty steel door creaked open.

The guard was a middle-aged man who wore a blue coverall almost identical—except in color—to those she had long been familiar with on the Orbitals and human Gypsies, although it was decorated with strips of metallic cloth that suggested girders. A heavy belt, kept from sagging much below his paunch by a single diagonal shoulder strap, supported his keys and a billy club. A single brass medallion, stamped with the profile of an automobile, was pinned to the strap.

The guard's cheeks were dark with end-of-shift stubble, a white-capped swelling marked the side of his nose, and his eyes and posture were weary, but he showed all the watchfulness of a professional prison warder as he stopped the door with his foot and peered through the crack to be sure the prisoner was safely out of reach.

The door swung wider. The guard stepped aside to reveal Hamid in the dimness of the corridor behind him. The kidnapper was holding a metal dinner tray.

The guard gestured. "Half an hour."

"I won't need that long." Hamid was grinning as if in anticipation.

"I don't have anything to say to you," said Pearl Angelica. Of her three captors, he was the one who had eyed her, pinched her, felt her. Suddenly, she could guess what he wanted. She also guessed that it was no rare event; the guard seemed quite unperturbed.

"That's all right." The door swung shut and clicked behind him. He set the tray on the wall shelf. "You don't need to say a word."

She stood up. "Then . . ."

He swung toward her, put one hand against her breast, squeezed, and pushed. As she fell backward on her thin mattress, he said, "I've heard stories."

She sprawled where he had hurled her. She glared, thinking of her father and Donna Rose, human and bot. Had he heard of them? Or did he mean other couples? "You haven't heard any about me."

"So you've still got nice tits." He took off his jacket and tossed it aside.

She tensed, knowing that she had not guessed wrong. She tried to push herself away from him, into a sitting position near the head of the narrow shelf that was her bed, but he grabbed her ankle and pulled her flat. Her voice trembled when she said, "How much did it take to bribe the guard?"

He didn't answer.

"Why don't you bring him in to hold me down?"

"Don't give me that. All you wear is leaves. No clothes. You flaunt it all, and you know you want it. I won't need him."

"You can't get a girl of your own sort?"

"I've got three." He was unfastening his pants. "But I've never had a bot."

She knew it would do her no good at all to struggle. He was stronger than she, and she thought that the guard outside her cell might be all too willing to hold her down if Hamid only asked. He might even want a piece of her himself.

She also knew it would not help to scream.

But though she lay still as her assailant wrenched aside her leaves, exposed her most private flesh, and assaulted her, she could not remain quiet. She cried in outrage, and again, again, again.

When he answered her rhythmic cries with a grunting "Shut up!" and an open-handed slap, she shrieked and glared and tried to claw his face.

He pinned both wrists in one large fist and used the other to pound her jaw and cheek and temple, grinning fiercely when

he split her lip and her red blood splattered across both their
chests.

She screamed with every blow and every unfaltering
thrust.

She screamed even though she knew it could not help,
not here, not on Earth, not in this cell that echoed with
her voice.

Her screams should have echoed beyond her cell, into
the corridor where the guard waited for Hamid to be done,
beyond the buried building and through the city of Detroit,
through all the continent and the Earth, to space itself and
all her friends and kin. They should have aroused the planet
and prompted the descent of legions of rescuers.

Certainly her screams echoed in the corridor beyond the
door of her cell. But no one came until the guard finally
opened the door, eyed her with the detachment of one who
has seen it all a thousand times, smirked tiredly, and said,
"Time to go."

The physical pain faded quickly, though bruises and scabs
remained. The pain of mind and spirit—humiliation and outrage, insult and fury—did not. She huddled on the thin pad
that covered her sleeping platform, picking at the leaves her
rapist had torn, smoothing others back into place, hoping desperately that his sperm would not take root within her. Other
bots mated by exchanging pollen, fertilizing the blossoms on
their scalps, setting seed that, when ripe, would be planted in
soil. She had been given more human features; presumably
she could get just as pregnant as any fully human woman.

Not that he knew that, her kidnapper, her rapist. If she had
a gun, a knife, anything sharp and long, oh, she would love
to penetrate *him!*

And there was nothing in her cell that she could use
to remove . . . the physical stain, the seed, the semen that
was now within her. She shuddered at the thought that she
might bear her rapist's child. Nor could she remove the stain
upon her mind, her spirit, her soul. She would bear that to
her grave.

She looked at the tray that still sat on the shelf across her
cell. It held a small piece of meat, grey, cold, surrounded by
congealed grease. There were vegetables, also cold, limp and

soft from overcooking. There was a glass of thin milk.

She gagged at the thought of eating. That, she thought, would solve her problem, her problems. If she could only starve herself, she would then escape the memory of rape and save her kin the need to pay any ransom at all.

She might even save her kin from rape and slaughter. She did not believe the Engineers would use the tunnel-drive just for trade and exploration. Earth might have recovered from the chaos and destruction of the revolution. The Engineers might indeed be building the mechanical civilization for which they once had yearned. But their minds remained the same. They would not leave the Orbitals and Gypsies in peace. They would be happy only once they stood alone on Earth, in the solar system, and among the stars, and perhaps not even then.

She gagged again at the thought of food. What she needed was soil and sunlight, sunlight and soil. The touch of Earth. And they had barred her from it. They had told her that if she left the pavement of the plaza above, if she but touched the soil of Earth, if she sank her roots into the planet's dirt, she would contaminate their world.

As if *she* were the rapist!

She wished she could be sure that her death would protect her kin, would confine the Engineers to Earth as she was confined to this cell. But she knew what von Neumann machines were. They had been conceived in the twentieth century, when computers were new, before the gengineers had found their ways to sidestep the shortages of minerals and energy that threatened the machine-based civilization of the time. They would be, if only they could be built, machines that could reproduce themselves. They would be able to mine the metals they needed, refine them, shape them into chips and motors and gears and structural elements, and assemble duplicates of themselves. Turned loose upon the Moon or Mars and later harvested for their valuable components, they promised an end to every conceivable shortage of materials. Programmed to build whatever their designers wished, they promised an end to labor shortages and an infinite ballooning of personal wealth.

They did, of course, require some compact power source. But given that, the payoff was endless.

So, she realized, was the threat to her people. Von Neumann machines could as easily be told to seek out and destroy enemies, or bots. And they did not really need a faster-than-light drive to reach the Gypsies. As machines, they could not die. An ordinary Q-drive would take them to the stars over the centuries and millennia, there to spread and seek and destroy. Tunnel-drives would only speed the process, shrinking the time to the extinction of the Gypsies and the Orbitals to mere years, or even months.

She still craved the touch of Earth's soil, but less than before. Earth was root-home, yes. It was also the home of the enemies of all her kind. It was the place where fate insisted on a dichotomy, an eternal conflict, between machines and life, and promised to extend that conflict wherever her own people might go.

She stared at her legs, her feet, her ankles, her roots and rootlets. Those branching tendrils varied in thickness, hair-slender near their tips, wormlike where they emerged from her skin. Prehensile tentacles, flexing, writhing. Could she have grabbed her rapist with them, stabbed through his skin, found his nerves, forced him to scream as he did her? Her stomach turned. It had never before occurred to her that she might use her roots in such a way. She was not sure she could.

What would the machines think of their mission? They would be intelligent. They would have to be, to handle the complexity of reproduction, the variability of the universe, the unpredictability of their target. They would eat, process energy, respond to their environment, reproduce. They would, in fact, share all the features of organic life. They would *be* alive, a form of life, different only in form and inorganic chemistry.

And their existence, by itself and aside from any mission of extermination the Engineers might lay upon them, would not disturb the Gypsies or the Orbitals, who coexisted comfortably with both machines and genimals. Yet what would the differences mean to the machines themselves?

Eventually, she realized what she was doing by thinking of such things. She was avoiding every thought of what had just happened to her. The von Neumann machines were really a threat. They would indeed be a kind of life, by any definition that really mattered. They would have their own opinions. They . . .

"I'm just distracting myself," she said aloud. "Trying not to think of how much it hurts." And it did, didn't it? She took a deep breath and admitted just how much pain she truly felt.

"I've been raped." No, it wasn't her fault. She didn't flaunt her body. She didn't ask for such treatment, and it had never happened, never even almost happened, among the Gypsies. Not that the Gypsies were so perfect. She had heard . . . But here, a prisoner, in a cell, at the mercy of the Engineers her kind had fled so many years before . . . She was helpless.

She knew she might be raped again. She *would* be raped again, if she stayed where it could happen.

"But how can I escape?" she asked the wall of her cell.

She focused again on her roots. Prehensile, yes, they were. They might be able to make Hamid pay in coin of pain for what he had done. They could squirm their way into soil, draw small stones to the surface and even hurl them aside. They could manipulate, and they were small, able to insinuate themselves into the thinnest of cracks.

She rose from the bed, stretched and heard her joints pop in protest. She examined the door to her cell. She looked at the meal Hamid had brought her. She thought of soil and—was it still day outside?—sunlight.

Finally, she lay down again, but this time on the floor beside the door. She raised her legs and propped one on the door and the other against the wall, beside the latch. Then she worked her roots as if she stood on bare ground, free and unmolested.

She closed her eyes to concentrate on those few signals of touch the nerves in her roots could send to her awareness. She felt the thinnest of her prehensile tendrils enter the crack between door and jamb. She made them twist and writhe, seeking further cracks and crevices, squeezing through the tiny space around the bolt, discovering the cramped interior of the lock. She flexed their very tips, probing for the mechanism, grasping, tugging.

Something moved, just a little. She focused her attention and strained. She poked and pulled. She gasped at the bright flower of pain when something shifted to crush a tendril. But she did not stop. She continued to strain until at last she heard a scrape and click and grind.

The door moved in its frame.

She withdrew her roots. She stood up. She pressed on the door with a trembling hand, letting it open just enough to show her the dim-lit corridor, empty and quiet, with not even the sound of distant steps.

With barely a glance at the cell behind her, she slipped out, free, and closed the door again.

Her memory served her well. She found the guard station, a small office with an all-glass wall that exposed to view the corridor and all who passed. But the guard was nodding, and she needed to wait only a little while before his eyes closed completely. She passed his station without incident. The corridors beyond remained empty, though once she stopped and stood stock-still against a wall, heart pounding, while a small robot scurried past. Soon after that, she reached the elevator that would lift her toward the surface.

She feared the noise the elevator made might attract attention, but when it stopped in the underground lobby there was no sound of pursuit, no sight of others, no sign that her absence had yet been noticed. There were only the stairs that stepped up to the plaza, dimly lit by scattered fixtures, with none of the warm glow of distantly reflected sunlight. She wished she knew how late at night it was, that she had a watch, that the Engineers had thought to mount a clock upon the wall. But she didn't. They hadn't. The only clue she had was the lack of traffic on the steps, and that hinted that the hour was late indeed.

Then perhaps she would not be free for long. Dawn would come, and soon someone would look into her cell, and they would learn she was gone. The search would begin.

The stone plaza, as empty as the stairway, was dark, shadowed by the monolithic building that stood to one side, the only light that shed by a quarter moon and distant stars through a tattered veil of cloud. She crossed it quickly to the wall at which she had stood earlier that day. Lights were visible beyond the river, their reflections shining broken white and yellow, red and green, on the water. More lights were visible on her own shore to left and right, marking where Detroit's Engineers lived and worked upon the surface.

She followed the scent of honeysuckle to where a sprig of vine and leaf and blossom poked above the line of the bordering wall. She swung herself over the edge, grasped the vine, strong and friendly and welcoming, and clambered down.

At last she stood upon Earth's soil.

Her heart leaped at the feel of dirt beneath her feet. She was tempted to stop right there and root herself, touch her mother world as deeply as she could, drink deep of all that heritage the Engineers had forced her kind to flee.

But she knew she did not dare. Turning her back upon the plaza, she groped through shadow-deepened darkness, pushing aside vines and branches, stumbling over blocks of ancient stonework, listening warily to the small sounds of nocturnal animals, wondering if she would meet a wandering Engineer, a honey bum, perhaps even another bot, overlooked in the pogroms of the past. She had not gone far before her hand touched a tree trunk, dew showered down upon her, and she realized that leaves obscured the sky. She was as hidden as she could hope to be from the search that would soon, too soon, begin.

She smiled and stroked the tree whose bulk had stopped her. She shifted her feet, luxuriating in the softness of dirt, the tickle of small growing things against her calves. She took a step, two, exploring the limits of the space she had found. She jumped when one hand met a curving surface as smooth as skin. As she explored it with her fingers, she realized that it was wood, wood carved into . . . what? Here was a cleft that could only be an armpit, here an arm, here fingers, nose, mouth. A statue, then, a wooden statue, hidden in the undergrowth.

She settled herself beside the unseen figure and finally let her roots unfurl to touch Earth's fertile surface and penetrate the soil, a dark loam rich with humus. She sighed at the touch of root-ease, wished for day and sun, and recognized the taste of honeysuckle vines. Her roots enmeshed themselves with those of the vines, and as her nerves found the plant's synapses, she felt herself merging with the world around her.

The honeysuckle had been designed long ago by bot gengineers to serve as a communications network. The nerve-bearing roots of all the separate vines merged together to form a single nervous system that permeated Earth's soil wherever honeysuckle grew. Once bots had used this network to send messages to each other. But the vines had simple senses too, and the bots had used them to watch for danger, to monitor events where no bots lived to formulate reports.

Her contact with the vines took form within her mind as a head-sized hole that pierced a solid wall. The wall was grey. The space beyond the hole was as black as starless space. Pearl Angelica knew there were no other bots on Earth, but she could not help herself. She leaned toward the hole, toward the image within her mind, and called: "Is anyone there?"

There was only silence, echoing in her nerves and brain as it must have echoed for years in the vast interconnected network that covered the continent and even stretched beyond, under the shallower seas to offshore islands.

She sighed resignedly. She opened herself to the slower, simpler flow of information generated by the honeysuckle itself. She began to see that threads of light and sound crossed the blackness of the hole, representations of the honeysuckle roots, datathreads woven into webs and cables, stretching forth across the landscape. She chose one thread, brighter and louder than the rest because its source was the immediate area, Detroit and its environs, and she let the senses of the vines report to her: The quiet streets of a city that once had roared with factories, automobiles, and hordes of people. Scattered lights marking the sway of neighborhoods and sketching the borders of fields and woody patches. Few people walked or drove abroad. Occasional robots trimmed lawns even in the predawn darkness, tilled fields and gardens, cleaned streets.

She chose other threads, dimmer, quieter, more distant, and she saw the world that she had sought, as peacefully idyllic as she had dreamed. Still other threads, still more distant, attenuated by the flux of information from an ever-growing host of vines, and she sensed forests, growing everywhere, replacing lawns and fields, surrounding and engulfing abandoned buildings. There were farms as well, seeming fertile, bountiful, adequate to the task of feeding the Engineer populace as they had not been in the years immediately after the Revolution.

Still she sorted threads, and now she found one that seemed brighter, louder, faster. As she focused her awareness, she thought the data seemed familiar. The signal seemed, in fact, not to come from the vines at all. She let it roll through her nervous system, and then it was clear: a lesson for young bots, a recital of how to flee, stay hidden, avoid detection, flowing from some forgotten bioform computer. Fugitives, refugees, had carried it with them, planted it in soil when they thought they had found shelter, and used it to educate their young. But then they had been discovered, or they had been rescued by the Orbitals. The computer did not say; it only repeated endlessly the task it had last been set.

Pearl Angelica closed her eyes against the darkness that surrounded her. Earth, she thought. Root-home. An empty house, abandoned by those who had loved it best, left to the rats in the walls. And haunted by . . . Tears spilled onto her cheeks at the contradiction between what this world once had been, a lifetime ago, and what it was now.

There were other threads as well. Some of them played still more somber notes to her mind. They spoke of ruins everywhere, signs of war, signs of death, signs that once many more people had lived on this world of roots. And the honeysuckle knew where they had gone. It answered her unspoken, almost unthought query by showing her the bones around which its roots entwined. Deep in the soil, in what had once been pits and trenches, the bodies had been piled. Here were the scorched and broken remains of humans, bots, Macks, Roachsters, Armadons, litterbugs, Cardinals, and many, many more. All the fruit of the gengineering technology Earth had birthed and its inheritors had rejected so violently.

Her tears became outright sobs, careless of whoever might hear.

And here were pits that held none but humans. Engineers, she guessed. Victims of starvation, of disease, of the war the Orbitals had waged in order to defend their escape from persecution, of the purges that had followed disagreements.

She sobbed again, shuddering, as the honeysuckle net brought to her mind what seemed the scent of death, even though she knew the flesh had long since left these bones.

Eventually, feeling as raped by knowledge as she had been by Hamid's flesh, she disengaged from the honey-suckle. Ironically, her withdrawal was as gentle as if she were sliding her fingers from a lover's hand. She sighed shakily and opened her eyes once more. Grey was just barely visible in the interstices of the leaves above her head. The sky was already lightening. She nestled her roots into the loam beneath her, wishing that she need not hide from the dawn, that she dared to venture into the open where the rising sun might touch her leaves.

The light brightened. Soon she realized that she could see the statue beside which she had stood for hours: It represented a naked man, kneeling, head bowed as if intent on the ground before him. Yet it hardly seemed to have been carved, for it duplicated every detail, every wrinkle and fold, even every pore and hair of its animal model. It was also covered with a skinlike bark as glossy smooth and dark as polished wood. A sturdy branch raised willowlike leaves above its head. Smaller branches sprouted from its back and sides and front.

She recognized it now. It was a fruit of sorts of the honeysuckle vine, whose creators had put in the nectar that pooled in the blossom cups a viruslike gene transfer vector. Those who succumbed to the wine and its freight of alcohol and euphoric drug would bit by bit see their genes modified until at last they took root wherever they happened to be. Soon thereafter all their flesh and bone, even their brains, turned to wood.

The only way a honey bum could ward off the fate of whoever had become this mindless statue was to stay on pavement, where roots could not find purchase.

There were honey bums on the *Gypsy,* she recalled. There might even be a statue or two like this, though she had never either seen or heard of one. She smiled and patted the stranger on what once had been a warm and fleshy shoulder. "Did you find *your* roots?" she asked softly. "Are you happier now?"

The sky was rose and gold and deepest blue. Light touched the trees around her and brought their greens and browns and blacks to life. Not far away, she saw that the trees gave way to a patch of brush, ferns and grasses and small bushes no higher than her waist. She sighed, surrendered to her craving, and pulled her roots from the soil. A few steps later, she sank her roots into the loam once more, spread her arms, and let Earth's sun bathe her leaves.

What had she sought in coming here? To the solar system, wishing for Earth, dreaming of a Mother, a world that would welcome her, a world perhaps where her kind lingered past all rumor of extinction. A sense of belonging, of family, of long-enduring context. Roots, and root-home.

Insects hovered over the blossoms of a nearby shrub. Black and yellow, buzzing. Bees. One approached and lingered briefly near her scalp.

What had she found? Nothing was left of her kind on Earth but bones and echoes and the stink of death. The soil was dirt much like any dirt she had ever found on the *Gypsy* or First-Stop or would someday find on other worlds. The sun, that ancient god of Earthly life, was a star like any other star.

There was the past, yes, but not a friendly past. Not belonging, but rejection. What she most truly sought waited for her in orbit, on the *Gypsy,* on First-Stop, at home.

A roaring whine overhead announced the long swing across her vision of a small airplane, the waggle of its wings, the bending of its course into a circle above her position.

She did not try to flee. She stood still, alone, face, front, and leaves offered to the morning sun, until the brush crackled behind her and people stepped into her brushy clearing. She made no move until Hamid held a knife before her eyes and said, "Pull 'em up, now. Or I'll cut 'em off."

She returned to her cell quietly, with neither struggle nor argument. She barely reacted when she saw that there was now a guard upon her door in addition to the guard at the station down the hall, except to think that they were taking no chances that she would escape again.

They did not know that the taste of root-home she had craved had been less than her dreams.

They did not know she craved it no more.

Chapter
Eight

THE GUARD WHO opened her door in the morning was the same man who had let Hamid in to rape her. But now he seemed more alert. His back was straighter, his gut pulled in, his eyes wide and searching.

"In here, Major Reiber." Before he stepped aside, his gaze lingered over her body in a way that made her wish for clothes. The man who stepped past him was lean to the point of emaciation, so lean that the sharp creases in his black trousers and white shirt seemed to ride the edges of his flesh as a tent rode its poles. Pinned to the shirt just below his left collarbone were three silver medallions Pearl Angelica recognized as depicting an ancient steam locomotive, an airplane, and the skeletal construction that had first landed men on the Moon. Glancing at the guard's single emblem of brass, she thought that the medallions must somehow signify rank in the Engineer hierarchy.

"I won't need you," Major Reiber said to the guard. His back was stiff, and his movements were as precise and abrupt as those of soldiers the bot had seen in old films. "Go."

As the cell door clicked shut, he said to the bot, "Stand up when I'm talking to you."

She sat up on her sleeping platform, watching this major. But he did nothing further, said nothing, made no threat. His confident stance said that he was no Hamid or 'Livrance or Prudence to be sent on distant missions, no agent to be sent hither and yon on others' errands. He represented this world's rulers far more directly, and he was absolutely sure she would obey his order.

His eyes moved the length of her body, though in a far colder, more impersonal way than had the guard's. She had no sense of the sort of threat Hamid had posed. She might have been a specimen in a laboratory.

She shuddered and thought that if she did not obey, he would surely remain there all day, standing stiff, staring, making her skin crawl and her throat ache to scream.

When she finally stood, she said, "Are you going to rape me too?"

His face twisted as if the very idea of sex with a bot turned his stomach. "Rape? A plant? No one has touched you. They wouldn't dare."

"One did."

"Don't lie to me. It won't help you."

"I'm half-human." ·

"Then it's only half-rape. At most. If anything really happened, we should punish you for contaminating . . . Who do you accuse?"

"Hamid," she said as she thought, *she* had contaminated *him?* Hamid hadn't treated her like a human being, but then he hadn't seemed to find her all that repulsive. Perhaps he had simply spent too much time among the Orbitals. "Ask him. Ask the guard."

"I will." The major nodded, and his expression promised that Hamid would not enjoy his immediate future. Then he looked her over once more and changed the subject, "You don't really want bees, do you?"

She blinked and nodded. He smelled of sweat despite the earliness of the hour and the crispness of his clothing. She wondered how often he bathed. "Of course we do. We've been using brushes, artists' paintbrushes, to pollinate our flowers, and . . ." She shrugged and used her hands to show him what she meant. "We left in a hurry, you know. Or they did. I wasn't even born until . . ."

"You're a spy. Admit it." The man sniffed, and she knew that he had barely heard her.

"What on Earth would I be spying for?"

He glared at her with an air of disgust. "Don't pretend to be so ignorant," he said. "I know you saw the robots on the way here." When she only looked puzzled, he added, "You don't have anything like that, do you?"

"Not quite. Not so small, but—"

"Ah. And you never will." He shook one fist before her

face. "We have learned to build artificial intelligences far, far better than anything the Orbitals can make."

Pearl Angelica nodded appeasingly. "I'm sure," she said. "They seem quite marvelous. But I don't think we need them when we have—"

"Abominations! But you will never have our robots. They will give us the universe! We will not trade them. We will not even trade their plans, nor their general principles. Not even for the star-drive you stole from our predecessors."

She said nothing, but her flinch at his words made her thoughts transparent.

"They were thieves! The Orbitals and your damned Gypsies. And now they send you to steal our latest discoveries."

His eyes now were so wide that the whites showed all around his irises, and there was sweat upon his forehead. But though Pearl Angelica had heard of such signs of rabid fanaticism, she had never seen them, never learned how dangerous it could be to argue. If she had, perhaps she would have kept her mouth shut. Or perhaps not, for his accusations were so blindly unjustified that her own eyes were widening, her heart was pounding, her palms were sweating.

"No!" she cried angrily. "I didn't sneak down here to Earth. You kidnapped me. It's *your* doing, not mine, that I am here at all. If you had left me alone, I wouldn't even *know* about your damned artificial intelligences."

He sighed with ostentatious patience. "But you *wanted* to be here. You *asked* to visit. And when we turned you down, you forced us to kidnap you."

"What . . . !"

"You are clever." He looked aside as if he could not quite believe his own words. "A very clever spy. You knew that your mere appearance in the solar system would be a taunt we could not resist. But it will not work."

"How can you say that?" But she knew the answer. She had read enough history to recognize the Big Lie in operation. The real question was who he was lying to. Not her. But himself? Or posterity? If he could extract a confession from her, he could then justify doing whatever he wished to her. And a mere unfounded accusation could serve nearly as well.

Or perhaps he merely hoped to rattle her until in confusion or self-defense she revealed her people's secrets.

"You proved you are a spy when you escaped. The only questions are how long you were free and how much you saw before you reported to your Orbital masters." Before she could protest that there was no way she could possibly have reported as he charged, he added, "We are searching for the radio you must have discarded before we caught you again."

She shook her head, unable to answer such audacious charges.

"Tell me," he said. "What did you find out before you hid so cleverly in our riverside thickets? What did you tell your masters? Where is your radio? Tell me . . ." He raised a hand as if he wanted to strike her. "Or . . . We have drugs, and other methods."

"I wasn't spying," she managed at last. She had no trouble imagining what "other methods" he meant. "Or hiding. I only wanted soil. Root-ease."

"Is that what you call it?"

"A taste of the world of my forebears, root-home."

His mouth looked as if her words tasted bad. "There is no such link. We expunged all your monstrous kind. Earth has rejected you, disowned you, and we have cleansed our world of all your traces."

Not all, she thought. There is still the honeysuckle. But all she said was, "You can't deny the history."

"It does not exist. And even your memory will vanish once we have the star-drive."

There, she thought. He had said it.

"What will you do?" she asked. "Use your robots? Send them out to hunt us down? You'll need an awful lot of them."

"They will make more of themselves. We have almost perfected that."

Von Neumann machines. Just as Hamid had told her. If the Engineers could make such things, the Gypsies might indeed be doomed. Dejectedly, she let herself slump onto the edge of her sleeping platform.

"Stand up!"

She stayed where she was.

The major only glared, as if he did not want to contaminate his hand by touching her.

"You foul the very air by breathing!"

"Will you have to destroy this warren when I am gone?"

"We will use a flamethrower on this room. We have already sterilized the plane that fetched you."

"Then why am I even here, if I am such a monstrosity? Such an intolerable nastiness?"

"You will not be on Earth for long. Only until the Council can question you. Then, if they decide to let you live, we'll move you to the Moon. Orbitals are sometimes permitted there."

"And how long will I be there?"

"Until your friends deliver the star-drive plans."

"If," she said. "They won't do it."

"Then we will finally kill you."

A moment later, he was gone. Pearl Angelica was left with the shock of his words.

They were going to kill her.

She would die.

Be gone.

Nevermore see her father, her friends, the Gypsies, First-Stop.

She had known that already. How could she not? She had been doomed from the moment the Engineers had decided to ask for a ransom that could not possibly be paid.

And there was nothing she could do to avoid that doom. There was no hope. No recourse or appeal.

Earth was ruled by fanatics. Perhaps it always had been. Or its nations, every one of which had at times been as much a closed society as was now the entire planet. Insular, sealed off from foreign contact, foreign ideas, fearing difference and seeing in it deliberate, malicious threats to the sole right way to think and believe and live. Fearing change. Fearing also spies and the implications of criticism, threat, and plot those secret agents must inevitably carry with them.

The Orbitals were far more open and less defensive. Perhaps they were more confident of the rightness of their beliefs. Certainly they tolerated difference better, and Engineers were welcome to move freely among them. If not many seemed to take the opportunity, that must be because of that very fear of difference that sealed off Engineer society on Earth. Perhaps as well the Engineer authorities blocked travel into space to keep the Orbitals from asking questions, spying, or even taking hostages. Perhaps they feared that those who did not share the official paranoia would defect if they had the chance.

Were there parallels to this situation in Earthly history? Pearl Angelica had read enough to know that twentieth-century Americans and Canadians and western Europeans had prided themselves on their freedom and openness and tolerance of diversity. Yet they had been nearly as defensive about the virtues of their institutions as their neighboring tyrannies. They had maintained immense armies. They had spied and hunted spies. They had controlled who could enter their nations and where their own citizens could go. The tyrannies had exerted even stricter controls.

As a Gypsy, she could understand some of that attitude. She fully agreed that the tunnel-drive should not be shared with the Orbitals, for fear that it would fall into the hands of the Engineers. Certainly it should not be given to the Engineers directly, not even in exchange for her life.

Yet she also saw that that attitude lay at the root of the very conflict it guarded against. She wished she could see some other answer.

"You're the first genny ever to enter this room. Did you know that?"

Except for his balding head and heavy abdomen, the speaker might have been Major Reiber's twin. His face was just as humorless, his posture as stiff, and he wore the same black trousers and white shirt, with very similar medallions on his chest. He was one of the twelve members of the Council of Engineers.

The Council Chamber was many levels deeper in the Earth than the cell that Pearl Angelica had occupied until the major had returned to escort her through locked doors, down elevators, and past guardposts to this encounter. The Councilors sat at a horseshoe-shaped table surrounded by tiers of plush seats. The tiers were empty now; Pearl Angelica supposed they were intended for spectators and those who had business with the Council. Inside the arc of the horseshoe stood a gleaming metal post topped with a backless seat. Her ankles were chained to rings that protruded from the sides of the post. A belt tight across her lap held her to the seat. Her hands were cuffed behind her back.

Inset in the gleaming wood before each Councilor was a silver button. There was also a small plaque bearing the Councilor's name. The speaker was Dubarry.

"Did you?" Only when she answered with a shake of her head did Dubarry laugh and go on. "In fact, I do believe you're the first one to be on Earth since it was built. Certainly, there aren't any wild ones left."

"We're not here for small talk." Her heart leaped as the stool spun on its stem. Pain erupted in her back, awakened by the abrupt, jerking motion. She gasped, and when she opened her eyes she saw that she was facing an older, dark-skinned Councilor.

The speaker was dressed much like Dubarry, though his shirt was pink. His name-plaque said "Kentaba." His voice was softer, more kindly, but his eyes were as stoney as a statue's, and his lips twitched when she gasped. By the way the others glanced his way as he spoke, she guessed that he was the Council's leader. "We need to know things. If it will tell us."

So to him Pearl Angelica was an "it," a thing, inhuman, as easy to destroy as a mosquito.

The stool jerked her painfully around to face Dubarry again as that Councilor said, "We should have let Reiber grill her. I'm sure the major's report would take less of our time. And . . ." He lifted one hand from the silver button that seemed to control the stool and fanned his face as if her presence fouled the air he had to breathe.

She tightened her hands on the edge of her seat. This time, when the stool spun the pain was less. She blinked, and she was facing a white-shirted Dostakovich, his jaw squared by the bulges of incipient jowls. He was not looking at her face, and his lips were wet. To him too, she thought, she was a thing, but not one to be destroyed immediately. It was clear that he had other lusts than the one for blood.

"We've heard rumors that you have a faster-than-light drive," he said. "Is that true?"

She did not think that anything she could say would make

the Engineers less implacable as foes. Their intentions were already as deadly as they could possibly be. She nodded.

"How does it work?"

"I'm a biologist." That was true enough as far as it went, though she knew just enough about the tunnel-drive's relationship to the ordinary Q-drive to reveal far too much. "That's not my field. I have no idea."

Her seat spun her to face a dark-haired, round oriental face and a "Kasumi" plaque. "What are you doing out there?"

Another spin caught her by surprise, and she gasped in pain. Dostakovich was saying, "Still corrupting life? Playing with yourselves? Making more monsters?"

Again, and Kasumi: "Or have you regained your sense?"

"They brought Armadons," said Major Reiber from the side. "And look at her."

"Ah." Kasumi shook his head as if regretting the obstinacy of those who refused to see the folly of their ways and return to the conventions of inanimate technologies. "Such a pretty girl."

"What *are* you doing out there?" asked Kentaba.

"We're still working on the *Gypsy*," said Pearl Angelica. But the expressions she faced told her that that was not the sort of thing they wanted to know. "And we found a species about as intelligent as chimpanzees."

"What are they?" asked Dubarry.

"Extinct." Kentaba raised one fist, pointed a finger at the other man, and showed stained teeth in an eloquent grin. "Boom."

"And?" Kasumi prompted her.

She closed her eyes and wished she could grip her head in her palms, bury her fingers in the cool waxiness of her petals. She could brace herself against the jerky spinning of her stool, but not enough. The spins and jerks that forced her to face each Councilor as he spoke were giving her a headache. "We call them Racs," she finally said. She told what the Gypsy gengineers had done.

"What?" cried Dubarry. "You made aliens!"

"It was only a matter of time before evolution did the same job."

Kentaba repeated "evolution" as if it were a dirty word.

"How much are you teaching them?" Dostakovich licked

his lips and eyed her breasts once more.

"Language and basic skills." She hesitated then, thinking that these Engineers would only be alarmed if she told them of the cache of history and science and other knowledge the Gypsies were planning to leave behind when they moved on. Yet she *wanted* to alarm them, to shatter their arrogant complacency.

No one interrupted the silence, perhaps because her mouth was still open. At last she did indeed tell them about the Tower.

The silence continued for a long moment until someone groaned. The stool did not spin her to see who had made the noise, but she thought it had sounded desperate.

"You are insane," said Kasumi. "All of you. Far more full of hubris than you ever were on Earth. Playing god. Out of control." He shook his head. "It is our duty . . ."

"Yes." She was facing Dubarry once more. He was nodding. "We must destroy them all. Orbitals and Gypsies."

"And the aliens." Dostakovich's lips were dry now. Fear seemed to have destroyed his lust.

"Or they will destroy us," said Dubarry. "They are making allies, future enemies for all humanity."

"Friends," insisted Pearl Angelica. "Companions, once they have advanced enough to climb the Tower and join us in space."

Kentaba snorted noisily. "We really do need that star-drive."

"They'll never give it to you."

"Then you will never see the *Gypsy* again."

Three days later, 'Livrance and Prudence appeared at her cell. They held cuffs and elastic bandages in their hands.

"Where's Hamid?"

'Livrance wore the same shirt of padlocks Pearl Angelica had last seen him in. At her words, he made as if to look over one shoulder, aborted the motion, and shrugged. Prudence, dressed in a light blue fabric printed with simple circuit diagrams, widened her eyes, said, "Gone," and clamped her lips between her teeth.

Pearl Angelica grunted in satisfaction. She would rather that he were being punished for raping her, not for contaminating his human sanctity with her disgusting slime, but at least he was being punished. It hardly seemed to matter that the two who had helped him kidnap her were once again cuffing her wrists behind her back, wrapping her roots, and pushing her into the hallway outside her cell.

A few minutes later, she was once more on the plaza under the open air, staring toward the overgrown riverbank and the river and cloudy sky, twisting her hands in their cuffs, wishing desperately for freedom.

But, she knew, the price of her freedom was far too high for her friends and kin to pay. She sighed and let her guards lead her where they wished her to go.

She had known her visit to Earth was almost over when Major Reiber came to her cell with a veedo recorder and a script. "Read this," he said. "Face the camera and speak into the mike. We'll send it out, and then it will be up to your friends in space. If they give us what we want, you can go home. If they don't . . ." He drew the side of his hand across his throat to show her what the Engineers would do to her then.

The script was quite simple. "I am a prisoner of the Engineers," it said. "As you can see, I am in good condition so far. They have not tortured me, and I have plenty of food."

When she added, "I have been raped," Major Reiber clicked off the recorder and said, "No. Try it again." He did not add, "As many times as it takes to get it right," but the implication was more than clear enough. She cooperated.

"But they will not let me leave," the script went on. "Until you deliver the plans for a working star-drive."

When her voice broke on the last word, the major smiled thinly and said, "Say good-bye now."

Reading the script had not shamed her. That catch in her voice and the tears she had almost shed did, for they made it seem that she was begging.

She hoped that that seeming would make no difference, that her friends and kin would know better than to buy her freedom with their own—and her—future extermination.

She could see by the plaza's edge the same long automobile that had brought her from the airport.

The Councilors had questioned her, though she didn't think they had learned anything useful. On the other hand, she had

certainly alarmed them with word of the Racs and the Tower.
Now, if the major had not lied, she was on her way back to
space. But not back to her friends and kin. She would soon
be delivered to other Engineers on the sterile Moon, captive,
prisoner, caged safely far from holy Earth and any possibility
of genetic contamination.

"We've got one small station," said 'Livrance. "But we won't
use it. We're the only passengers. There's no cargo. So we
can go all the way in this."

He meant the spaceplane. But though he and Prudence
were just as snugly strapped into their padded couches, they
were not prisoners. Their right hands were not cuffed to their
couches' frames. Their legs were not wrapped in tight elastic
bandages to conceal unnatural roots and cramping worse with
every moment that passed.

Pearl Angelica wished the spaceplane had a porthole. She
knew she would not be able to see Munin or Hugin. They
were simply too small against the empty vastness of space.
And the Engineer crew would surely have chosen a course
that carried the craft's three passengers as far as possible
from those Orbital bases, or even the Engineers' own station,
and any rescue attempt the Orbitals might dare.

She did not want to look once more upon the Earth whose
call had summoned her across the light-years. Yes, the Gypsies
needed bees, but really, if she were as honest as she should
be with herself and others, the brushes and ladders worked
just fine and provided useful employment for youths who
might otherwise invent rebellion and offense as they had
always done when history left them idle. And if the Gypsy
gengineers could not adapt First-Stop dumbos, then surely
there would be something at the next world they visited, or
the gengineers could modify some Earthly creature.

Earth had rejected her. It had been the lure of root-home
that had drawn her, and root-home was not there.

But the stars. They would be there, all around. Perhaps she
would even be able to see Tau Ceti, around which orbited
First-Stop and the *Gypsy,* Frederick and the Racs, all her
friends, all her kin.

There was her true root-home. She should have known it.
Thrusters banged and rumbled beneath her seat. Accel-

eration pressed her briefly into her cushions and let up. She floated against her straps while 'Livrance and Prudence released themselves and moved about the spaceplane's cabin, pulling themselves from empty seat to empty seat. Both of them were grinning as if they loved space more than Earth, though whether that love was based in the freedom of zero-gee or distance from their bosses Pearl Angelica could not tell.

No one spoke until finally, growing bored, Pearl Angelica said, "Prudence?"

Her guard spun in mid-air, her face shifting instantly from unguarded joy to sour watchfulness. "What?"

"Where were all the women?"

"What do you mean?" A gesture said that Prudence was a woman, she was there, there was no mystery.

"Yes, there's you, of course. And I saw a few on the street, walking. But that was all. There were none in the airport. No woman Councilors. No . . ."

"They're all at home," said 'Livrance. "Where they belong."

The woman's sourness increased, though it did not now seem aimed at Pearl Angelica. "Making babies," she said. "Keeping house and wiping noses."

"Anyway," said 'Livrance, "you couldn't have a woman Councilor. They haven't got the brains . . ."

"Shut up," said Prudence.

"Such a waste," said the bot.

"It's important work." The woman's tone seemed defensive now. "We lost so many people. We have so much to rebuild. And the Council insists, unless . . ." She held a cupped hand near her lower abdomen, a surprisingly eloquent hint that for some reason she could not do that important work.

'Livrance smirked at them both. "And we have the robots for the scutwork."

Chapter
Nine

EVEN AS THE roar of the belly rockets that had cushioned the landing on the Moon died away, another engine in the spaceplane's tail began to whisper, pressing the passengers back into their seats but only gently, as when an automobile accelerated down an Earthly road. The ship rolled forward, turned, and finally halted. There were noises—clanks, hums, and rumbles—and the ship's hatch opened to reveal the glass-walled end of a tunnel much like those that on Earth linked airport terminals to airplanes. Rubbery accordion folds mated the tunnel to the side of the spaceplane.

"Let's go."

Prudence was already unfastening the prisoner's seatstraps when 'Livrance spoke. "Just a minute," she said. She pulled the chain from the front of her shirt and produced a key, which she then used to unlock the cuff that chained Pearl Angelica to her seat. She promptly clamped the cuff around the bot's other wrist. "Now," she said. "Come on."

As soon as she stood up, Pearl Angelica noticed the Moon's light gravity. Her feet rose higher when she stepped, and her spirits lifted at being this much closer to her kin. But though she was free of Earth, she was not free of the oppression she had found there. Her spirits fell again even as her gait took on the slide and shuffle she had first learned long ago, when she was just a toddler.

The bot stopped walking when they reached the tunnel mouth, stiffened her legs, twisted against the hands that held her elbows, turned to stare through the glass. For a moment, 'Livrance and Prudence stood beside her, just as fascinated by the broad plain marked by spider-webbing vehicle tracks, intersecting ridges with clamshell doors set in their flanks, and dish antennae. Low hills marked the horizon, weathered into crumbly regolith by eons of meteorite bombardment, solar winds, and changing temperatures. Unwinking stars above those hills, painfully familiar, brought tears to Pearl Angelica's eyes. She wondered if Tau Ceti was visible from where she stood.

No Engineers were visible on the lunar landscape, but she had no doubt that they were waiting for her just beyond the end of the boarding tunnel.

"Come on," said 'Livrance at last.

She strained to see as much of the base as she could. "Is this the same . . . ?"

"God knows." They jerked her into motion once more, but not before she glimpsed between two ridges the lines of what could only be a mass-driver, a railgun, perhaps even the very one that had provided the rocky makings of the projectiles with which the Orbitals once had hammered the Engineers on Earth. Beside it scurried several small robots much like those she had seen on Earth.

She remembered what she knew of that time when the Gypsies had not yet become the Gypsies, when the *Gypsy* had not yet been built, when they had not yet fled the solar system. First they had had to flee Earth's pogroms, seeking safety in space. Her father, her mother, Donna Rose, Uncle Renny, they had been among the first. Later Uncle Renny and Aunt Lois had flown the first Q-ships on rescue missions, plucking bots and gengineers and other refugees from beneath the Engineers' boots.

When the habitats and stations in orbit had proved too small for the horde of refugees, tunnellike shelters had been prepared on the Moon, metal-ribbed, plastic-sheathed, insulated by layers of regolith.

She remembered those crowded shelters. She had seen them, lived in them, and they had been much smaller and cruder, even to a child's eye, than what she had just seen. They had still to have been in place when the Engineers reached the Moon themselves. Over the decades since, they had been enlarged and interconnected. Now that portion of the lunar surface must be honeycombed with tunnels. Briefly she wondered if the material that sheathed their frames was still plastic or the webbing she had seen the robot Spiders weaving in Detroit.

One man was waiting in the drably painted room at the end of the boarding tunnel. He wore blue shirt and trousers unadorned with metal trinkets and, one hand on his holstered sidearm, he was bouncing gently, impatiently, on his toes, untiring in the Moon's light gravity. He was of middle height, stocky, brown-haired without a sign of grey. His age showed in his face, where lines of skepticism seemed permanently engraved.

"Hrecker. Chief of Security." He neither smiled nor offered a hand as he spoke to 'Livrance, ignoring both the woman and the bot. "Come with me."

He led them into a tunnel so much larger than the original refugee shelters that Pearl Angelica was immediately reminded of the distant *Gypsy* even though the passageway was straight and level, not winding up and down and to the sides. Small electric carts and robots replaced the genimal vehicles she was used to. In the bare metal walls were doors, some of which bore signs that marked them as shops or laboratories. Others, she thought, were offices or homes. The curvature of the roof suggested that the central corridor could be no more than a third of the tunnel's width. Stone urns beside many doors held small trees and shrubs and flowering plants.

The pedestrians seemed stranger, for not one wore the coveralls of the Orbitals and Gypsies and though some smiled at her as if she were not a prisoner, most scowled. One even spat. No one spoke to her.

"They compost everything they can," said Prudence. "From dead leaves and bodies to sewage. Then they mix it with regolith to make their soil. They grow almost all their food right here."

"Just like the Orbitals," said Pearl Angelica.

'Livrance had one hand on her upper arm, as if he feared the cuffs alone were not enough to keep her from escaping. "They get a lot from Earth."

Pearl Angelica guessed that the Orbitals would say much the same about the lunar Engineers. The difference between "growing *almost all* right here" and "getting *a lot* from Earth" must be a matter of perception.

Where their corridor met another, the ceiling rose and the urns were replaced by larger troughs. A faint buzzing drew Pearl Angelica's attention to yellow-banded insects that hovered and darted near the flowers. "Bees!" she cried.

Hrecker snorted as 'Livrance jerked her onward. "That's what you came for, right? We go left."

Other pedestrians were more numerous now, and many stared at Pearl Angelica as she was hustled along the passageway. "Haven't they ever seen a bot before?" she asked, but before any of her guards could speak, she answered her own question: "Of course they haven't."

More women were visible here than in Detroit. Most wore the same blue shirts and pants as the men. Many of them had children in tow or carried shopping bags; the children and the bags provided the only trace of brilliant color not found on plants. A few of the women carried toolkits, briefcases, and portable computers, suggesting that the Engineers on the Moon were at least slightly more egalitarian than their kin on Earth.

Hrecker stopped them at the next intersection, where an elevator dropped them to a lower level of the base and deposited them before a wall with only one door. Above the door a sign said, "Construction Bay 1."

The Security chief punched a code number into the keypad mounted in the wall beside the entrance. A moment later, the door slid open to reveal a vast, brightly lit cavern and fifty meters of spaceship, held erect by massive staging. Through the tangle of catwalks and cables, Pearl Angelica could see a needle prow, gleaming white paint, blue lettering, gold bands of trim. Just above the ship arched steel girders and glistening sheeting. Above that, she guessed, must be the thin layer of regolith that covered all the base's tunnels.

"It's ready to go." Hrecker pointed at the two fat cylinders that bracketed the ship's lower half. "Fuel tanks," he said. "They're already loaded with powdered regolith. As soon as the other four are installed and filled, the *Teller* will fly. And it will fly just as well as anything *you* have."

Beside the ship stood a rack that seemed designed to lift the missing tanks into place, but Pearl Angelica gave it only a glance. She was staring at the pristine ship. It was not quite the same shape as the Q-ships she was familiar with, but it was close enough. The largest difference lay in its sleekly aerodynamic nose; the *Quebec* and its sister ships were blunt, knobby, far less oriented to Earth. She was sure that if she knew how to appraise the engines, she would see that they would work. The *Teller* would indeed fly.

"It's the same technology." She had not seen the other Engineer approaching; Hrecker did not introduce him. "Did you know that a vacuum can produce particles spontaneously, out of nothing?" Not waiting for their answer, he turned and pointed toward the base of the ship. "It can. They come in matter-antimatter pairs, so there's no net production of matter, and they usually annihilate each other immediately. This can yield energy, though the only way to get very much energy is to increase the probability of the necessary quantum fluctuations. Your people found out how to—"

"They stole it," growled Hrecker.

"Of course." The other gave the Security chief a wary look. "And then we stole it back. We even improved it, and now we have a probability warp drive even better than their Q-flux drive. Space is ours!" He delivered his last three words with the fervor of a slogan.

"It's only a matter of time," said Hrecker. He faced Pearl Angelica. "We'll have more ships, more men, better men. We'll get the star-drive. And then we'll push you to the wall and replace you all. Mechanical technology is superior."

Pearl Angelica gently shook her head. "You seem to think we don't use it too." When it's appropriate, she did not add. There were things it could do best, and things it could not. And the biological technology was self-reproducing and needed only relatively simple fuels.

He did not seem to hear, although she noticed the unnamed spokesman for the shipbuilders suppressing a smile as Hrecker growled, "Let's go."

"This is yours. Give it a try."

When Pearl Angelica had asked if there were more construction bays, no one had answered. Hrecker had only led them down the corridors until they reached an intersection of four tunnels where the ceiling rose until it was lost in darkness. Perhaps it rose as high above their heads as it had above the Q-ship in Bay 1. In the center of the concourse, surrounded by stone pots of intensely fragrant roses—red and yellow, pink and white—and mock oranges, stood an oblong dais about a meter high. One end of the dais supported a larger version of the stone plant pots on the floor; the other end held an inert veedo set.

Hrecker jumped to the edge of the dais, turned, grabbed the bot by one upper arm, and pulled her up beside him. He held out one hand and said, "The key." When Prudence pulled the chain over her head and handed it to him, he undid the cuffs. Then, while Pearl Angelica rubbed her wrists, smoothed rumpled leaves, and grimaced at the pain, he said, "Undo those wraps."

'Livrance promptly began to remove the bandages that confined her roots. While he worked, his fingers far less gentle than her own would have been but still a blessed relief, the bot looked at the oversized plant pot. It was as high as the dais and a meter and a half in diameter. Its flat rim was decorated with inset disks of polished metal, and it was almost full of dark, rich soil.

"Go on," said Hrecker. "Climb in."

She turned and scanned the concourse while her roots writhed as if delighted to be free at last. Some of the pedestrians, mostly women with children, had stopped to watch what was happening on the dais. The rest were moving from corridor mouth to corridor mouth, glancing toward her and then away, scowling at the sight of gengineered anathema, pretending they saw nothing out of the ordinary in what was being offered her. Only the robots in the flow of traffic ignored her completely.

"I'll need light," she said.

Hrecker gestured, and a brilliant beam speared out of the shadows overhead.

She looked at the beam, the dirt, the concourse around them, and the reflections awakened on the metal walls. She realized just how much on display she would be, like a specimen in a zoo. Or worse, a specimen of some endangered species, or of one the zoo's managers intended to endanger as soon as they possibly could.

She shook her head. "I'd rather have a room. Even a cell."

"This is it. Climb in." The Security chief's voice was less inviting, more commanding. It was clear that she had no choice.

She drew herself over the edge of the massive pot and stood erect in its center. Her roots twisted around her ankles and reached for the dirt. She could hear someone in the distance hissing: "Snakes!"

Her roots touched and burrowed, stretched and branched. She found and twined about a narrow pipe that trickled water, just enough to meet her needs. She tasted the moist richness of the soil and closed her eyes as she identified human wastes, decayed remnants of hair and meat and bone, flowers and peelings and stems, all composted into humus. She felt as well the gritty lunar soil, rich with mineral nutrients that had never been tapped by roots before, reeking of dry vacuum, solar wind, and black, star-spangled sky. And there, she thought, was a banner for the Orbitals or Gypsies if they ever decided they needed one, stars on a black field not a blue. Blue was the sky seen from Earth, the color of the Engineers. She would tell them if she ever saw them again.

The hum of gears and the rub of metal against rock snapped her eyes open once more. Hrecker was holding a black oblong studded with buttons, a remote control unit. The metal disks in the rim of her planter had risen to reveal themselves as the ends of steel rods. They surrounded her as a circular enclosure, now just knee-high like a picket fence but still rising, still sliding upward, emerging from their concealment in the wall of the planter and in the dais below.

They were waist-high, and she thought that in the light lunar gravity she could easily climb or jump over them. But the Engineers knew that as well as she. They still rose, and so rapidly that the moment when escape seemed conceivable passed more quickly than she could possibly have withdrawn her roots from the soil.

The bars were shoulder-high now, head-high, higher, and she was trapped in a cell. She had soil rich with nutrients. She had light for photosynthesis. But she was trapped, on display in a steel-barred cage.

Yet she no longer felt quite like an ordinary zoo specimen, not even of a soon-to-be-endangered species. She felt like a sample of vermin, carefully isolated to prevent its escape and infestation of the surrounding community.

Worst of all—if there were anywhere for her to flee—there was no lock for her prehensile roots to pick.

She blinked to prevent the tears from overcoming her self-control.

She supposed the point must be to prove the superiority of the Engineers. *She* was the one in the cage. Therefore she and all her kin, bots and gengineers, Gypsies and Orbitals, must be inferior to those who stood outside the bars.

Hrecker adjusted the veedo set on its stand, turning it so both she and her audience could see the screen. He turned it on, and then he said to 'Livrance and Prudence, "Your ship should be refueled by now. You can go back to Earth." He sounded envious.

The villains were mad gengineers who plotted to release plastic-eating microbes, poison reservoirs with transplant vectors, give Council chieftains the heads of pigs. Game shows offered antique automobiles and air conditioners, reconditioned household appliances and brand-new vacation tickets to the Moon. Heroic astronauts rescued Orbitals whose jury-rigged space drives failed, killed their air plants and Slugabeds and even bots, and converted them to Engineering holiness. Comedians told gene jokes.

Propaganda for the glory of machinery, thought Pearl Angelica. And the news was no better.

She grew quickly tired of seeing herself on the veedo screen and hearing herself called spy and traitor and an example of the horrors of genetic engineering. "Spy" she had heard already. But "traitor"? What could she be a traitor to? What had she betrayed? She was a Gypsy. She had never touched the Earth until just a few days before. Certainly she was no member of the Engineer polity. She was loyal to her own group, and no traitor to it.

But the Engineers saw it differently. She was of Earth, and she had betrayed her heritage simply by being born what she was, a gengineered bot, illicit mingling of plant and human. If she wished to prove her loyalty, she would as willingly as any vegetable lay her head upon the block.

That was nonsense. Sheer pig-headed, demagogic non-sense. Even the Engineers who wrote and read the news could not possibly believe it. She was a trophy, nothing more, and a tool with which to try to extort a starship from the Orbitals and Gypsies.

And "horror"? Humans lived longer than ordinary bots, but bots had roots and leaves and, like any plant, needed only soil, water, and sunlight, not farms and markets and kitchens. She herself was a hybrid, able to survive in either mode, by eating or by photosynthesizing.

Did that make her such a horror, such a monster? She thought it an advantage herself, and in the biological, evolutionary sense of course it was. But even though she was no blood-sucking vampire, no gore-splattered murderer, she was not normal, not usual, in this world of animal humanity. She was different, and that was enough for some people to brand her enemy and monster.

Or prey.

For her first few days in the cage, she was rarely alone. Every morning, nozzles in the ceiling above her cage showered her and her surrounding roses and mock oranges with water, welcome despite the pipe buried beneath her. Soon after that, the first groups of lunar Engineers appeared in the concourse. Most of them had obviously never seen a bot; they stared and parroted the names the veedo called her. Only a few ignored her. Even fewer eyed her sympathetically or pityingly. Children dashed close and yelled, "Look at the plant lady! Why don't you wear any clothes?" Their mothers yanked them back and cried, "Stay away! Or she'll turn you into things like her!"

From time to time a robot with a camera for its head would wheel out of a corridor mouth. It would pan the crowd, squeeze among the men and women and children, and focus its lens on her and the bars of her cage. If she watched not it but the veedo set, she saw that it was feeding live coverage of her plight to the broadcast system. She could also hear what those near the periphery of the crowd were saying.

Occasionally, Engineers with clipboards and tape recorders approached while Security guards channeled traffic toward the edges of the concourse, well away from her. "What do you know about Q-ship design?" "Is it true that the Orbitals are plotting to attack the Moon before our ship can be completed?" "Are the gengineers really raising armies of monsters to avenge their expulsion from Earth?"

She sighed. Were they journalists? Or government intelligence agents? Were they local? Or did they come from

Earth? It did not matter. She denied all knowledge of spaceship construction or operation. She laughed at the thought of attacking the Moon or Earth. The Engineers had them both, and they could keep them.

In time the questioners stopped coming. Even the spectators thinned as the charm of a plant that looked like a human being with her feet buried in a plant pot wore off. It was not long before most of the Engineers passed by with no more than a glance, as often at the yammering veedo set or the massed flowers as at her in her cage. Yet some still did stop, and at least one returned again and again, though he always kept his back against the wall between the corridor mouths. He was a man of about her own age, dressed in the blue of the Engineers. His eyes were intent. His hair was black curls that looked always freshly wetted.

She opened her eyes at the sound of breathing. She shuddered when she saw thin lips and coldly speculating eyes, as grey as cloud, not at all those of the man who had left his vantage point not long before though he had remained a question and a mystery in her mind. She thought she had noticed this man before too, but always surrounded by other passersby. Now he was standing among the plants that encircled the dais, studying the dais's rim as if looking for a control panel. When he found nothing, he shifted his stare to her body, stepped close to reach through the bars, and . . .

He drew back at the hum of tires on pavement, winked, and disappeared. She shuddered at the thought that he might return, perhaps at night when no one would be likely to interrupt his hands. Then she looked for whatever had interrupted him and found the veedo robot, its camera swinging to track the man as he nearly ran from the concourse. It had stopped just outside the mouth of a corridor.

From time to time, she noticed Hrecker standing by the concourse wall, watching both her and whatever audience she had at the moment. That was when the looks of sympathy and pity vanished entirely and the laughs and threats grew louder.

Usually she did not respond. But once, when a small boy had taken a pebble from a rose pot and hurled it at her, she withdrew her roots from the soil and turned to face him and his mother. She put her hands on the bars as if she intended to bend them aside. She opened her mouth and growled.

The boy clung to his mother's leg. The mother screamed and backpedalled as if Pearl Angelica's mouth were full of fangs. Others screamed as well. Someone began to run.

Seconds later the concourse was empty except for one man, Hrecker. He was laughing.

He was a stocky man with a flattened, narrow face and a receding hairline, and he wore the coverall of an Orbital.

Pearl Angelica leaned toward the bars of her cage. "Who are you? What are you doing here?"

"Marcus Yamoto." He spoke softly as he inclined his high-browed head in her direction.

"I haven't seen any Orbitals here!"

"They don't welcome many. But I'm a trader. I have things they want."

A wave of suspicion suddenly made her draw back. Was he truly an Orbital? A trader? Coveralls were cheap. Had the Engineers thought they could win her confidence with an imposter?

"What would they have to gain?" He chuckled, and then he added, "Your thought was obvious."

"Then what are you doing here?"

"Shh. A message, but not one we want them to hear." His mouth twisted when he saw the hope flare in her eyes. "Not that. Sorry. We've told them that only the *Gypsy*'s people know how to build a starship." She nodded; that was true enough. "And the *Quebec* has gone back to First-Stop to report the ransom demand. It won't be back for at least six weeks."

"What's the message?" she whispered urgently.

He suddenly looked far more sympathetic and pitying than any Engineer had managed. His voice turned even softer. "They let me wander around, but I'm sure they're watching me."

She scanned the concourse. It was empty, and the veedo was displaying a late-evening show.

"Back in the tunnel," Yamoto said. "I didn't see anything, but there could be hidden cameras and directional microphones. That veedo robot could be lurking just out of sight.

There could even be mikes in these bars." He touched one. "Or overhead."

"I don't care," she said. "Tell me!"

"The Orbitals have no intention of trading you for the drive. They're just stalling."

Her face and spirits fell even though his words did not surprise her.

He nodded. "Yeah, it's tough."

"But we really can't afford to turn them loose."

He shook his head. "Not the way they are now. Maybe in a hundred years."

"Then . . ." Then they would kill her. The only question was how long they would wait before they did it. And what method they would use.

"You have six weeks," said Yamoto. "Maybe a little more."

She moaned.

"No comfort, eh? I suppose not. But that's six weeks when you can be useful. If you wish."

"How?"

"Pretend to be a tree. It won't be long before they're sitting on this dais and talking to each other as if you *were* a tree. Listen to them. Tell me what they say."

"A spy."

"Even a femme fatale. I've seen the way some of the men look at you. Encourage them. Play up to them. Maybe you'll get out and be able to move around."

"You want me to be a whore."

"If that's what it takes. We're at peace now, but . . ." He bit his lip and shook his head. He didn't think it would last.

"I don't have much choice, do I?" She paused; he said nothing more. "You know about their robots?" He nodded. "Their plans to make von Neumann machines?" She explained when he looked puzzled and grinned mirthlessly when his oriental complexion turned pale.

"That's the sort of thing we need to know," he said. "It won't make the Orbitals change their minds about ransoming you, but we need to know it."

"Can you stop them?"

"I don't know."

Chapter
Ten

THE AIR WAS cooling toward autumn frost, but the valley's purple moss was still speckled with the white of blossoms and berries. Yet there was also change, for the yellow lines of paths were more numerous now. Most of the paths radiated from a single point, that watching place the Racs had laid out with stones, and they had been worn through the moss just in the most recent weeks.

As evening fell, straggling lines of Racs descended from the bluffs and wound along those many radiants as they did each evening. They came from every one of the villages in the vicinity. They were males and females, adults and youths. No children were among them.

No more than a tenth of the local population was on the move in any one evening. That tenth was chosen by strict rotation, omitting only the females with young cubs, the elderly, and the ill or infirm. The villages remained occupied by most of their adults and youths.

They each brought a stone, just as they did every night, and when they approached the watching place they set their burdens in a pile near the entrance. The next day, other Racs would fit these and other stones in place.

Only one seemed to think it strange that Wanderer, Stonerapper, and Shorttail, the strangers who had come to see the tree that held up the sky, joined in the community's efforts. "Stop!" cried Leaf in her smoothest tones when she saw them pick up their stones each night and step into line. "Go away! Just sit and watch! Better yet, go home!" she cried in the morning, when they took stones from the waiting pile, passed some to other Racs, and set some on the walls themselves.

Blacktop's growling voice could calm her only briefly. "Hush," he said. "Let them help. We need every hand. And

remember, every stone they move gives them a greater sense
that this watching place is theirs as well as ours."

"That is the trouble."

"They will never lead their people here to destroy it."

"But they will claim the right to watch with us. To attempt
to climb the Tower." Three small Racs clustered near their
mother's knees, looking up at her as if to ask what distressed
her so. She cupped their heads in her hands. "To seize our
children's future."

"Yes," said Blacktop. "And no. Not seize. But share."

Leaf snorted at him and pointed. "Look. They *will* destroy
it. Already he takes our stones."

When Blacktop followed her finger with his gaze, he
snorted himself, but more in amusement than in outrage.
Stonerapper had picked a small slab of shale from the pile
and was studying it carefully, slanting it against the light.
As they watched, he nodded and put the rock in one of the
pouches that hung from his belt.

"A bone-rock," said Blacktop. "You have picked them up
yourself."

Leaf snorted once more and turned away from both Blacktop and the strangers he inexplicably tolerated.

The watching place had grown. The arc of stone was narrower
and deeper now, less like a parabolic dish antenna than a
round-bottomed letter U. The triangular stem was gone, its
stones scavenged for more important aspects of the construction. An observer, noting the smell of dust, mossberries, and
many bodies, might have guessed that decades or centuries
hence, the moss would long since have lapped across the bare
dirt path that rimmed the wall outside, but the floor inside
would be as bare then as now, every trace of moss worn away
and kept away by the repeated passage of many feet.

The walls were higher, stone fitted carefully to stone, the
meter-high edges as straight and even as if the Racs were
New England dry-stone masons transported from another
age, another time. Single rounded blocks of stone stood
within the enclosure, arrayed to repeat the line of the wall,
U within U within U, leaving empty only a central aisle.
In the opening of the arc was a pyramid of stone steps,
constructed to surround and brace a bark-stripped pole four

meters tall. Atop the pole was a wicker basket woven to mimic the bulbous tip of the Gypsies' Tower.

The Gypsies were careful not to interfere, but those whose business it was to observe the Racs had noted the resemblance of the pole to the staff Blacktop once had planted in the soil atop the bluff, of the basket to the fruit he had scooped and hollowed. Yet this pole resembled even more the Tower, which was now stripped wholly of its bark, smoothed of branch-stubs, polished so it glowed red and orange beneath the setting sun. The pumps that were filling the wood's pores with mineral still throbbed. Bioblimps still hovered above and around the tip, while crews installed the first of the ceramic plaques that would someday reveal secrets of origin and nature to the Racs.

The congregation filed into the watching place and sat upon the blocks, revealing their function as simple pews. They waited patiently, silently, unmoving, until every seat was taken and no Rac was left standing except one. That one then stepped onto the lowest step of the pyramid that held the miniature Tower. Anyone who stood or sat at the back of the stone-walled U could see him in line with and superimposed upon the base of the pole, while the pole itself and its basket were superimposed precisely upon the Tower beyond.

The priest's light yellow pelt stood out in the dusk as he lifted each hand in turn to his muzzle and scratched a formal greeting to his congregation. When they had replied in kind, he raised both arms to his sides until they were level with his shoulders. "Do we have offerings?" His voice was deep, rough, comforting to his fellows though to both bots and humans it sounded like a promise of mayhem. He beckoned with his fingertips. "Come. It is time. We cannot yet climb the Tower our gods have made to challenge us. But we can show them we stand ready to obey, to find the secrets of the world, to learn all that we must to build or climb or fly to reach the chamber of secrets so high above."

Arms still extended, he searched the congregation with his eyes. Then he turned, showing them his back and the dark stripe that ran from the top of his head to the end of his spine while he faced the pole and the Tower, their own simulation and past it the real one, so far unattainable. Blacktop bent his head back and up, staring at the Tower's tip, snarled exultantly, and cried, "Who will be first?"

One by one, the members of the congregation stood, opened the pouches that hung from their harnesses, and produced their offerings. Treasures in hand, they formed a line down the middle of the watching place and filed toward their priest.

The first, a burly female with a scarred leg and a limp, stepped past Blacktop to the second step of the stone pyramid and held out a sheet of paper for his inspection. The priest, his arms still horizontal, nodded even though he could tell the paper was nothing but an outdated duty roster. The female then immediately put one corner of the paper between her lips, climbed the two remaining steps, and leaped halfway up the pole. Her claws sank audibly into the wood as she climbed, and in a moment her face was even with the opening of the basket. Her motions as she placed her paper within the basket seemed reverently slow, but it was only seconds before she was once more on the ground and walking back to her stone seat.

Others followed her with books, computer cards and disks, instruction sheets, and a dozen other bits of human "knowledge" they had found dropped, mislaid, or simply set aside for a moment. The one exception was a young Rac whose creamy fur was marked with orange on his shins, belly, shoulders, and forehead. Known as Firetouch, he held out to Blacktop a length of bark covered with drawings of dumbos' wings, leaves blowing on the breeze, and a flattened, tilted hand that bristled with narrow lines.

"Garbage!" cried a menacingly smooth voice behind the priest. "That is not knowledge! Only pictures! Scribbles in the dirt!"

Someone else laughed and added, "He has been doing that ever since he was a cub."

A third said, "How could he find true knowledge? He never ventures near the Tower."

Blacktop's arms and shoulders fell. He turned to face the speakers. He shook his head.

"Is this true, Firetouch?" His voice was as rough as ever. "Is this something of your own? Did you devise it?"

Behind him, the other was still holding out the strip of bark, seeming confident and resolute. He nodded. When he spoke his voice too was rough. "Yes."

"Tell us, then, what it is."

Firetouch's deep breath was plainly audible. "Dumbos' wings," he said. Now his tone was touched with the smoothness of apprehension. Would his gift to the Tower be rejected? Was it too crude? Too simple?

"Like leaves in wind," he said. He pointed with one clawed finger at the sketch of a hand. "Hold hand, your hand, in wind. Feel it push. It wants to move." He indicated the bristling lines. "Up," he added. "And up."

Clearly, Firetouch was one of those whose minds did not lend themselves to speech. Yet that did not mean his mind was useless, and he was after all articulate enough for his purpose.

Blacktop bowed his head. Then he said, loud enough for all to hear, "You dream of flying."

"Yes."

"Then it is you, and those like you, who will lead us to the Tower."

"But the humans already know how to fly!" cried the one who had already denounced Firetouch's offering as garbage.

"That is *their* knowledge," said the priest. "We must learn it for ourselves, just as every cub must learn to walk."

"We teach them! As the humans should teach us!"

"No," said Blacktop. "No cub needs a teacher, but only encouragement. That . . ." He spun to point at the Tower with an outflung arm. "That is *our* encouragement."

He then gently pushed Firetouch toward the pole. "Go," he said. "Make your offering."

Once the youth had leaped up the pole and down again to vanish in the congregation, once the few remaining Racs had deposited their scraps of paper or plastic in the basket, Blacktop turned back to them. Slowly he scanned his eyes across all the Racs in the enclosure of the watching place. He hesitated when he saw the visitors from that distant tribe to one side, near the wall. Near them, not an arm's length away, sat Wetweed. Blacktop sighed at the thought that only two of his tribe, Firetouch and Wetweed, looked at the world to learn, and not just for what the Gypsies mislaid, dropped, and left behind.

Stonerapper held something in his hands, something flat and heavy, a stone of course, perhaps the very stone Leaf and Blacktop had seen him pick up earlier.

The priest waited patiently. Wetweed's hands were empty. Would the visitor make of his stone an offering?

Could a stone be knowledge?

Other Racs realized where he was looking and turned their own eyes toward the visitors. Wanderer poked his companion with a stiffened finger, and Stonerapper jerked. He looked at Blacktop, at what he held, and then he shook his head. No. Not yet.

The priest sighed and broke the expectant silence at last. "Only one of you." He raised his hands imploringly. "Only one. All the rest of you believe that all the knowledge we must seek belongs to our Gypsy Makers. That finding knowledge means picking up their leavings. That what they already know, there is no point to finding for ourselves.

"They have told us that every star is a sun. Many suns have worlds. Many worlds have life. Some of that life must be as intelligent as Racs and Gypsies. And every such intelligent kind must learn the workings of its world for itself. Secrets are always new to those who have not met them before."

"But we have the Gypsies," someone called from the growing shadows within the watching place. "They are here. They could tell us everything! But they refuse!"

"No," said Blacktop. "They have told us much already. They promise even more in what the Tower will hold when they leave us. Yet they also say that we must learn some things by ourselves, without help."

"Why?"

"So that we will also learn how to find secrets *they* have not found. So that someday we will be able to surpass our gods."

The congregation had heard this all before, yet still it grew more hushed. Eventually one Rac stood up. The light was too dim to reveal his markings, but his voice identified him as Firetouch. "Then the Tower is not our final goal. It is only the edge of the bluff we see from the valley. Beyond it . . ."

"We cannot know," said the priest. "Maybe even the Gypsies cannot know. But if it is the edge of a bluff, then there are forests and mountains and more bluffs beyond."

After a moment's pause, he added, "And you are the first to offer up a secret of your own."

"It was only a question."

"Questions are the most desirable of secrets, for without them there can be no answers. And this one was your own." Blacktop was silent for a long moment while he stared toward the other. From the corner of his eye, he registered a change in Stonerapper's posture: straighter, prouder, less uncertain. Next time then, perhaps, he would offer up the question he had found.

"The more questions we ask, the more answers we find," he continued. "The more offerings we can make. The sooner we will be able to climb the Tower. The sooner we too will be gods, and perhaps even more than gods."

He scanned the congregation. "I hope others will soon set foot beside you on the path out of our valley."

The Bioblimp hovered, one tentacle anchoring it to the shaft of the Racs' miniature replica of the Tower. Another tentacle snaked through the open hatch of its control cabin to curl around Caledonia Emerald's legs and hold her fronds against her chest. "Is he still there?" she asked.

Lucas Ribbentrop sat at the console, his hands ready to work the controls that would make the Bioblimp pluck the bot from the cabin and lower her toward the ground. A screen before him showed a single source of infrared within the watching place. It occupied a stone seat beside the aisle and about a third of the way back from the opening of the U. It moved only as if to shift its weight from one buttock to the other.

"Blacktop never misses," he said.

"Wants to make sure we come clean out the Lost & Found box."

"If we didn't show, he'd have to do it himself."

"Couldn't let it get choked up."

"Not a chance. I want Leonardo's scribbles for the museum."

"Gil Abenden just wants his little black book."

"If they found it, he's got it."

With one hand Ribbentrop moved a slide and touched a pressure pad. With the other he reached for a joystick. "Ready?"

"Ready."

* * *

The Rac Surveillance Office occupied an entire pumpkin not far from the base of the Tower. One room was devoted to monitoring the tiny cameras and microphones that clung to trees in the Rac villages and to the basket that overlooked the watching place. Another room was where, during the day, a technician made and repaired the bugs. A third was a storeroom. The fourth and largest held the broad table on which Caledonia Emerald was dumping the Racs' evening offerings. Firetouch's strip of bark was already propped on a shelf.

"At least they keep the place picked up," said Ribbentrop. He was crumpling sheets of paper and throwing them toward a wastebasket.

"So do litterbugs." The bot was sorting through the trove as well.

"But they never give it back."

"Do you think Firetouch'll start a fad?"

"Get the rest of them thinking for themselves, you mean?"

"Some of them, anyway." As the bot bent forward, a blue petal, streaked with orange, fell from her scalp. It too wound up in the wastebasket.

The man snorted. "Maybe a few. Most of 'em—litter, most *people*—just can't. They pick up scraps of knowledge all their lives. They haven't a clue how to make it."

"But people are always being told, 'Take my word for it.' In school, at home." She picked up a palm-sized notebook covered in brown plastic; when she fanned its pages, she saw it was half full of names and numbers, many of them scratched out.

"Religion too."

Caledonia Emerald laughed and set the notebook aside. "Not very human, is it? A religion that doesn't insist on keeping its worshippers on their faces in the muck, that says here's a leg up, come on, join your gods, even go beyond them."

"We're *not* gods, dammit."

"That's what they're calling us in that baby cathedral out there."

"Huh."

"We should have known we couldn't prevent religion."

"We never mentioned it, never taught it. It was just too easy to invent."

"And look what they invented," said Caledonia Emerald.

"It's embarrassing is what it is. Who the hell wants to be a god?"

"Our kind, anyway."

"That's it."

The sorting was done. The useless, outdated papers were discarded. The rest were arranged in rows upon the table.

"We can get things back where they belong tomorrow."

"Gil bunks next door to me. Did you find his little black book?"

"It's brown." When she handed it to him, he laughed and added, "The *Quebec* is back."

From a Rac, her snarl would have indicated a very good mood. "I've heard. What a screw-up. If Pearl Angelica had asked . . ."

"The bot council?"

The bot's answering nod was curt. "She'd still be here."

"You'd have had to tie her up."

"Such a waste. She had so much potential."

Some bots aboard the *Gypsy* chose to put down their roots in the spacecraft's parks. Many lived alone, as family units, and as small groups of friends in apartments that were much the same as those the humans used, though their floors were dirt and their ceilings were banks of sun-mimicking lights. Many more lived in the large chamber that had been set aside for the bots to build a community of their own if they wished. The community had never developed because the bots had found much more acceptance here than on the Earth they had fled, but the chamber remained, brightly lit by artificial sunlight, the ground covered with grass, vines, shrubs, and trees, some of them always in bloom and the air oppressive with honeysuckle and other scents.

The three oldest of the bots, not one of whom was old enough to remember Earth, were gathered in this chamber, in a clearing whose bare dirt testified to repeated churnings by bot roots plunging in and out of the soil. Two showed their age in lined skin, fading blossoms, and worn fronds.

One, Crimson Orchis, the youngest of the three, still had vivid petals.

"She must have reproduced?" asked Boston Lemon. Her fronds were edged with brown, and her blossoms had once been a brilliant yellow.

"No." Titian Thyme—once red-flowered, still pungent-scented—furled her fronds tightly, defensively. "She never did."

"Why not? She's old enough ten times over."

"I need the honeysuckle to answer that." Titian Thyme let her roots enter the soil and synapse with the living cables that would link her to the records preserved in the computers that were rooted elsewhere in the chamber. She was silent then for several minutes. "The last time that subject came up, she said she wasn't ready for a family, she hadn't yet found anyone—bot or human—that she wished for a mate, and besides, she was too busy."

"At least," said Crimson Orchis, "she gave us bits of her tissues for the freezers."

"So we've got tissue samples," said Boston Lemon. "It'll still take years to grow up any clones."

"Better to lose the time," said Titian Thyme, "than to lose her genes."

"They're crucial," said Crimson Orchis, and the flowers that gave her her name shook as she nodded. "She has lived so much longer than any of the rest of us. If she would only mate . . ."

"Then we would have an Eldest."

The others nodded. The title of Eldest did not go with age alone, else Pearl Angelica would have the title already. Lacking that, one of them would bear it. But it also called for experience and wisdom, and the bots had long ago realized that Pearl Angelica would accumulate more of both age and experience than any other bot. When the last Eldest died, even before the *Gypsy*'s departure from Earth orbit, they had chosen to wait for the wisdom.

Some thought her wise enough already. Once "Eldest" had meant nothing more than "Oldest"; that bot with the most life experience had been as well the wisest, or close enough. But Pearl Angelica had been older than the oldest while she was still a child. Granting her the title of "Eldest" had seemed ludicrous. Yet now that she was an adult, she still seemed far too young for the title.

Some said she was reluctant to grow up, to assume her responsibilities to her kind, to mate and reproduce. She had a duty, they said, to pass on and spread the genes that lengthened her life and diminished her leaves and flowers and thereby made her more similar than any of her ancestors to the humans. As long as she shirked that duty, she should not be Eldest.

"We should start the cloning now," said Crimson Orchis.

Titian Thyme nodded in agreement, but Boston Lemon said, "Not yet. She is not dead. She may return to us."

"No," said Crimson Orchis. "Lois McAlois has reported that the Engineers want a tunnel-drive. She says we cannot give it to them. So she *is* dead, or she will be soon."

"She could escape."

"How? She is not human enough to pass among the Engineers."

"We could rescue her!"

Titian Thyme shook her head. "No. That would surely cost too many lives, and we already have her tissues and her genes. Her most important parts will not be lost, no matter what."

"But all the living she has done so far *will* be lost. And we will not have an Eldest."

"We've managed well enough so far."

Chapter
Eleven

THE MAN WITH the black curls was by the concourse wall again, his stare seeming as hot as summer sunlight on the scalelike leaves that covered her skin. He continued as always to keep his distance, wary either of her, so strange, so alien, officially anathema, or of his own kind, the Engineers, as represented by Hrecker and his security force.

Pearl Angelica ignored him. Her hands gripped the bars of her cage. Her knuckles were white. Her eyes ached with the strain of staring at the veedo screen so long, so hard. Yet she remained aware of the several Engineers who stood nearby or sat on the edge of the dais that held her planter, all of them watching as intently as she.

Hrecker had come to her the evening before, standing close, holding his hand where she could see the black plastic remote and its promise of at least temporary freedom. His other hand held up a pair of long black socks with their feet cut off. "Cover your roots. Then come with me," he had said. "We have more questions."

"No handcuffs?" No such things were visible in his hands or dangling from his belt.

"Where would you go?"

He had led her through corridor after corridor until they reached an innocuous-seeming chamber, the size of an apartment living room, carpeted, furnished with a metal table, upholstered chairs, and even a sofa.

"The Minister for Education." Hrecker had indicated the only one of the four waiting men who was not wearing solely the typical uniform of the Engineers. His blue shirt was mostly hidden by an old-fashioned grey wool sports coat whose breast pocket held several pens in a plastic sleeve. His hand grasped an unlit pipe. A sunburst medallion was visible on his shirtfront beneath one lapel. The other three men wore lapelless jackets such as Pearl Angelica had seen on other Engineers; the colors were light pink and orange, and the collars were padded arcs.

Hrecker had then pushed her toward a straight-backed, unpadded seat. She did not sit until she had rocked it on its pedestal and seen that it was not built to spin and jerk. One of the others then actually handed her a cup of coffee.

She had felt absurdly grateful for that small indication that someone, anyone, saw in her a fellow human being. Yet that gratitude had not lasted long. It had vanished as soon as it was clear that there would be no more introductions, replaced by a watchfulness that told her the unnamed three were just as confident in their manner as the Minister for Education. They were neither aides nor toadies but men of status in their own right. She faced, she guessed, the lunar equivalent of Earth's Council of Engineers. She wished she knew their names and positions; their metal ornaments provided no clues.

Now she stared at the veedo screen intently, as if she thought it might relieve her ignorance. That same room was laid out before her. She was visible, captured by hidden cameras as she faced the others. Hrecker was standing by the room's only door, and someone was saying, "Tell us about the Racs."

She obeyed, once more describing the raccoonlike near-sentients the Gypsies had found when they reached Tau Ceti IV and the decision of the gengineers to try to raise their intelligence to human level. "We were disappointed," she said. "The smaller ships had visited several worlds by then, and though they had found life, there were no signs of intelligence at all. We were feeling lonely."

"Arrogant, you mean. You had no business—"

"Monsters," said someone else.

"No," she answered. She hoped the man meant the Racs but she knew he would apply the same word to the Gypsies. "They're builders, not destroyers. They love their mates and children. They look at the stars and yearn. And they're covered with fur, not slime. They have arms and legs just like us, not tentacles or claws."

"You taught them everything you could," said the grey-jacketed Minister for Education.

"No." She shook her head, though she knew it was useless to argue. "Not everything. Not at all. They wouldn't be able to use so much. But fire, yes. Basic survival skills. Language. We wanted them to have the basis for building a culture of their own. We didn't want just to hand them ours."

"Why not?"

One of the Engineers who had not been introduced smirked. "Don't you think it's good enough?"

She shrugged at her interrogators. "We wanted neighbors, friends. Not clones. We thought they would be more interesting, maybe even more valuable as allies against whatever we might someday find, if they developed in their own way for a while."

"How long? Are they supposed to come find you when they learn how to build spaceships?"

She nodded.

"That will take centuries. Millennia!"

"So you built the Tower to speed the schedule up."

"All of human history. All of human knowledge."

"Hypocrites as well as arrogant. 'A culture of their own,' eh?"

"We gave them only Stone Age technology," she said. "They have to develop much more on their own before they can climb the Tower."

"That's not that hard," someone said. "They won't need helicopters. Balloons will do. Or towers, skyscrapers."

"It took humans five thousand years to go from the Stone Age to hot air balloons," she said. "Just a few hundred years ago. We won't speed up their development that much."

Friends, she thought in her cage. Neighbors and allies. That was what the Gypsies craved, and there was no guarantee that the Racs would ever be such things. They might become Engineers and enemies. They might even destroy themselves as humans had nearly done. But the Gypsies had decided the Racs had a right to their own destiny.

She remembered the debate among the Gypsies. "Help them now," some had urged. "Teach them everything. Make them Gypsies and take them with us if they'll come."

"No," had said others. "That would rob them of their heritage, just as long ago on Earth we robbed other, more primitive peoples of theirs."

"What heritage?" her father, Frederick, had asked. "They haven't got one. They haven't been a people long enough."

"But . . ."

"On the other hand," he had said, "if we interfere too much too soon, we can only weaken their pride in themselves as a people, make them dependent, rob them of potential. Grow the Tower high, so high no one can climb it easily, and they will have time enough. Time enough to grow a culture of their own quite rich enough to stand the shock of whatever they learn from what we leave behind."

"These Racs will never have a chance. We'll cleanse them from the universe just as we have cleansed the Earth." The voice from the veedo was stern and unforgiving, unrelenting, righteous.

"Yeah!" The voice snatched her mind from the screen to a mustached man sitting on the edge of her planter. He was glaring up at her, lips parted, teeth showing.

She shuddered just as she had the night before, just as her image was now doing on the veedo screen. "Get away from me," she hissed. Grains of soil bounced from the Engineer's shirt as a root tendril popped out of the soil and stretched toward him. She wriggled it. "Or I'll push this root up your—"

"You wouldn't . . . !" But he scrambled out of reach and found another perch from which he could watch the screen.

She hadn't dared to say a word the night before, much less threaten violence. Knowing she was powerless, she had forced herself to clamp her lips between her teeth. But then the Minister had rapped the stem of his pipe against the table and spoke what at first seemed much more reasonable words. "We're not really that different, are we? Some people might have given your Racs all the education that was available just as soon as they showed they could talk."

When she nodded, he went on. "Fortunately, that sort of soft-headed liberalism is long, long past. It nearly destroyed twentieth-century America, you know. You don't? No matter. We do." He waved one hand dismissively. "My point is that we, both the Engineers and the Gypsies, know that knowledge should not be freely available to all who ask for it. It must be held close, restricted, reserved for the advantage of society. Though you don't hold it close enough." He shook his head. "That Tower."

"Research too," said Hrecker from his post by the door.

"Ah, yes," said the Minister. "You had to arrest—" He chopped the sentence off when Hrecker gestured as if toward the camera. "Ah, yes," he said again. "Unrestricted access to knowledge. Unrestricted, unregulated research. They are what led to the evil of the gengineers, the loss of the first Machine Age, and the destruction of so much of Earth."

He leaned toward the Pearl Angelica on the veedo screen. "Genetic engineering should have been banned at its very beginning."

The bot in the cage shuddered as the people in the concourse around her murmured in approval of the Minister's statement.

"You would have burned Gregor Mendel at the stake," she had said sourly.

"Not that perhaps. Some good came of his discoveries, after all. Better crops. Cures for diseases. But . . ." He shook his head. "You do understand. We cannot permit another such disaster. We will not permit it. And we will destroy whatever we must to ensure that it does not happen. Certainly we will destroy your Tower as soon as we can reach Tau Ceti IV."

Once more the concourse murmured with agreement. Pearl Angelica glanced toward the man who had fled her threatening root. He was nodding vigorously.

"And the Racs," said another of the bot's interrogators on the veedo screen. "They are abomination."

The Minister for Education smiled at the bot. "It should be enough to leave them in their Stone Age, confined to their world. We don't have to live there with them, after all."

"But they are evil!"

"Unnatural!"

"Destroy them!"

When the veedo image was suddenly replaced by a commercial for a line of sextants and steam engines and other clothing ornaments that celebrated the dawn of the golden age of mechanical technology, Pearl Angelica understood that that was the last note her captors wished to sound for their audience. A goad to tell every Engineer on the Moon what was the proper way to think. A threat to the Orbitals and the Gypsies so far away. A compact with doom for Pearl Angelica herself.

And the audience had not missed the point. There were mutterings around her, dark glances. Someone threw a pebble. The man who had fled the edge of her planter cursed. A mother turned her child away from the wicked bot, glared over her shoulder, and fled the concourse.

She wanted to cry, but she knew that tears would only please the Engineers. She clamped her eyelids shut and held the water back.

"It's not fair."

Pearl Angelica was taking what pleasure she could in the artificial sunlight that inundated the small leaves that covered her body. She refused to open her eyes, though the voice came from close by. Someone—male and rather past his youth—was sitting on the edge of her planter even though most of the lunar Engineers were keeping their distance after the threats the Minister for Education had made. "What isn't fair?"

"Everything." There was a pause and the sound of cloth rubbing rock as a body sought some more comfortable position. "The schools teach us only what we need for our jobs. Anything else, they say, is wasted effort. And dangerous. Like he said on the veedo."

"You were watching." It was not a question.

"Everyone's seen it. They've shown it several times. And the way they treated the gengineers and the bots. There are rumors . . ." The voice hesitated. "Mass graves. Mass murder. Do they really want to wipe you out *that* way?"

"It's true." She opened her eyes and was not surprised to see a head of dark curls leaning against a bar of her cage. "They don't admit that?"

The curls shook in negation. "I never heard it discussed at all until I was in high school, and then the textbooks and teachers all said it was a political thing. The Engineers won elections everywhere. When they passed laws to regulate gengineering, the gengineers and their sympathizers fled the planet. Then they destroyed all the Roachsters and other bioforms."

"What's your name?"

When he looked up at her, surprised at her interest, she saw a light brown skin, dark eyes, and a long, angular face that, with the hair, spoke of eastern Mediterranean ancestors. He seemed no more than a little older than she. "Anatol. Anatol Rivkin. I don't remember it that way, you know. But I don't remember murder either. I was just a kid. My mother never talked about it."

"Your father?"

"I barely remember him. Maybe he . . ." He fell silent, though his voice was rising at the end as if he were about to ask, "Maybe he was murdered?"

"I didn't see it myself," said Pearl Angelica. "I wasn't even born until after we left."

"But I do remember . . ." He paused, licked his lips, looked around the concourse as if wary of being overheard. "We must be bugged. They do that all the time, you know."

"They watch you all?"

"Not really all the time, I suppose. Though they could, especially if they used the computers." He shrugged. "If they do, or if they just happen to have heard me, you'll never see me again."

"But why?"

"I didn't accept the official line. I'm asking questions."

"Then you shouldn't say anything else."

"It's too late." He hesitated as if wondering whether he were right. "I remember the bioforms," he said at last. "We had a Tortoise. A pig under the sink. Snackbushes and hanky bushes. And then . . ."

"The Revolution."

He nodded. "Yeah. We lost it all. Things got pretty tough. They're better now, but it took a while."

"Was it worth it?"

He shook his head and fell silent as others entered the concourse. They were only passing through, but they paused long enough to examine the specimen in its cage and say to Anatol, "Unnatural thing, ain't it?"

"Perverted," said Rivkin. "I hear they're all female. Makes you wonder what those gengineers do with them at night."

The others laughed. Pearl Angelica turned her face away and wished her feet were not anchored by her roots. Anatol Rivkin rose from his seat and followed his fellow Engineers from the concourse.

Pearl Angelica knew why Anatol Rivkin had said what he did before he left. The words had hurt her, but she knew that if he had not sounded like any other Engineer he would have been suspect.

Was he suspect anyway? Would he be arrested, charged with treason to the holy cause, jailed, executed? It depended on . . . *Were* there mikes and cameras trained on her? Did Security's people or computers watch her all the time? Did they listen to everything those around her said to her and to each other? Or was it spot checks only? Did Security see only what that roving camera-headed robot showed them? Might Anatol have spoken safely as long as the robot was not present? And if he had been overheard, did Security really care that much what people said?

She felt pleased to learn that the Engineers were not as unified in their ideology as they would like the Orbitals and Gypsies to believe. For a moment, she thought of 'Livrance and Prudence, who had seemed at least capable of sympathy, and wondered whether it was the contact with space that made the difference. There was more freedom there. Even confined to tunnels beneath the surface of the Moon, in spaces much the same as those beneath Detroit, she could sense . . . It was the buoyancy of lighter gravity, she guessed, that spoke of the closeness of vast distances and three dimensions in which to move. There was also more exposure to other ways of thinking in the occasional Orbital an Engineer might meet. Or perhaps there was simply more need for thought in an environment that let one take nothing for granted.

Certainly some of the lunar Engineers were as bigoted as anyone she had met on Earth. And some, such as this Anatol Rivkin, were not. She wondered if Anatols existed there, if she would have found sane and reasonable Earthlings if only she had been able to meet more people on the planet.

She had said nothing about her thoughts then. Nor did she mention them the next day, at noon, when Anatol returned.

By then the worst of the public's avoidance reaction had passed. Several Engineers had even brought their lunches to the concourse and found seats along the edges of the dais that held her planter. Anatol ignored them when he arrived, stepping between the rose and mock orange bushes and climbing up to touch the bars of her cage. He had a sandwich in his fist; lettuce, tomato slices, green pepper strips, and something unidentifiable were visible between the slices of bread. As soon as he sat down, she asked, "What's—?"

He didn't wait for her to finish. "Soy sausage. It's not bad. Do you eat? Is that enough for you?" With his free hand, he indicated the spotlight that illuminated her leaves.

She shook her head, and her stomach growled. He laughed and tore the sandwich in two.

"You came here because you wanted bees?" He murmured the words as if trying not to be overheard by his fellow Engineers or Security's eavesdroppers.

"I told you. I wanted to see Earth."

"But officially."

"Then yes. Officially. And we really do need them."

"Do you think you'll get them?"

"What difference would it make? I wouldn't be able to take them home with me." She curled one hand tight around a bar. "I'm never going home."

"But . . . They're asking for a ransom, aren't they? Won't your people—?"

"They want a star-drive. You don't think we'll give it to them, do you? We can't, not as long as you want to kill us."

He winced at the change from "they" to "you," but he did not try to argue with her. He fell silent. He bit into what was left of his sandwich and chewed. "Yeah," he said at last.

"So I don't need any bees, do I?" Her own portion of the sandwich was gone, and her voice was rising. "I'll never go home. I'll never see my people, my friends, my father, again."

Anatol made a sympathetic noise. "He was dying when I left," she added. "He may be dead already. And I won't live much longer. I'll die right here. Just as soon as they realize they aren't going to get what they want."

"How long?"

"I came with my aunt, you know. Now she's on the way back to the *Gypsy* to say what happened. To say what ransom your people want. And as soon as she gets back here . . ."

"How long?" he asked again.

"Another month," she said. "A little more. A little less. That's all I've got."

Anatol bowed his head. "And there's no way out of it, is there?"

"You want us *all* dead."

Pearl Angelica did not think that his silence was only because there were others nearby who might overhear his words. He simply could not answer her.

She did not see Anatol again that day or the next. But the lunar base followed the rhythms of Earth. When night came, the corridor lights dimmed and the traffic in the base's corridors diminished. A few people worked night shifts in control rooms and administrative offices, but most ate and socialized and eventually slept. In time even the veedo shut itself off. Silence reigned in the concourse as Pearl Angelica twisted her roots again and again through the recycled soil that filled her planter, tasting it, loosening it, plowing it. She hadn't really needed, she thought, to come to Earth for bees. Paintbrushes worked, after all. And eventually they would find or gengineer something to serve the purpose. But she had wanted to see the home of her ancestors.

Root-home.

Folly.

Doom.

Earth was so unlike her dreams that she felt . . . No, disappointment was not the word. She felt *foolish*.

Frederick, her father, might be dead already. Or he would die before she could get home even if she left right now.

But she couldn't leave. Her foolishness had cost her the chance to say a last good-bye to her father.

She had been kidnapped and raped and imprisoned, caged like a beast in a zoo. She was being held for a ransom that would—that *could*—never come. She was going to die here, a long, long way from home. Among strangers, and worse than strangers. Among enemies.

And all her other dreams and yearnings, all the potential that her fellow bots so treasured, would be forever lost.

The sound of feet sliding quietly across the concourse's rocky floor brought her eyes open. The dim light was enough to let her recognize the head approaching her. "Marcus."

Marcus Yamoto stood between two rose bushes near her feet. He smelled of beer and garlic even over the strong perfumes of the flowers. "I saw the show."

"Didn't everyone?"

He nodded. "Have you learned anything else since we talked?"

"Only that they're not all as awful as I thought."

"I could have told you that. They're a little saner here. Some of them even realize that they have more in common with the Orbitals than with Earth."

"Not very many."

"The ideologues are still in control. And that doesn't seem likely to change." He shook his head. "I didn't really expect you to have anything new for me this soon. But I've got to go away for a while. I'm a trader, right? So, back to the Orbitals."

She grasped the bars of her cage with both hands and put her face as close to his as she could manage. "Tell them . . ." She stopped, not knowing what she wanted him to say for her, or who she wanted him to say it to. Lois McAlois could not yet be back. She took a deep breath.

He covered one of her hands with his own, squeezing it against the metal bar. "I'll tell them you're alive."

"No." She blinked as tears curdled her vision. "Or yes. That too. But say, say I'm not expecting to be ransomed. They shouldn't. It's not worth it."

"Yes." He nodded, squeezed her hand once more, and was gone.

She was still gripping the bars of her cage, teeth sunk into her lower lip, when Anatol Rivkin's quiet voice, almost a whisper, made her open her eyes.

"Who was he? An Orbital, I know, but . . ." He was looking up at her, his pupils wide in the dimmed light.

"A trader." She looked away from him, toward the corridor into which Marcus had disappeared. "A contact. A friend, I hope. He'll tell them I'm okay. Alive, anyway."

Anatol grunted as he sat on the edge of her planter, wrapping his own hand around a bar to help him keep his balance. "When you were talking to the Council down there . . ." He glanced briefly upward as if he could see Earth through the concourse's ceiling. "Down" had two meanings on the Moon, at least for those who had come up from Earth. "You said you were looking for root-home. That's why you came here."

"The land of my forebears. You saw that on the veedo too."

He nodded. "Yeah. I can understand that. I want it too."

"But you're already home."

"The way things used to be," he said. "More like that, I guess."

"When the Engineers were just a crank cult. When there was a Roachster in every garage and a pie plant in every kitchen."

"A Tortoise. But yeah. The Good Old Days."

"I never knew them."

"A lot of us remember. Vaguely, anyway. And we aren't all like . . ." His gesture included the Minister for Education and his anonymous colleagues, the Council of Engineers on Earth, and all the rest of his culture's rulers. "It was nice then. There weren't many machines, but there were a lot more people."

"That's why there weren't—"

"I know. They don't teach us that, but it's easy enough to see. The resources had been drawn down too far and spread too thin. The bioforms really were the only way to meet people's needs."

"Birth control could have done it."

"That would have solved some of the discontent too. Unemployment was bad enough even before the gengineers made carpenters and mechanics and miners superfluous. Afterward, there was a lot of anger."

They fell silent.

He was leaning against the bars, one shoulder touching her knee, looking downward, studying the way her roots sprang from her shins and calves and burrowed into the dirt, the way her toes curled and dug as if they too could be roots. She leaned against the other side of the bars, her forehead pressed against one cold metal rod, her eyes ranging along the walls of the concourse from corridor mouth to corridor mouth, watching for anyone who might interrupt them, listening for approaching footsteps. For a moment, she thought, if he were caught being too friendly . . . But then she remembered that they were surely bugged. Hrecker and his men surely knew that Anatol was there, although perhaps his quiet voice had not been clearly heard and his face, kept distant during the day, now shadowed by night and bowed as well, had not been seen.

"They didn't really want me there," she said at last. "Even though they kidnapped me. They weren't about to give me any tours. They didn't even want to let me taste Earth's soil. But I escaped just long enough."

"Was it what you expected?"

She looked down at him and rocked her forehead against the bar she held. "No. It wasn't home. It must have been once upon a time. But it isn't now."

"Maybe I should take a lesson from that. If I defected . . ."

"I *can't* defect. I'm a bot. I couldn't even visit, until they decided to kidnap me."

"No one's going to kidnap me."

"Then give it up. Stop wishing. Settle for hidebound, oppressive, irrational . . ."

"It's not that bad!"

"Oh?"

"Yeah. We're innovative enough. We just don't do things the way you do."

"And there's room for both of us in the universe?"

He nodded silently. "I don't see why they want to wipe you out."

"They're afraid we'll prove they're wrong."

Chapter
Twelve

THE CORRIDOR MOUTHS held small clumps of young Engineers, three here, four there, none much older than boys. They peered toward Pearl Angelica, pointed, waved at their friends across the concourse, talked, and laughed. Then they vanished, only to appear again a little later.

Robots, oblivious of tension, scooted out of the corridors and across the concourse, swaying on their wheels. Other Engineers, men and women both, hurried through like planet-dwellers who sensed a coming storm. Few lingered near the dais and the cage. None spoke to the captive bot.

Pearl Angelica tried to ignore the situation, but as the day wore on that grew harder and harder. She guessed the youths were working up their nerve to approach her, the gengineered monster, and taunt, torment, even kill her. She did not know their actual plans or when the crisis would come.

But before anything could happen, the camera robot appeared in the one corridor that held no cluster of young men. Beside it materialized two Security guards, identifiable by their holstered sidearms and watchful air. Across the concourse, Hrecker emerged behind one group and spoke to them using gestures that let Pearl Angelica construct his words in her mind: "What are you doing here? We know she's scum and worse, but we can't do anything to her now. She's our only hope of getting a starship, don't you know? Queer that deal, and we'll make compost out of you. C'mon, clear out, get lost."

The strut went out of the group and its members vanished up the corridor Hrecker had used. When he moved along the concourse's rim to a second group, the scene played out again, and then again. Yet Pearl Angelica's state of mind did not improve when all the youths were gone. She found herself wishing that Anatol Rivkin would appear, but though she studied carefully every passerby, she saw no sign of him.

The lights dimmed. The traffic through the concourse grew sparse and sparser and finally stopped entirely. No one came, and she began to wonder whether Security had indeed been listening to their conversations, whether Hrecker had decided that Anatol was no longer a loyal or reliable Engineer, whether her sole friend on the Moon had been arrested, imprisoned, executed, or sent back to Earth.

The morning shower announced another day that crawled past, bringing night again in its wake. Still there was no sign of her only friend. She found herself thinking of him constantly. Was he safe? Where was he? Would she see him again? When?

Gradually, other questions grew to dominate her thoughts: She had known him so briefly. Why was she so obsessed with him? He was the only Engineer who had offered her a friendly word. Was that enough to account for her obsession? Or was there something more? Would she care so much if he were another Gypsy?

Struggling to control her mind, she forced herself to think of the last words she had said to him: "They're afraid we'll prove they're wrong."

Were they wrong?

It was mechanical technology that had raised the human species from savagery, wasn't it? That had fed and clothed billions and tied a global economy together with rapid transportation and communication?

But what had made those billions possible? Not transportation or communication. Not industry. But agriculture—that had enabled the birth of civilization. Antibiotics and vaccines and Green Revolutions. Greatest of all, perhaps, sanitation, the simple realization that sewage and drinking water do not mix.

Mechanical technology had played a role. Of course it had, and for a while it had been by far the more visible of the two. But the greater impact on human life had always belonged to biological technologies, even though few people had ever recognized them as such. And when the machines had run short of fuels and raw materials, their latest versions had filled the gap.

Yet biology could not do everything. Even the Orbitals and Gypsies had to rely on machines for some things, such as space travel.

And the Engineers were buying Macks and Sponges.

In time, perhaps, the two groups would meet in the idea that a single civilization could use both kinds of technology, each in its appropriate place, for its appropriate purposes.

She thought that future might have much more in common with her own peoples than with the Engineers, for the Orbitals and Gypsies already freely used machines when they were better suited to a job than bioforms, although the Gypsies at least did have a distinct preference for the latter. If a larger difference remained, it would be rooted in the natures of Engineers as people who craved control of others and of Orbitals and Gypsies as enablers. The group versus the individual. Authority versus freedom. Duty versus responsibility.

Over the next two days, Security guards strolled through the concourse frequently. When the constantly blaring veedo set said nothing about their presence, Pearl Angelica guessed they were on guard against any recurrence of youthful fervor, any danger to official plans to acquire a starship, perhaps even any risk that a riot might damage their contained environment. Other Engineers did not linger near the dais but rather hurried past, heads down or turned aside.

The situation slowly shifted toward normal. The intervals between Security patrols grew longer. Passersby slowed their pace and once more recognized the bot's existence. A few paused to sniff the flowers and indulge in longer covert stares. At last a couple shared a lunch while sitting on the edge of the dais that held Pearl Angelica's stone planter, ignoring the bot until the man picked a cluster of mock orange blossoms, held them toward her, said, "With your permission," and tucked them into the woman's hair.

When Anatol finally appeared just before dawn, he peered furtively from the empty corridor mouth, scuttled across the concourse floor, and crouched among the bushes beneath the rim of the dais. His face was grey with fatigue, his eyes hollowed. "I heard about the kids."

"Where have you been?" She pushed a hand between the bars but could not reach him.

"Busy. Did I tell you I'm on a tunneling crew? Yeah. Rush order. Back-to-back shifts. No time for anything but sleep."

"I missed you." Her smile was relief and frustration and pain. "What are you doing down there?"

A fading rose blocked her view of his face. He brushed it aside and grinned back at her. "The kids pulled in their horns very nicely, but the halls are still full of Hrecker's troops. I don't want to be chased back to my room."

She withdrew her roots from the soil, knelt, and tried again to reach him. This time their fingers touched. "Just one room?"

He shook his head. "An apartment. But that's what we call it."

"If I could get out of here . . ."

His expression said that he understood what she was offering.

"I think I know how to do it," she added. "But I'll need your help."

"Not now. Wait till the cops go back in their holes."

It was two more days before the Security guards vanished from the concourse entirely. That night, Pearl Angelica said, "They can't be watching me, can they? No cameras, no mikes."

"Or they'd have arrested me already?" When she nodded, he said, "I suppose so. Does that mean we don't have to worry about what we say? Or I say?"

"Uh-uh." She reached between the bars to pat his arm. "I'm not worried for me. I can't be any worse off. But you . . ."

His answering smile was strained. "Just tell me what to do."

"Stand there, Anatol. Right against the bars."

He obeyed, but he asked, "What good will that do?"

"I can't squeeze between the bars. They're too smooth to climb. And they're too high to jump over, even in this gravity. Now bend your knee. Put your hand on your hip."

"Ah," he said, and she set one foot on his knee, the other where his hip braced his wrist. The next step put her on his shoulders. The last perched her on the top of his head.

"Straighten up now," she said. "Grab the bars, and brace yourself. I think I can jump from . . ." There was a grunt of effort. The joints of Anatol's spine popped, and he swayed from the force of her push-off.

She was sliding down the bars, gripping them with both arms and legs, but now she was on the outside of the cage and grinning broadly. Her teeth gleamed in the dim light. "We'll know soon enough if they're watching. If they catch me . . ."

"They'll make the bars higher. Or they'll add a roof."

"I'll worry about that when it happens." She did not look as if she thought it wouldn't. "But you . . . you're risking a lot. Everything. I wish you had someplace safe to go."

He gave a soft bark of laughter. "So do I."

She patted a bar with one hand. Her eyes seemed to probe the corridor mouths on the borders of the concourse. "Is there anywhere we can go where no one will see us?"

"You can't hide out. They'll turn the place upside down. They'll find you for sure. And then you'll never get loose again."

She laughed. "Then I'll have to get back here before dawn. Before anyone sees I'm gone. Where's your room?"

"It's too far away. Too long a hike. Dawn's not that far off." He did not say there was too much chance of meeting someone, for she had planned for that. By his feet was a sack containing a blue shirt and pants. Now he helped her don the clothes and cover up her leaves. When she was dressed, he reached into the sack one more time and said, "I thought of shoes, though I didn't know your size." He held out a pair of sandals.

"I'm not used to these." She frowned in concentration as she fitted them to her feet. When she was done, she stamped her feet and laughed again. "Now let's take a walk," she said. "I need to stretch my legs."

"I wish we had something to cover your head."

"My petals? The light's not bright. We'll be okay."

They almost ran from the concourse and into the nearest corridor. Then they walked, taking turns almost at random, peering into empty, darkened rooms, picking apples and oranges and apricots from dwarf trees in their pots, sniffing flowers, seeing no one other than a few robots trundling by on mysterious errands. Eventually, and far too soon, Anatol was saying, "The night is almost done. We've got to get you back."

Her face fell. "Can't we get a peek at the *Teller* first?"

"No," he said. "That's shut up much too tight."

"Then . . ." She stopped when she remembered Hrecker tapping numbers into a keypad lock. "Okay." She pointed at a left turn just ahead. She had been trying to build up a map of the base in her head as they explored. She did not think they had used that corridor before, but it seemed to go toward familiar ground. "Will that get us back faster?"

"It should. Why do you want to see the ship?"

"I'd like to know how close it is to flying."

He indicated another turn. "I heard two more fuel tanks have been delivered."

"Making four?"

He shrugged. "As far as I know."

They stopped at the border of the concourse and looked at each other. Footsteps sounded faintly in the corridor behind them. "Hurry!" she said, and a moment later she was climbing his sturdy frame once more. The clothes she had worn were hidden under a mock orange bush.

The footsteps were closer now. "Tonight?" she whispered from within her cage. Anatol gave her a curt wave of one hand and vanished into a different corridor.

The concourse lights brightened and the sun-mimicking spotlight above the cage flooded her with brilliance. Water began to sprinkle from the ceiling. The footsteps stopped. She turned, afraid of who she would see in the corridor mouth. But no, the thin-lipped face belonged to no one that she knew. Certainly it was not Hrecker's.

When Anatol returned the next night, he had a wig of black hair long enough to cover Pearl Angelica's ears. With it on, and dressed, she could be betrayed only by the green cast to her skin. Yet, they thought, that would matter only in brighter light than was available in the nighttime corridors. They felt free to explore the lunar base, pausing by viewports, inspecting dark and empty dining halls and libraries and game rooms, avoiding footsteps whenever possible. And when they rounded a corner to confront a cleaning crew, they were delighted to find how well her Engineer disguise worked. Not one of the night workers showed the slightest sign of recognition or alarm at seeing her.

"At least I'm getting exercise," she said three nights later. They were standing beside a viewport that revealed a grey and dusty square of lunar surface tracked by feet and wheels, littered with scraps of twisted metal, cast-off machine parts, and even a forgotten tool or two. The view was surrounded on three sides by the ridges that marked buried tunnels. The fourth side was blocked by a row of sturdy pillars that supported a thick roof; in the black-shadowed space beneath the roof were parked three balloon-tired ground vehicles. Two space-suited workers and a trio of robots were working near the rear of one of them.

"The roof keeps the meteorites off the trucks," he had told her. "We bring them inside only for major repairs."

Her arm brushed his. Their fingers met, and they were holding hands. "I know my way around the base now," she said. "But there's no way out of here."

"Of course there isn't," he said. "We don't keep spaceships here, and if we did . . ." He shrugged. "You'd have to deal with locks and crews. You'd be caught for sure."

She sighed. "I haven't seen your room yet. Do we have time tonight?"

Anatol's "room" turned out to be more than ample for a single man. One room of the apartment held shelves of books, veedo tapes, and music disks, as well as a comfortable reclining seat; one wall was nearly covered with photographs of friends, lunar landscapes, and spiral storms on Earth, viewed from orbit. Another was a bedroom with a small bathroom off one corner. The third room held a small refrigerator and microwave oven, a single glass-fronted cupboard full of dishes, a table, and a computer terminal. "Mostly I use the dining halls," he said. "This is where I study. I don't want to dig tunnels all my life."

"What are you studying?"

He touched the keyboard, and the screen lit up with diagrams and words. "Project management," he said. "Someday I'll be telling the diggers where and when to dig." He looked at his watch. "We've got to get you back."

She made a face. "Can we come here earlier next time?"

Pearl Angelica began to remove her pants and shirt as soon as the apartment door closed behind them.

"Wait a minute!" cried Anatol.

"Bots don't wear clothes," she said. Nor were they ever as celibate as she had been forced to be among the Engineers, and she was a bot. A bot who had never chosen a mate with whom to produce children, though she had had lovers enough.

She threw the shirt on the floor. The wig followed it. "You know that."

"But you're a woman! Aren't you?"

She lifted a single leaf to expose a nipple. "The last time I looked. All the parts are there. And you're a man." She reached for his shirtfront and grinned when he blushed. There was nothing accidental about the effect she was having on him. "You're the only one here to be nice to me. You're sweet. So go ahead. You strip too. It'll be a nice way to pass the night."

"But . . ."

"It's taboo? I'll contaminate you? That's what they said on Earth when I complained about being raped. No one would do such a thing! But Hamid did."

"He's probably dead now."

"Are you afraid they'll find out?" When he nodded jerkily, she said, "I won't tell if you won't. I like you."

Later, she said, "No. No 'Baby.' Call me Pearl if you want. Or Angie. That's okay. But not Angie-Baby."

He grinned and ran his fingers gently under the leaves that covered her stomach. "Angie, then. Angie. I wish I didn't have to take you back to that cage."

"If you don't, we'll never be able to do this again." Her hand was as gentle as his.

"Maybe someday."

"But for now . . ."

Pearl Angelica froze in the doorway. The room was full of Engineers she had never seen before, unless they had visited the concourse to see her in her cage. So many had done that, she told herself. So many she had seen so briefly that it was no wonder she could not remember any of them.

Anatol pushed her abruptly from behind. "Someone's coming. I've got to close the door."

That made her move, even if it did bring her closer to the strangers who were now turning toward her. She heard footsteps on the other side of the door behind her. Were they hesitating? No. They were going past, and now she must face the room before her.

"Want to meet some people tonight?" Anatol had been standing beside her cage when he asked the question that made her back away. His knee and hip and shoulder had already been positioned for her to climb.

"You mean here?"

"Uh-uh. A private party. Maybe a dozen people, and you can trust them all."

"They're Engineers."

"So am I. And you trust me. Don't you, Angie?"

"But I don't know them."

"I do. Come on." He had pointed at his knee, urging her to take the first step. "You say your friends can't ransom you. So you're doomed. So what do you have to lose?"

"You." She had lifted her foot slowly, reluctantly. Was he really that precious to her?

"Ah, well." He had gripped the bars to steady the ladder he was. "And I'd hate to lose you too."

She had landed beside him. "There has to be some risk."

"I think it's worth taking."

And now here she was. Taking that risk despite her better judgment, facing strangers who thought it a lark to invite a prisoner of war among them.

Or did they think it a lark? They held drinks. Trays of snacks occupied shelves and tables around the room. But they were sipping only rarely from their glasses and eating not at all, while the sound that emanated from them was sober, quiet, quite unlarkish. Nor, she suddenly realized, had the sound been any different when she first opened the apartment door.

She patted her wig. She plucked at the waist of her shirt. "Now what?"

"Over here." He led her to a bowl of pretzels and poured her a glass of something bubbly. "Hard cider. It's the closest we can come to beer. Apple trees grow well here."

Pearl Angelica laughed at the thought of an orchard on the Moon. "Are there enough of them in the halls?"

"And greenhouses," said another voice. It belonged to a small, round-faced woman whose only ornament was a trio of tiny gilded washers that dangled from one ear. Her skin was dark, and her hair was the color and texture of steel wool. "Whole tunnels full of trees and vegetables."

"He hasn't shown me those."

"If he doesn't, I will. You don't look dangerous to me."

"She doesn't, does she?" murmured still another voice. People were now clustering around Pearl Angelica, leaning toward her, handing her tidbits from other trays, refilling her glass. Many of them wore no mechanical ornaments at all. When she looked for Anatol Rivkin, she saw him on the other side of the room, looking on with an expression that was both amused and proud. His people were making asses of themselves, but the center of their attention was someone he had brought. His girl. She grinned anxiously at him, and he raised his glass in salute.

"Quite human," someone said. "Is that a wig? Take it off, please. Oh, look at the petals!"

"Too bad they're all gone on Earth."

"But bots have fronds!" Waving hands indicated the long leaves the speaker meant. "I've seen them on Munin. She's not a bot. Not the same thing at all!"

"I see leaves under her shirt."

"Maybe she's the Mark II."

"More like Mark VI," said Pearl Angelica. "Or maybe Mark X."

"Are you really hybrids?"

She nodded.

"But how?" asked the woman who had mentioned greenhouses.

Pearl Angelica shrugged. If she said as much as she knew—which was by no means enough to repeat the work—it would just be wasted on Engineers. "I don't know, but it all began on Earth. It's in the literature."

A man snorted in disgust. "Which doesn't exist anymore. Unless it's under lock and key somewhere."

There was a moment of silence, broken only by a few mutters that suggested others shared the man's disgust. The bot sipped her cider and said at last, "Is it my turn now?" Her smile was tentative. These people were Engineers, but they were not much like the others she had met. They were more like Anatol. There was so much she wanted to ask about them. "Who are you? What . . . ?"

"He didn't tell you?" There was quiet laughter. Another man stepped forward, tall and thin, dark-skinned. He wore thick glasses, and a thick cuff of grey plastic covered half his forearm. "Technical sorts, mostly. We like to think we're forward-looking. Mostly, we don't believe that a person or a creature can be evil just because they contain genes from more than one species."

Now that the talk was on familiar ground, the others turned away, back to whatever conversations they had been having before she had arrived. "You don't believe in names either?" she asked.

"Only in *noms de guerre,* to slow Security down a bit if they catch anyone. Me, I doubt it will slow them much." He offered her a half-bow. "You can call me Esteban." He did not say whether that was his real name.

"Are you one of those technical sorts you mentioned?" she asked. "Anatol's a tunnel-digger."

"Who's always looking for novelties. Like you. And me. He saw this one day . . ." He indicated the cuff on his forearm. "And followed me. We had to let him join us."

"What is it?"

"Look." He slid aside a cover plate to reveal a speaker grille, a screen, and a rectangular time display. "There's a keyboard too, but it's not really necessary. Speak up, Stan."

The answering voice had a ripe and fruity sound: "Whaddaya want, Ollie?"

"I want you to meet someone," said Esteban. "She's a bot."

"You shouldn't make cracks about the poor woman's figure, Ollie."

"Bee—oh—tee." He spelled it.

"Ah, one of the flower people! The one from Tau Ceti?"

"Her name's Angie."

"Pearl Angelica," said the bot. Anatol was approaching now, and he was the only one she had told to call her Angie.

"Tell me!" said the machine. "Tell me everything about—" Esteban slid the cover plate back into place and the voice cut off. "It's an artificial intelligence," he said. "That's my field. Robotics."

"I've never heard one that sounded so human," said Pearl Angelica. "Or seen one that small."

"He's a helluva programmer," said Anatol.

"The big problem was the power supply. Batteries were too bulky and didn't last long enough. Photocells couldn't generate enough power. But I managed to miniaturize a Q-flux generator." Esteban spoke the words as matter of factly as someone else might say he had replaced a screw. "It'll run forever."

"So will everything else," said Anatol. "As soon as you publish. And you'll be rich."

Esteban made a face as if that was the last thing he cared about. Pearl Angelica thought of all the things the Engineers—or the Gypsies—could do with an eternal energy source so small. When Anatol's hand touched her arm, she shuddered. The von Neumann machines were now all too real a possibility.

Pearl Angelica could and usually did—at home—sleep like a human, in a bed, flat on her back or curled on her side. Yet she was part plant; if a bed was not available, she could root herself in soil and lock her knees, close her eyes, and sleep as soundly as any tree.

She had been tired when she returned from the party, and she had entered that state as soon as the artificial sunlight flooded her cage. Unfortunately, it was less than an hour before a muttered, "Where the hell were you?" shocked her awake once more.

"Come on. I know that woke you up." The voice seemed familiar now, but still she struggled to feign sleep, to ward off the moment of discovery and the final closing of the trap she suddenly felt around her. Someone had seen the empty cage. Someone knew that she had been loose in the Engineers' lunar base. Then her breath caught in her throat as she thought that she had—of course!—been with Anatol, and he shared the trap with her. If she was caught, so was he.

"I'm not a mechin' Engineer."

She opened her eyes. The face before her was narrow, flattened, sallow. Water from the morning shower was still visible on the pavement beyond it. "Marcus!"

"Damn right. I'm back. And the first thing I find out is you're out of your box and wandering around somewhere. I hope you're learning something useful, because—"

A rapid clatter sounded from the mouth of a corridor. Marcus Yamoto and Pearl Angelica both snapped their heads to look as three Security guards ran into the concourse. Their guns were in their hands.

"Freeze!" one yelled.

"Litter," Marcus said quite conversationally. "I'm supposed to tell you, the Orbitals would like to rescue you, but—"

There was a shot, and a bullet spanged off a bar of the cage.

He didn't even try to finish what he was saying. He leaped from the dais and begun to run toward a corridor. More shots brought him down long before he reached his goal.

The body was soon removed. The first gawkers arrived to study the bloodstained floor and crowd among the roses and mock oranges. A pot toppled, and then another. Pearl Angelica wondered how long it would be before someone discovered her disguise. But she was safe. Someone discovered thorns instead and swore. The crowd drew back a bit, though still it stared and jabbered.

She did not understand a word of what they said. Instead, her mind was whirling round and round Marcus Yamoto's last "but." What might have followed it?

But she was surrounded by too many Engineers for a rescue raid to succeed?

But they didn't have the troops or weaponry?

But they didn't think her life worth as many of theirs as the raid would cost?

But they didn't want to antagonize the Engineers who sold them food?

But they wouldn't or but they couldn't. For whatever reason. She was stuck unless the Gypsies would part with the secret of the star-drive. But they wouldn't. They couldn't.

Her own life was the price of safety for all her friends and kin.

She knew that.

She wished she could be sure no Engineer would ever invent the tunnel-drive on his own.

And where was Anatol? Hadn't he heard? Didn't he think she needed reassurance and comfort? They couldn't speak, of course, not with so many people all around. But his mere presence would help.

The day passed. The gawkers trickled away, satisfied for now and eager to tell all their friends who had not been there what they had seen. The very spot where the alien spy had been killed! His very blood! The monster he had been talking to. Perhaps he had been telling it when to run amok and slaughter them all in their beds!

Her imagination failed as the lights dimmed as they did every night. She bowed her head and closed her eyes and wished she could sleep for a while. But one more set of footsteps said she could not yet rest.

She peered toward the edges of the concourse. Was it Anatol at last? No. The approaching man was not her friend, though he did seem familiar. He wore standard Engineer clothing; his belt buckle was an oval medallion bearing the word "Ford." His nose was large. The valley in his upper lip was deep. The lips themselves were thin and pale.

When he was close enough for her to see how light were his eyes, he winked and said, "Do you know what they're going to do to you tomorrow?"

He had reached through the bars, hadn't he? He had stared then just as he did now, stripping her leaves away with his eyes, wanting . . .

"They're going to take you out of this cage and strap you to a table in a small room. They will attach wires to your body. They will ask questions. And if they do not like the answers, they will . . ."

She understood. "Why?"

He came closer and laid a thin-fingered hand on a bar at the level of her face. "What did Yamoto tell you before they shot him? That's all they want to know."

She shook her head.

"They have drugs too. They might use those first, but they'll get to the wires eventually." His hand darted forward, and he had her shoulder. The other hand approached her chest. He tore leaves away. He poked and squeezed. "But

I have influence, you know. I can tell Security to leave you alone. All you have to do is come with me."

When he pulled her toward him, she stiffened. "No!" she cried as she pushed against the bars and tried to claw his hands from her shoulder and breast. "Get away from . . . !"

But he knew he was right, for he was the one outside the cage. He had all the strength and confidence of the righteous, and she was quickly losing the struggle.

Both of them were so intent on what he was doing with his hands that they did not hear the footsteps, so much softer than his own had been, coming up behind him until hands gripped his ears and pulled.

He groaned and let go of Pearl Angelica.

"Anatol!"

Anatol's knee was in the small of the Engineer's back. His face was distorted by effort and anger and hate as he continued to pull on the man's ears, bending him backward. Hands found his wrists and gripped, tugged, strained. Nails dug into his skin. A mouth opened and a voice began to bubble toward a scream of agony.

It took Pearl Angelica only a second to see what she had to do. Then she stepped closer and slammed the heel of one hand into the man's chin.

There was the snap of breaking bone.

Anatol let go, and the man fell to the dais. He was not dead, for life battered its wings against the inside of his head. His eyes rolled. His lips worked. A thin keening emerged from his throat.

"Get me out of here."

Anatol positioned himself. Pearl Angelica climbed and jumped and said, "He'll tell them about you." Then she raised one foot above his throat, ignored the terror that suddenly bulged his eyes, and crushed his larynx.

"You can't come back here," said Anatol. "You'll have to hide."

"But where?"

"My room."

Chapter
Thirteen

NEITHER ANATOL NOR Pearl Angelica slept that night. Nor did they make love, for though they both undressed and lay down on Anatol's bed, they did so only briefly. Neither was able to lie still. They held hands and paced.

She told him the man they had killed had said she would be tortured. They huddled in each other's arms on the couch, shivering even though the lunar base was never cold.

Anatol said that Security did indeed use torture when it wanted answers, even though drugs were more reliable. They stood pressed together as if each could find safety and concealment inside the other's body.

"I've never killed anyone before," said Pearl Angelica, more than once.

"Me neither," said Anatol. "I didn't know I could."

"I couldn't let him live."

"I never saw him before. He couldn't have recognized me."

"He would have described you, and then . . . You should have left him alone."

"I couldn't . . . I saw your leaves falling to the floor. I had to stop him, Angie."

"I'm glad you did."

I'm glad *I* did, she thought. She had never had a lover for whom she would have killed. Never one she could hold so close so long. Never one she wanted to keep for the rest of her life. Never one she thought she could accept as the father of her children.

But was it him? Or was it only that she was so alone among the Engineers that he was her only friend? Did she really love him? Or was she only clinging to the only thing that floated in this alien sea? What would she think of him if she could only take him home and see him among the other Gypsies?

Toward morning they lay down again, but only to play through their script once more. There were minor variations, but it began as always with "I've never killed anyone before" and ended with "I'm glad you did."

Only after his computer terminal chimed and called from the kitchen, "Time to get up! Time to get up!" did she add anything really new. "I'll have to wear that shirt all the time." She made a face. "It'll be two weeks before I can replace those leaves."

"What happens then?"

"The buds will open. See?" She pointed. "Under every leaf, there's a replacement waiting." On her skin, faint lines traced the shape of each leaf, an up-pointed heart. At the tip of the point between the heart's two lobes, a tiny, intensely green bud emerged from a pore.

"Time to get up!" cried the terminal more loudly.

He propped one elbow on the mattress and leaned over her. "Are they sensitive?" The tip of his tongue grazed a bud. When she shivered, he smiled for the first time all night. "It's too bad I have to go to work."

"If you don't, someone will come looking for you?"

He nodded despite the arm she had around his neck.

"Then they'd find me."

"Time to get up!" The terminal was now downright strident.

"Then I have to go. Willy-nilly." He pulled away from her and left the bed. He touched the wall, and a veedo screen lit up with an image of the cage Pearl Angelica had fled just a few hours before. There was no sign of any body.

A voice was saying, " . . . was only a clerk in the Security department. If Crocin had called for trained help when he spotted the Gypsy agent, he would surely be alive today. His assassin would be in custody."

The image changed to one of Pearl Angelica herself. "And the escaped prisoner would still be in its cage. We believe that prisoner and assassin are both hiding somewhere on this base. Keep your eyes open. If you see this *thing,* call Security immediately. Do not try to catch it yourself. Chief Hrecker says the assassin will surely not be far away."

The voice was replaced by music, but her picture remained on the screen. "They don't want anyone to forget what you look like," said Anatol.

"I wish there *was* a Gypsy secret agent. Then there'd be a hidden ship, and some hope of getting away from here."

He shook his head. "They'd have spotted a ship. So they have to know there's no Gypsy agent hiding here. They'll admit it eventually."

But the veedo emitted only music while they drank tea and ate biscuits and honey. After breakfast, he said. "Don't open the door. If the phone rings . . ." He flipped a switch on his terminal. "You'll be able to hear whatever the caller is telling the answering machine. If it's me, go ahead and answer. But I won't call unless they double-shift me again."

They held each other for a long moment then, and he was gone.

After a while, the image on the veedo screen changed. Pearl Angelica's face was replaced by her empty cage, and then by the broken body she and Anatol had left on the dais. Lettering across the bottom of the screen identified the body as that of Luther Crocin. The camera's angle clearly showed Crocin's angled neck, crushed throat, and glazed eyes. A few minutes later, Pearl Angelica once more occupied the screen, but this time her full figure showed. She was in her cage, her roots unfurled to anchor her to the tiny plot of soil they had given her. As she watched, the Engineers' image-processing computers materialized Luther Crocin's body just outside the bars that held her in and twisted the face of her image into a demented snarl.

From time to time a voice repeated the news that an Engineer was dead, an assassin was hiding somewhere in the lunar base, and a bot was loose. Toward noon, a panel of experts appeared on the screen. One of the panelists was the Chief of Security, Hrecker. Another was introduced as a historian specializing in the many things the engineers had made before they left Earth; he was therefore the closest thing the Engineers had to an expert on bots. Two more were a journalist and the lunar consul, the local representative of Earth's distant rulers.

"It had to have help," Hrecker was saying. "It couldn't have climbed those bars all by itself."

"So the assassin has to be real," said the journalist. "Or at least, there had to be a third person on the scene. She might have murdered Crocin herself." He emphasized the "she" that Hrecker had refused to use.

"She could have," said the historian. "Bots are strong devils."

"It didn't resist on Earth," said the consul. He eyed both the journalist and the historian as if their humanization of the enemy verged on treason.

"It got away from you," said Hrecker.

"It said it wanted to taste the local dirt. They found it easily enough."

"It can't be the same thing here," said the historian. "There's no soil."

"The greenhouse tunnels."

"We're searching those now," said the Security chief.

"You said the other guy came from outside?" asked the journalist.

"We don't think so anymore," said Hrecker. "There are no hidden vehicles on the surface. We searched for them first."

"Then he has to be one of us?"

Hrecker nodded. "It must have seduced him."

"It did that on Earth," said the consul. "Ruined a good man."

"Is that where she's hiding, then?" asked the journalist. "How many apartments are there in this base?"

Hrecker shrugged, his face as impassive as ever. "Twelve hundred and fifty eight." He did not say that Pearl Angelica did indeed have to be hiding in some disloyal Engineer's living quarters, but the implication was clear.

The bot found the controls for the veedo set and turned it off. She swore. Half the people who had seen that panel would not believe that someone had rescued her and killed Crocin and was now sheltering her in his apartment. No Engineer could possibly do such a thing, after all. But yes, she could be in an apartment, perhaps in theirs or a neighbor's. She could be hiding in a closet or a bedroom, ready to leap out and kill again. There was no reason to think one death had slaked the monster's thirst for blood.

The least unusual of sounds or sights would be enough to rouse suspicion—or even panic—and provoke a call to Security.

She scarcely dared to move.

Could Anatol's neighbors hear the sounds she made? She could hear them, faint murmurings beyond the apartment's walls, muffled steps and voices in the corridor outside the door. She could make out no words. She could not even tell whether the quieter sounds came from straight ahead or right or left, up or down.

Of course, they could hear her too. But would they hear anything they were not used to hearing when Anatol was home? Would they be suspicious? Would they call Security?

She decided it did not matter. It was a risk she had to take, for she had to know what was being said about her on the veedo. She had to move about. And she was hungry.

She wondered whether anyone could tell that even though Anatol was gone his veedo set was turning on and off, the water was running in the sink as she filled the kettle for another cup of tea, the refrigerator was opening and closing as she found more of the biscuits they had shared at breakfast and a slim packet of cheese slices. A computer *could* monitor such things, she knew.

But none did, or someone would have been at the door already.

She was almost sure of that by the time she turned the veedo on again.

The panel was still on the screen. Hrecker was saying: "The thing is far too good at hiding. I've posted extra guards on the power plant and air supply. It wouldn't do to let it sabotage those."

"What about the *Teller?*" asked Earth's consul.

"We covered that first. If it's a spy, that must be high on its list of targets. The Orbitals and Gypsies don't want us out there with them. They don't even want us on the Moon."

"You really think she intends to destroy the *Teller?*" asked the journalist.

"Or the base itself," said Hrecker. "The bot might actually have a bomb buried in its belly. We never thought it necessary to X-ray the thing. We should have. I'm sure our foes would consider one life a very cheap price for such a victory."

"No," said Pearl Angelica even though she knew they could not hear her. She thought of the Racs. "We are builders, creators. We aren't killers. We won't give you a star-drive, but we don't slaughter. Not even you."

She wished she really believed what she said. Unfortunately, she had heard too many times the tale of how the Orbitals had pounded Earth with rocks to aid the escape of the gengineers. She knew her people *could* kill.

The sound of an opening door spun her around, her heart hammering in her chest.

"I'm early," said Anatol. The sack in his arms bulged with packages. "I picked up food."

Pearl Angelica's relief at seeing him safe, at seeing *Anatol* come through the apartment door instead of some agent of Engineer authority and vengeance, nearly dropped her on the floor. But he was beside her even as she sagged, and their arms were around each other, his so tight her ribs creaked, her own so tight she wondered why his ribs didn't.

When they could talk, he told her he had heard more than was on the veedo. There were guards on every exit from the base and at every major intersection of corridors. No ships, not even ones from Earth, were being permitted to land for fear that she and her unknown ally would hijack a ride to freedom. No vehicles of any kind were leaving, not even supply trucks for outlying mining stations. And a room-to-room search was being planned for the next morning.

"What can we do?" she asked. "They have to catch me that way."

"Us," he said.

"Me." She smiled and shook her head. "You don't need to get in trouble. I'll step out that door and walk down the hall until I find one of those guards you mentioned. You'll be safe."

"No," he said. "If you do that, I'll call them up and confess everything. I seduced you. I killed that man. I spirited you away and hid you."

"But you didn't!"

"Crazed infatuation, that's what it was." His tone was jok-ing, but his smile was strained. Though their relationship was not that intense, what he said had an element of truth. They both knew that if it did not, there could be no relationship at all between an Engineer and a Gypsy, much less a half-plant bot. "It had to be. Innocent by reason of insanity." His face twisted, and his tongue lolled like a beast's. "Maybe then they won't torture you."

"But they will. They won't believe you, no matter how much you drool. And they'll kill me anyway, no matter what."

"I won't let you surrender like that."

"They'd question me anyway, wouldn't they? And find out about you?"

He nodded sadly. He was doomed either way, whether she surrendered or he confessed. He was also doomed if they found her. "We need a better hiding place for you."

"But where?"

Neither of them sounded hopeful.

They made love that evening with all the desperate, feverish intensity of two people who fear they may never have another chance to see or touch or hold each other. Yet neither one forgot what they had to do.

"I'll bet you didn't know we had an amateur theater group here." When she shook her head, he opened a cupboard in the wall and began to rummage.

"I've been Rosencrantz and Eglamour and Pinch. Once we did a version of 'Modern Times,' and I was Charlie Chaplin. Ah, here it is." He produced a rack of small jars and bottles and cotton swabs. "I wish we could pluck the rest of your leaves . . ." When she looked alarmed, he laughed and added, "But no. Uh-uh. Can't do that. We'll have to see what we can do with this."

"What is it?"

"Makeup," he said. "Your skin's a little green. A stand-out in bright light. But . . ." He opened jars, dipped swabs into their contents, and daubed at her cheeks and forehead, nose and chin, even ears and neck. When at last he held a mirror for her to see what he had done, she gasped. Her face was fair with an overlay of tan, and her lips were pink.

"Now your hands," he said. "Your wrists. I don't think your ankles will show."

He found her wig and put it on her head. He stood back and stared at her. "I saw a picture once," he said. "A woman from a myth. Feathers covered her just like your leaves, though they were white instead of green. And both her breasts were covered."

When she covered the exposed flesh with a hand, he laughed. She snorted. "I'll need my clothes too."

"Right here." But first he handed her a narrow towel and said, "Put this around your chest." He helped her draw it snug and pin it into place. When she had donned her shirt and pants, he pulled a jacket from his closet. "It's a little big, but . . ."

The sleeves were only slightly long. The shoulders sagged. But the arc of the rolled and padded collar behind her neck made her look, she thought, like a genuine, human Engineer. She would pass in the corridors outside Anatol's apartment. She might even be able to avoid the searchers just by staying in the halls, walking on and on until the fuss died down.

When she said as much, Anatol shook his head wearily. "You're not that perfect. Someone would surely see. And the makeup rubs off on your cuffs and collar. It dries and cracks. It wears far too thin."

"At least I don't look like a bot." She stared at herself in the mirror. "Or a woman, except for the hair."

"Then no one will recognize you."

"Now what? Where do we go now?"

"I don't know," he said. "But we can't stay here."

"You mean *I* can't."

He sighed as if growing used to her refusals to let him share her risks. "Okay. *You* can't. *We* have to find you someplace to hide." He opened the apartment door. "They haven't dimmed the lights yet. But there's no one around here right now. Let's go."

Anatol had said that only the major intersections were guarded. That may have been true earlier in the day. Now, however, there were guards wherever one corridor met another or an elevator connected the base's levels. Fortunately, they seemed content merely to peer at the passersby, looking for green skin or leafy scales. They said nothing when Anatol and Pearl Angelica brushed past them on their way toward the surface level. They demanded no identification.

The guards in the bays that surrounded the entrances to airlocks *were* asking all who wished to enter or leave the base for their documents. Pearl Angelica shuddered at the thought of how easily such a demand would reveal her. She was grateful that the guards had not imagined that she might disguise herself with more than clothes.

Did she imagine that she and Anatol drew a suspicious glance when they passed one airlock for the third time? Was she right to fear that once the lights dimmed for night and traffic disappeared from the corridors they would be far more conspicuous? That *every* guard would want to know who they were and what their business was?

They passed another lock, larger than most, and the floor turned gritty. In spots the grit was visible in patterned strips. "Tracks?" she asked.

"Tires," said Anatol. "There's a maintenance shop just ahead." He pointed toward a wide, double-leaved door under which the vehicle tracks seemed to pass. The left-hand panel held a smaller door for people to use.

She looked over her shoulder. The guards by the airlock were hidden in their recessed bay. Those at the intersection beyond the lock seemed more interested in conversation than in distant pedestrians.

"We have to find someplace soon," she said.

"I know," said Anatol. "But . . ."

"Is it open?"

Instead of answering, he tried the small door. It swung inward on well oiled, silent hinges, and they stepped into a broad, high-ceilinged space dominated by a single flatbed moontruck. The bed was at head height. The huge tires, which would be tautly swollen balloons in the lunar vacuum, were flaccid now that they were immersed in pressurized air. Its cab was as large as a small room, and both doors to its airlock were open. So was its motor housing, revealing a tangle of heat exchanger tubing, electrical converters, and cables surrounding a massive electric motor. Behind it all they could see one end of the massive cylinder that shielded them from the small nuclear reactor that powered the truck. Brackets, wires, tools, and electronic modules lay scattered on the floor beside the vehicle. A clipboard hung from a metal stand.

At the back of the room, a single door opened into a tiny office that offered no concealment at all. There were no storerooms, no ladders, no catwalks. One wall held a rack of deep shelves full of metal sheets, slabs, and bars, pipes, rolls of wire, and unidentifiable shapes. In a nearby corner stood a dormant industrial robot that seemed capable of lifting and even bending the heaviest pieces. Not far away, a cabinet's many drawers held nuts and bolts and other fasteners. More tools hung from the walls.

"You can't hide here," he said.

"What about the truck?" She indicated the open airlock.

"They'll be working on it in the morning," said Anatol.

There were two ladders on the side of the cab, one leading to the flatbed in back, the other to the lock. Pearl Angelica was already climbing the latter. Inside a padded driver's seat faced a viewport and a rack of display screens, knobs, and switches. The viewport stretched the full width of the truck's cab and arched from the top of the instrument console nearly to the ceiling. Its material was darkened by the reflective coating that outside the base would temper the glare of lunar day. A horizontal strip of angular digits glowed just below the level of a driver's eyes. One set of digits flicked and flicked and flicked, counting seconds and minutes, hours and days.

From one of the knobs on the console hung a radio headset that had been repaired with silver duct tape. Most of the truck's controls were mounted in the seat's broad arms. Behind the seat was a sliding partition, a narrow bunk, a toilet hidden by a curtain, and a small refrigerator. "There's food," she said when she emerged again.

"But they'll catch you right away!"

"It's my only chance," she said. She took the clipboard from its hook and studied the sheet of paper it held. "And it may not be a bad one. Look."

He took the clipboard. "It needs a new drive controller."

"Which is on order." She pointed at the paper. "From Earth."

"And they aren't letting any ships land." He shook his head. "But that won't last."

She grinned at him. "I'll stay out of sight. While you try to find something better."

Chapter
Fourteen

PEARL ANGELICA SHIVERED when the maintenance shop's small personnel door closed behind her friend. Would Anatol return before the maintenance workers showed up for their workday? If he didn't, would the workers find her? Until the drive controller arrived from Earth, they would be unable to fix the truck, and until it was fixed, the truck wasn't going anywhere. So the workers would have no excuse to enter the truck. She would be in no danger of discovery as long as she remained within its shell. But . . .

Would he return at all? Maybe he would decide that his own safety was more important than hers. He would go back to his work, risk no more discovery by Security and the punishment it would mete out to a traitor. She would have to hide for as long as she could manage, with no hope of escape from the base. Eventually they would find her. And her fate would be no different from what it would have been if she had remained within her cage.

The silence in the maintenance shop was disturbed only by the rustle of a paper fragment stirred by the slightest of air currents. She could hear her own breath, her heartbeat, the hiss of cloth sliding over cloth, not the rustle of leaf on leaf, as she moved an arm against her side. She wished she were home, outdoors on First-Stop, no clothing, leaves exposed to sun and wind, watching a Rac scratch his muzzle and listening to his rough voice say, "Winter comes."

There really wasn't any way, she told herself, that Anatol could find a better hiding place and hope to move her to it before night came again. Until then she would have to hide as best she could, just as she had promised him.

The question was, where?

She reentered the truck cab and began to search in earnest. The space beneath the bunk? It was large enough, but it was occupied by storage drawers. The toilet was hidden only by a curtain. There were no cupboards large enough to hold her.

Eventually she thought to try the grille in the wall opposite the head of the bunk. To her surprise, it came free in her hand. When she looked at it closely, she found that it was held in place only by strip magnets. Screw heads were merely glued into their holes in the grille's rim.

She smiled at the picture of a smuggling trucker that sprang to her mind. A girl friend? "Slide in here, dear. It's just till we're out of the base, just in case of an inspection. We don't want anyone catching you." Or girls for the miners in the outer camps?

Or could this be a route in and out of the base for Orbital agents or contraband? Then perhaps there could be a way for her to escape, if the base were not sealed and if the trucker could be found and if he did not think bots were agents of the devil.

Sounds outside the truck announced that someone had just entered the maintenance shop. Pearl Angelica ducked reflexively away from the truck's port before remembering that ports had sun-reflective coatings. No one could see her if she just stayed out of the line of sight through the airlock. Yet she could see outside the truck: Three men had entered the shop, each one carrying a large thermos. And they were walking toward the truck.

She probed the heating duct behind the grille with one hand. There was a sharp bend and then a straight run beside the wall, extending as far as she could reach. She fitted her feet into the opening and twisted her body, pulling, pushing, straightening at last with a gasp of relief. She tugged the grille back into position and pushed herself a few feet down the duct.

The clank of tools and rattle of voices came to her from outside the truck. No one entered the cab. She told herself that she should have taken some of the food in the fridge. She had had time. Perhaps she should even have stayed out of the duct. As long as she stayed away from the cab's entrance no one would see her. She would have been safe. Would she have had time to hide if anyone had begun to enter the cab?

No. She would have made noise too. She would have shaken the machine, as huge as it was. Someone would surely have noticed and found her, and then . . .

She shuddered. She did not want to go back in her cage. Nor did she want to be killed.

She wanted to stay free. She wanted to go home. She wanted to see her father, Frederick, one more time before he died. She wanted to see Aunt Lois and Uncle Renny and the Racs.

She could feel the impact of tools on metal wherever her skin touched the interior of the duct. Scrapes and clangs, some soft, some loud, assaulted her ears.

A voice was suddenly clear through the open airlock: "Motherless bastards! Gotta take the whole friggin' thing apart to get at the one piece that ever fails, and then we don't have it in stock." After a pause while—she thought she could hear the sound—someone answered the speaker more quietly, he said, "Of course that's why it's out of stock! But at least it came in before they froze the landings."

Her heart leaped in her throat. They had the drive controller she and Anatol had thought was still on order. The truck would be repaired today. Then it would be put back in service. Or it would be parked outside, perhaps even under the same slab of roof she had seen from one of the base's ports.

Either way, she would be trapped in her hiding place, unable to leave the truck and cross the vacuum all around it because she had no suit, forced to surrender to the first Engineer who entered the cab.

Could she overpower a driver and handle the truck herself? There would be only one man, his back to her as she crawled from her hiding place, and she had driven similar vehicles on First-Stop. But there were no guarantees. If a driver needed to know secret passwords or numbers to start the motor, like the number Hrecker had used to open the door to the *Teller*'s construction bay, she would be helpless.

But if she wasn't . . . She remembered the patched headset hanging from the console beneath the viewport. She grinned as she thought that once she was far enough away from the Engineers' base, she might be able to use the radio to call the Orbitals. This was therefore the best of all possible hiding places.

Yet if she escaped, she would never see Anatol again.

Her grin vanished. She sighed. She lay her head on her arms and listened for hours to the muttering and swearing, the clanking and scraping. Eventually silence fell. She crawled from her hiding place, moving as cautiously as she could, and peered from the truck's broad port. The workers were near the door to the shop's small office, bent over a game of cribbage while eating their lunch.

She continued to move cautiously, afraid that one of the men might look up just in time to see the truck quiver on its springs, while she found something to eat and used the toilet. She wasted a few minutes taking off her shirt and wig and letting the truck's interior lights bathe her leaves. She sighed as a trickle of photosynthesized sugar reached her blood and brain. She wished it were more, the rush that proper light could give her when she was down. Finally, reluctantly, she covered herself once more and crawled back into the darkness of the heating duct.

It was not long after lunch that she heard a satisfied grunt and a slam that might have been the lid of the truck's motor compartment. The vehicle rocked as one man clambered into the cab, and then again as a second joined him.

"Think it'll start?"

"It had mechin' better." This voice sounded older than the other, but there was no way Pearl Angelica could tell whether it belonged to the first man or the second to climb aboard.

"And then what?"

"We leave it right here." The driver's seat creaked, and the truck's electric motor began to hum. The vehicle lurched and rolled. It turned in a tight circle. It backed up. "Works fine now." It stopped. "Right here. They ain't lettin' 'em out and they ain't lettin' 'em in. So we're a parkin' lot for the duration. Goddam lockdown."

"They'll find something for us to do."

"Probably give us a gun and put us on a search party. I hear they haven't found that bot yet." The voice wobbled as if the speaker were shaking his head. "Or that murderer. You think there is one?"

Hot air began to move past Pearl Angelica's feet and over her body toward the grille. She grimaced. It was too hot. Her leaves, already stifled inside her disguise, were wilting. But she told herself she wasn't dying. She wasn't in danger. She was only uncomfortable, and that she could stand as long as she had to. No one would discover her. She would not be trapped outside the base, caught by a driver she could not overpower, stuck in a vehicle she could not drive.

She *would* see Anatol again.

"She couldn't have done it herself, could she? She's just a plant."

After the workers left for the day and the shop was quiet once more, Pearl Angelica ate again. She wished she dared step out of the truck to stretch and walk and test the personnel door to see whether it were unlocked as it had been the night before. But she did not. She wanted Anatol to come through that door, but she knew that someone else—searching Security guards, or a stranger who would cry alarm— might precede him.

She stayed in the truck, sitting in the driver's comfortable seat, fingering the buttons and slides that controlled the vehicle. Her eyes moved between the view of the shop's cavernous interior through the thick-paned port and the ever changing display of the truck's heads-up clock. She was waiting as patiently as she could, though she cursed and shifted her weight more often as the hour grew later.

Her breath froze in her throat. Was it opening at last? Was that a crack of light around the jamb? Yes, someone was coming in, but . . . Her heart hammered in her chest. Sweat sprang to her palms. Air rushed from her lungs and back again. She thought of being outside the truck, in full view, and she was glad she wasn't standing up. Her legs would not have supported her.

That wasn't Anatol. A woman. Small. Grey-haired. Was she familiar? Had Pearl Angelica seen that round face in the concourse? Or . . . ?

A hand appeared and pushed. A man came in behind the woman, turned, closed the door, and searched for a lock. Was that . . . ?

The sigh that emptied her lungs marked her recognition of Anatol. But before she could get out of the truck driver's seat, the door to the shop began to open once more.

Her heart leaped. Her stomach rolled. Her mouth went dry. Her hands spasmed on the arms of the seat, and her leg muscles cramped. This time the man who appeared wore a Security uniform. But the woman moved close to Anatol, put her arms around his torso, and buried her face in his chest. Anatol shrugged at the guard. The guard scanned the interior of the shop, as devoid of hiding places as ever, winked, saluted, and turned away.

The "fight or flight" reaction has two components, one coordinated by the nervous system and quick both to flood the body with a galvanizing energy and to drain away, leaving the muscles limp and the breath gasping. The other, managed by the adrenal glands and the hormone adrenaline, is slower to take effect and slower to leave, so that even in the post-crisis letdown, the heart may still pound and the mouth stay dry.

"Angie!" called Anatol Rivkin. "Are you still here? Are you okay?"

Pearl Angelica was still laughing when she was finally able to stand and walk toward the truck's open airlock. By then, Anatol and his companion were already at the entrance. She looked down at them, focusing on the woman. She still seemed small, but now it was her brown skin that dominated the image she cast. The bot's mind linked a flash of green to her face. "Now I remember you," she said. "You were at that party."

"Cherilee Wright." She looked far more worried than Pearl Angelica felt at the moment.

"She can help," said Anatol.

"If we can get you to my greenhouse," said the woman. When the bot looked puzzled, she added, "You have leaves, don't you? They're green? So if we surround you with greenery, you should blend right in. With a little luck, they'll never notice you."

"If we can get you there," Anatol repeated. "The room-to-room search is half done, and Security still hasn't found you. They're frustrated. They aren't being nice to people anymore."

"But . . ." The bot descended to the floor and gestured past the two humans toward the door to the maintenance shop. "That one was."

"You should have heard what Doctor Wright said."

The woman blushed. "I told you before. I'm Cherilee."

Pearl Angelica made a sympathetic face. "It sounds like you'd better be. A 'Doctor Wright' would never say anything that embarrassed her."

"And if I would, he shouldn't insist on being so formal."

Anatol indicated his embarrassment by turning away and clearing his throat. "As I was trying to say, they aren't letting people pass them in the halls anymore. ID checks. They're also making people take off their shirts to show they don't have leaves."

"Then we're stuck here?"

"They'll get around to searching it sooner or later. Probably as soon as that guard decides to be suspicious."

"I don't think they'll find me."

"They won't be able to miss you," said Anatol.

"In a heating duct?" She explained where she had spent most of the day.

"They'll probably take the truck apart," said Cherilee.

"Even after they've just put it back together?"

"You mean they fixed it?" asked Anatol.

She nodded. "It works fine now."

The truck's flatbed had a low curb or sill around its edge. As soon as Pearl Angelica had opened the maintenance shop's large vehicle door, she clambered up the ladder on the back of the cab and threw herself flat behind the curb and beside Cherilee Wright.

"Did you see anybody?"

The bot shook her head and gripped two tie-down rings as the truck began to roll into the corridor outside the shop. Its electric motor was as quiet as when the workers had tested it. Most of the noise came from the limp tires, thudding as they flexed, grinding fragments of regolith into the pavement, hissing as they rubbed on the side of the door. "I hope he remembers where the brakes are."

"Brakes we don't need. I want to see where we're going." The greenhouse manager raised her head as the truck straightened out. When Pearl Angelica rose on one elbow to pull her down again, she saw the shop's door gaping behind them. Metal screeched against rock as the truck met the corridor's far wall. "Shit!" said Cherilee as the sound brought a Security guard into view by the airlock.

The guard had his gun in his hand. More guards were erupting beside him. "Get your head down!" cried the bot. She wished the curb that sheltered them were higher. As it was, she was all too aware that part of her was visible, a target.

Shouts and flat reports punctuated her words. Bullets whined overhead and spanged off the truck. There was no sign of damage, for the truck, even its tires, had been designed to withstand occasional blows from small meteorites.

Light and movement drew her gaze upward. A red laser beam was pointing at a tiny spot on the arched ceiling, and a Spider much like those she had seen on Earth was racing toward it. Projectile weapons, she thought, would be insane aboard a ship like the *Quebec*. The only thing that made them usable here, where despite even careful aim ricochets could puncture the barriers between air and vacuum, was instant repair.

The women grunted as the truck lurched over the pots and planters that lined the corridor. The truck's motor whined louder. They rocked around a curve. Pearl Angelica winced when Anatol scraped the side of the vehicle against the wall again. The tracks that had led them from the nearby airlock to the maintenance shop were what had given her the idea: The lunar base's corridors were wide enough for the truck. Now she wished they were even wider.

But neither rocky obstacles nor tight scrapes could stop them. The truck would protect them on their way to Cherilee's greenhouse. It would distract the guards, draw them away from any post that might let them see its destination or interfere. It could even run them down if necessary. Then, when it passed the entrance, it would slow and the two women would jump off the flatbed.

Now the shots came from ahead, stopping as the truck lurched to one side. There were shouts of alarm, a crunch, a thud, and Pearl Angelica risked raising her head just in time to see a guard stagger to his feet behind the truck. A short-barreled gun with a large grip and magazine lay two meters from his outflung hand. The ruins of a planter and the shrubbery it had held were scattered near the wall.

"Soft tires," said Cherilee. "He's only bruised."

"Then how . . . ?"

"There shouldn't be any guards. They'll never see us get off."

The accelerating truck so nearly filled the corridor that it compressed the air ahead of it. What passed around the cab and under the flatbed whistled and screamed now, but not loudly enough to drown out the Klaxons that announced emergency. Booming noises announced the slamming of pressure doors as Security tried to cut off their paths and trap them in some sealed compartment. They leaned into another curve, rising as the wheels rose over the planters, thumping down, and scraping, yes, again, a shriek of metal on rock. There were more guards, more shots, more shattered urns and spilled dirt, more flickering laser beams spotlighting punctures in the roof, and Cherilee said, "One more turn. If only they don't . . ."

The brakes almost made them lose their grips on the tie-downs. "Now!" she screamed, and she was rolling over the flatbed's curb before the truck was nearly stopped. Pearl Angelica followed her, and the truck immediately accelerated again. It was barely two lengths away when a pressure door slammed shut behind it.

Cherilee opened a door, snatched at the bot's arm, and yanked her out of the corridor. "Will he get away?"

"There aren't as many pressure doors downstairs. If he can reach the elevator, he should be okay. If he can't, well . . . You showed him that air duct. He has a chance. But now we need a hole for you."

Cherilee slammed the door. The bot saw that it was set in an oversized truck door just like the one in the maintenance shop. The room they were in, however, was smaller. Dominated by ranks of stacked crates and parked forklifts, it looked more like a warehouse than a greenhouse. Yet it did smell of fruits and vegetables.

"Will they know he slowed down?"

Cherilee shook her head. "But as soon as they find the empty truck, they'll start backtracking. They'll search every room it passed." She led the bot down an aisle between tiers

of crates. A moment later, they were passing through a door
of ordinary size. "No trucks in here," she said. "We get the
crops out on a conveyor."

Ahead of them stretched a tunnel that had not lost
two-thirds of its width to rooms walled off along its
sides. Bright lights flooded the ceiling, even though elsewhere in the base it was officially night. The broad
expanse of floor was marked by a grid of paths surrounding raised beds of soil. Some of the beds were
bare, some barely fuzzed with seedlings, some choked
with the greens and reds and yellows of mature growth.
Set near the ends of several beds were white cylinders about
a meter tall.

"Where is everyone?"

"Home. Asleep. Follow me." Pearl Angelica recognized
tomatoes, beans, peas, beets, lettuce, potatoes, carrots, cabbage, broccoli, corn, eggplant, cucumbers, squash of several
kinds, and more. It was no wonder that this tunnel, and the
others like it, could feed the lunar Engineers with relatively
little help from Earth.

Yet the tunnel was not given over entirely to food
crops. Ahead of them was a stand of bamboo, palms, ferns,
and other tropical plants. Cherilee led the bot to a bed that
was largely covered with a tangle of vine. "Some of my pets,"
she said, pointing to three short, stout trunks that rose from
the mat of vegetation. "Cycads. Now strip. They could be
here any minute."

Pearl Angelica understood just what the other wanted. She
quickly removed her disguise. Then, with no more than a
glance at Cherilee for confirmation, she stepped among the
vines, chose a spot touched by the circle of shade cast by
a cycad's feathery fronds, and lay down. Seconds later, her
wadded-up clothes and wig were under her head, a sheet
of loosely woven green cloth covered her face and scalp
blossoms, the vine leaves had been arranged to blend with
her own, and her roots were telling her that the black soil
beneath her back was rich with years of loving care.

There was no change in the light to mark the time, but the
coming of day was still obvious. There were voices, rattling
containers, the sounds of tools touching the stone floors and

the sides of the soil beds. Most of the noise was distant. Some was near and growing closer.

"Don't worry. I don't let anyone else work on my pets."

"You didn't get much sleep," murmured Pearl Angelica. She could see nothing but the dim green light that filtered through the vine leaves and cloth that covered her face. Her only connection with what surrounded her was sound, the scents of soil and growing vegetation, a hint of sweat.

"Shh. Don't talk. I'm going to weed a bit, just to look busy. They'll be coming over here, the foremen."

A moment later she was speaking more loudly. "Chop the residues in section A32 and till them under. The onions in C12 should be ready. Check the melons in C18. B27 is ready for planting. Lentils this time."

Sound was enough to tell Pearl Angelica when the others withdrew. She waited long enough to be sure no one else was approaching, and then she whispered, "Weeds?"

"Shh. Yes." The vines rustled, and there was the scrape of some small hand tool in the soil, the scritch of roots being pulled out of their nutrient matrix, a strange buzzing in the air above her head. "People used to think gardening in habitats or on the Moon would be weed-free. After all, the soil is sterile, and the only seeds are the ones you plant. They forgot that many weeds have evolved to imitate crop plants. There's one—the wild variety bears its seeds close to the ground. But the variety that grows in wheat fields lifts its seeds to the same height as the wheat. Then, when farmers harvest the grain, they get the weed seeds as well. And when they plant the crop, they plant the weeds."

"Natural selection. What's that sound?"

"Of course. What sound?"

"Zzz-zzz."

"A bee. Several bees. They must be smelling your petals, even under the vines and cloth." There was a pause. "You'll have to tell me how genetic engineering works." Pearl Angelica imagined a shrug. "It has to be a lot faster than natural selection."

"I don't know enough."

"Shh. I wish I dared to experiment. But selective breeding is all I can get away with. The Revolution produced a few sports, mutations from the radiation. I can work with those."

There was a pause. "This vine. Do you know what it is? No, don't answer. Shh. I see someone coming."

There was the slightest of foot sounds, a shuffle, a pad. "Do you want something, Sanjan?"

"We have orders to fill, Dr. Wright. And the onions have not been picked."

"They're working on that now. You can see." Her joints creaked faintly as she stood. Pearl Angelica imagined her pointing toward section C12. "Is there anything else?"

"What are those bees doing there? There aren't any flowers."

"Who knows? Maybe they're scouts, and one of the hives is about to swarm. I'll have someone check on it."

The man grunted. "Did you know there are guards at the door? They say they're making it a checkpoint. They also say they will have to search all our crates."

"It doesn't surprise me." Cherilee's tone changed from stiffly formal to worried disapproval. "I hear that bot escaped from her cage."

Silence stretched out then until Pearl Angelica wondered if the other woman had left as silently as Sanjan. But then there was a muttered curse. Her tool stabbed the soil. "He runs the warehouse out front," she said. "He thinks he's my supervisor because he's a man. And I guess we aren't going to sneak you out of here today. That's the only exit."

"Shh," said the bot. "Tell me about the vine."

There was a sigh and a forced chuckle. "Of course. Do you know what kudzu is? It grows ferociously. Covers everything. This one's more restrained. As well-behaved as ivy."

As if they somehow knew their presence might betray her, the bees disappeared from over Pearl Angelica's head shortly before Security finally searched the greenhouse that afternoon. Guards marched two abreast down the aisles between the garden beds, searched among the cornstalks and between the rows of potato vines, and rummaged through the lockers in which the tools were kept. One even used a rifle butt to ruffle through the kudzu leaves less than a meter from where the bot lay concealed. Another joked that the search had taken longer the first time they searched the place. Now they knew all the hiding places.

Not one of them found a thing, but when Cherilee Wright appeared beside the kudzu bed the next morning, she said, "The guards are still there."

"I could tell," Pearl Angelica murmured from beneath the vines. Tools had banged more loudly as work began that day. Voices had been tense. She guessed that people were being stopped, their papers checked, their bodies searched, as they went in and out of the greenhouse. Perhaps even at every intersection and elevator.

"And your bees are back."

"I can hear them. Did you know they're why I'm here?"

"It was on the veedo."

"I really just wanted to see Earth. But we do need them, and that was my excuse."

"You could have all you wanted if it was up to me. A whole hive."

"Thanks." Pearl Angelica appreciated the thought no matter how empty, futile, useless, it had to be. Even if she had a hive of bees under her arm, there was no way she would ever be able to get it to the *Gypsy*. Or the Orbitals. Or even off the Moon. "How many bees in a hive?"

"Twenty thousand or so."

"I don't need that many!"

"Shh. There's no one close by, but . . ."

"I'd only want a few. Just enough to breed."

The other chuckled. "They don't come that way."

"What do you mean?"

"Do you know about queens?"

"Yes, but . . ."

"There's just one to a hive, and she's the only bee that reproduces. All the rest are there to take care of her, and they produce new queens by feeding larvae a special food."

"Then you can't just clone them."

"I think it would be tricky. You'd need a mated queen. They mate as soon as they emerge from the pupa, and they store all the sperm they will need in their lifetime. And then you'd need some workers too."

Pearl Angelica said nothing more. She was a biologist. She knew First-Stop's biology. She understood plants and pollination. She knew what bees did and how necessary it was. But she had never really studied the bees themselves, not in books, not in the memories of her fellow bots, some of whom must surely have preserved the knowledge, handed down from earlier generations.

"Are you embarrassed?" When the bot remained as silent as the garden she was pretending to be, Cherilee laughed gently. "It's only ignorance, you know. A very curable condition."

Chapter
Fifteen

A THIN CURTAIN veiled the room's only window. It gentled the light of Tau Ceti and provided just enough of a visual barrier to keep passersby from spying on the man whose life was ending within the pumpkin house. The barrier was not enough to keep those inside from seeing the valley and its carpet of moss, white now with frost instead of berries, or the nearly complete Tower.

A glass bottle hung upside down from the rack beside the bed, a thin plastic tube leading from it to a Y-shaped junction. The other arm of the junction was sealed by a rubbery membrane. From its stem, another tube passed to a bony wrist marked by normal spots of age, small hillocks grown from aberrant cells, and scars where tumors had been cut away.

Monitor screens displayed the rhythms of the man's life, slow now, sedate, far less regular and reliable than once they were. His shallow breathing stopped entirely for seconds at a time. When it restarted, there were faint gurgles deep in his throat and his chest would quiver. There was no sign of life at all in his arms and legs.

A nurse aimed a hypodermic half full of golden fluid toward the ceiling, squirted a miniature geyser, and eyed it judiciously. Then he thrust the needle through the membrane on the free arm of the tubing junction, pressed the plunger, and let the medication mingle with the IV fluid.

"It's only a mild stimulant," he said. "Anything stronger would kill him. So he may not wake up at all. If he does, it won't be for long. He's nearly—"

"We know," said Lois McAlois. She sniffed. The room smelled of medicines and disinfectant cleansers and a musk, not quite a human body odor, that made her think of the pig

Frederick had been before the gengineers gave him the body of a man, long before she had first met him.

Her husband was holding Frederick Suida's unencumbered hand. "He'd hate it if we didn't tell him."

"She is his daughter, after all." The nurse shook his head sympathetically, turned, and left the room.

"We've waited too long," said Lois. She had known she should tell him as soon as she returned to the Gypsies, but she had dreaded the task. Better, she had told herself, to wait for an official decision on whether to pay Pearl Angelica's ransom and then to wait for the *Quebec*'s tanks to be refilled and a new cargo assembled. Better to wait until she could board her ship and flee the knowledge of the distress her news must cause her friend. Or would have caused, when his mind was whole. Might cause, for a few minutes or an hour if she could tell him while his mind was briefly lucid.

"Will he even know we're telling him?" asked Renny. "Or what we're saying? Will he remember it?"

Lois brushed at a speck of lint on the blanket that covered their old friend. "That doesn't matter, does it? He would want to know. And we would know if we failed to tell him."

A gurgle became a snort. A muscle moved visibly in Frederick's neck. A finger twitched.

"For us, then." Renny nodded. "For him, if he can grasp it. But for us, at least. We won't have to feel guilty. We'll know we did all we could."

Eyes opened and revealed whites turned yellow by a failing liver, blotched with red by burst capillaries. There were clouds beneath the pupils, in the lenses, and a hazy film over one cornea. Yet life remained, weary and near its lowest ebb though it be. "Donna?" The voice was weak, the word almost a grunt.

"Lois." Donna, she knew, had been his wife. Pearl Angelica's mother. The thought flickered through her mind that she was glad she and Renny had had no children if this was what could happen, and then that it was good that Donna Rose was dead.

"Renny?"

"You got that one right."

"Unh. I . . . feel different."

"They gave you some extra vitamins, Freddy. We've got news you've got to hear."

"Bad n . . . ?"

Lois nodded, though she knew he could barely see her. "It's Pearl Angelica." She paused while Frederick's eyes closed and his face signalled all the alarm it could now manage. Then she told him about the kidnapping and the ransom demand.

She stopped when the water began to fill Frederick's eyes and run down his cheeks. Renny reached forward with a tissue to blot the tears. The dying man rolled his head slowly from side to side on the pillow.

"No!" said Frederick.

"I'm afraid so," said Lois.

"No! Don't. Can't . . . do it."

She hesitated. "No," she said at last. "We can't give them a tunnel-drive. No starships for the Engineers." They would have to invent their own. Unfortunately, Lois was sure they would, in time. They already had the basic Q-drive.

"No." He smiled weakly, while the tears increased their flow. "Not even if . . ." For a moment, he seemed to have lapsed once more into unconsciousness. But then his lips parted to show the tip of a thick tongue. "Rescue?"

Renny nodded. "We'll try."

"I'm starting back tomorrow."

"We don't want her to die."

"Or you," said Lois. She blinked against her own tears. She looked at her husband. His eyes too were wet. "We love both of you, you know."

There is a tension to a living body even when it is asleep or in a coma. As long as the nervous system is functioning at all, it sends signals to the muscles to maintain muscle tone and snug the bones against each other in their joints. The result is a readiness for action that persists until the link between the brain and spinal cord and the muscles is lost. If that loss leaves the body living, as it does in a paraplegic or quadriplegic, the unlinked muscles lose their tone. The joints go loose. Yet there then remains a different sort of tension, one born of moving blood, of inflation, of turgor like that which keeps a leaf of lettuce from wilting. When it too is lost, the body wilts indeed.

Frederick closed his eyes and gasped for breath. "Some th . . . things," he managed to say. "Important. More important. No matter. How much it . . . it hurts."

Renny nodded. "I think we've learned that lesson." He spoke very softly. "The Nazis taught it. The Palestinians. Others too. And then the Engineers. When terrorists make demands, the price of giving in is always worse than the price of resisting. In the long run."

"It's not easy," said Lois. "Not easy to say no. To refuse the ransom. To let someone you love die."

"Hurts!"

Frederick Suida's fingers twitched at last. Renny squeezed the hand he held. Lois McAlois took the other hand, being careful not to disturb the IV tubing, and squeezed that as well. Both were crying, their cheeks as wet as Frederick's had been not so long before.

Yet now Frederick's cheeks and eyes were dry. He gasped once more, said, "Hea . . ." and fell silent while his eyes opened for what seemed to both Lois and Renny must be the last time. "I see," he whispered hoarsely. "Tower. Tower of . . . the gods. Stair . . . way. Heaven."

Did he mean that Tower that soared into the sky outside the pumpkin? He was staring at them fixedly, ignoring the window and its view, seeming to see something quite other than anything in this world at all, and to see it more clearly than he had seen anything for years.

A moment later, he said quite flatly and reasonably, in a perfectly normal tone, "Shakin' my anther for you. It hurts."

The tensions of muscle and blood that had marked his life ever since his birth vanished. The lines that had danced across the screens of the monitors beside the bed went flat. A light began to flash.

"Hurts," said Lois. "No matter how much it hurts. We can't give them the tunnel-drive. They're too strong to raid. We have to let them kill her."

The word spread quickly. On First-Stop, it drew the Gypsies from their tasks, from installing ceramic plates in the Tower's treasure chamber, from polishing a few last spots on the Tower's flanks, from farming and fishing, from research in laboratories and libraries, to gather outside the pumpkin in which lay the body of the man who had conceived the monument they would leave behind them when they departed this world. In orbit, the labors of pollinators and cooks, technicians and managers, engineers both physical and genetic, came to a halt. Classrooms fell silent. People—both humans and bots—froze where they stood, and then they went home to be alone with their thoughts. Traffic briefly bloomed in the tunnels, and then it disappeared.

It had been years since Frederick had played much of a role among the Gypsies, but his people revered the memory of what he had done and the mission he had given them for their wanderings among the stars.

Many Racs knew only that the Gypsies were their Makers. They drew no distinctions between the gengineers and all the rest. But a few did realize that some Gypsies deserved worship more than others. Of that few, some knew who Frederick was and what his role had been in the genesis of the Tower. They held him just as high as they did the gengineers responsible for their rise from nonsentience. All the rest could see how the Gypsies responded to the news of his death and sense a reverence much akin to that which Blacktop preached for the Tower and the gods.

They gathered in and around their watching place until no scrap of dirt was visible. They stood quietly, none sitting upon the pew-stones. Some, as was their custom, faced the Tower or its smaller representation that was their icon. Most watched the crowd of Gypsies near Frederick's pumpkin as the body was brought out and laid in a coffin. The crowd shifted its attention then toward the graveyard on the Tower's north side, while the Gypsies produced shovels and dug a hole.

When the bots and humans dispersed at last, Blacktop climbed slowly to his usual post on the lowest step of the Racs' pyramidal altar. From that vantage point, he stared out across the sea of faces that was his tribe, his people. And yes, there, to one side as they were for every evening service, were the strangers who had come to see the tree that held up the sky and stayed to carry rocks and build the walls of the watching place. Wanderer, Stonerapper, Shorttail, each as attentive as any one of the tailless Racs surrounding them.

What would they tell their own people when they finally returned whence they had come?

And there was Leaf, a little further from the front, glaring at the strangers' backs, her fur bristling. The priest could not see her children, but he knew they were old enough to leave Leaf's hut and accompany her. They surely stood beside her knees, awed by the atmosphere surrounding them, puzzled by their mother's ferocity. Her slightly hunched posture said her hands were curled protectively about their heads.

Blacktop sighed. Her attitude was as fixed and unchangeable as a mountain. If it spread—and it might—there would be war. That was something else he had discovered in the Gypsies' library.

At last he raised his arms until they extended from his sides like wings, and he said, "Even the gods are mortal."

The smooth susurrus of response bespoke anxiety.

His hands moved as if he were beckoning his congregation. "A god has died," he said, and then he let his voice grow rough and calming. "Call him the god of knowledge, for other gods have told me he was the one who thought of building the Tower before you, whose secrets will one day be ours."

He glanced at the trio of visitors, and then at Leaf. "No matter who climbs the Tower." Then he stopped. He let his arms fall to his sides. He said, "The gods live even when they die. There is a part of them that flies to a land of milk and mossberries if they have served *their* gods well. There they live in bliss forever. If we pursue the Tower well, we will someday join them.

"Yet pursuing the Tower need not always mean offering it whatever knowledge we can find. Today there is something more important we must do. Frederick faces a long, long journey. If he will reach its end, he must have food and water. We must provide them." His pause was just long enough to be sure every ear was aimed his way. "Bring Frederick's journey rations with you to the evening service."

Several faces within the compass of the watching place's low walls looked skeptical. Blacktop chose one and pointed. "You think the dead do not eat or drink. But the books that tell of the gods that *our* gods worship are very clear. The part of them that lives forever is no more solid than a scent. They call it 'spirit.' And it gains strength from the similar 'spirit' of what the living offer for its sake."

He stared over the sea of faces. At last he nodded as if approving their acceptance of his addition to the doctrine they were still learning how to follow. Then he raised his arms once more and beckoned to them. "We cannot know how long it takes a spirit to reach the land of its gods," he said. "Not until we undertake that journey ourselves. As each of us surely will. We must therefore feed it for as long as we possibly can. Tonight bring dried meat and berries, nuts, jugs of wine and water." He turned and held both hands toward the pole at the peak of the altar, and the basket at the peak of that. "Enough to fill the treasure chamber on this image of the Tower."

He held his pose for several minutes before stepping down to join his congregation in staring toward the graveyard and the mound of yellow soil that marked where Frederick Suida's remains now lay at rest.

Lois McAlois and Renny Schafer slumped on opposite sides of the table in their small kitchen. Before them rested tumblers, empty except for eroded ice. The man held a bottle of amber liquor, the best the Gypsies could produce by way of scotch.

"Did you know?" he asked. "When I first met him, I was just a genned-up dog. A big-headed shepherd."

She nodded. She knew. She had met her husband well before he had become a human being.

"They wanted to put me down. My Makers hadn't got a license for me. No genetic impact statement. So PETA sued. People for the Ethical Treatment of Animals. Making me smart wasn't ethical, they said. An insult to animalkind. Human genetic imperialism."

He refilled their glasses carefully. "And Freddy saved me. He was working for BRA, the Bioform Regulatory Administration. That's who PETA was suing. But he sneaked me out of their jurisdiction. Into space. And I met you."

She lifted her glass to him. "No regrets."

"Hell, no. They've been good years. For Freddy too, though the last few . . ." He shook his head. "They say my new genes are holding together okay. I won't go the way he did."

"But you'll go," she said. "We both will."

"He had a good run, didn't he?"

She was nodding when the apartment's door scanner squawked, "To arms, to arms! Prepare to repel boarders! You got callers, folks!"

She set her drink down and climbed wearily to her feet. "We should reprogram that mechin' thing."

He answered as he always had. "One of these days." Then he too was standing. "Shall we?"

When they opened the door, they found themselves facing three bots who were obviously near the ends of their lifetimes. Two had fading blossoms. The fronds of all three were browning and frayed at their edges, and their faces were lined.

"Boston Lemon," said one as they entered the apartment. "Titian Thyme."

"Crimson Orchis," said the one with the bright red petals.

"I know who you are," said Renny. "I've heard those names. Some sort of governing council for the bots."

Their nods were simultaneous. "Once our people would have called us 'Eldest,' " said Crimson Orchis. "But your niece is so much older than us that . . ." She shrugged. "We have all been waiting for her to *seem* as old as she is."

"To gain wisdom," said Boston Lemon.

"To fulfill her potential," said Lois McAlois, and Renny laughed. "You don't know how much she hates being told to do that."

"Even so," said the bots together. "But we need a leader, and she has been the best candidate for many years."

"The most potential," said Titian Thyme.

"Vast potential," said Boston Lemon.

"I quite agree," said Lois.

"You have to get her back," said Crimson Orchis.

"We can't," said Renny.

"We understand," said Boston Lemon. "It would be suicide to pay the ransom the Engineers demand."

"We need an army," said Titian Thyme. "Humans and bots and even Racs."

"We have fought when we had to," said Lois. "We surely will again. But the *Quebec* is too small to carry troops, even with the help of her sisters. And the Engineers have railguns and heavy lasers and missiles."

"Rescuing Pearl Angelica," said her husband. "It could not possibly be worth the losses we would have to take. No matter how much we want her back."

There were tears in his eyes as he turned back toward the bottle in the other room.

"Would you believe they asked me to come up to the *Gypsy?* And only partly to wash bottles in the greenhouse lab?"

Lucas Ribbentrop snorted agreeably. "Why you?"

"I was her friend. And I've had a bit of experience in the lab. 'Good hands,' they said, and all the better for having something of a personal interest. I said that wouldn't really make much difference. They'd be growing new bots, not old ones. Even if the cells did come from . . ."

"I told them no," Caledonia Emerald added. Then she kicked the pile of sacks toward her coworker. They had never thought they would have to haul so much away from the Racs' "cathedral." "You don't have any fronds to get in the way. You clean it out this time."

The man laughed. "I did it last night. We take turns, remember? Even if we are running late."

The bot pointed forward, through the windshield of the Bioblimp's cabin. The view had the eerie sheen of infrared, and in the distance a line of Racs, the last of the congregation to depart, glowed brightly. "But this time they packed it full."

"And then some. Food galore." Ribbentrop smacked his lips loudly. The pyramid of steps at the base of the symbolic Tower was nearly invisible beneath the heap of offerings. He stroked the controls. The Bioblimp's tentacles snaked into view ahead, grasped tufts of moss and stray blocks of stone, and pulled. "Maybe it'll catch on."

"You heard the tape. It's for Frederick. One time only."

"I wish it would." A tentacle lost its grip as wind rocked the genimal, and they lurched backward on their path. He swore. "Then we won't have to . . . Why we can't use the engine . . . He knows we're here. He *waits* for us!"

Caledonia Emerald leaned toward the glass. "I don't see him yet."

Ribbentrop grunted as the Bioblimp regained the ground it had lost. "If it does, no more Lost and Found."

"We'd still have to come. If we didn't, the basket would fill up and they'd think we didn't love them anymore. They'd feel rejected."

"So they'd get mad? Attack us? Tear down the Tower?" He snorted. "They'd need a nuke." He struggled with the controls as wind made the Bioblimp lurch again. "Or mass suicide? I've heard the guesses."

"If they're going to do that at all, they'll do it anyway when we leave."

"Naah." He shook his head and indicated a hot spot on a pew-stone just inside the entrance to the watching place. "There he is. Blacktop's a pragmatic fellow. He'll empty the basket himself if we don't show up. That's why he's there."

"Do you really think so?" She pointed at three other hot spots toward the back of the stone-walled enclosure. "He's not alone."

"He's bright enough to invent religion, isn't he?" He touched a control, and the infrared image in the windshield enlarged. "Those visitors."

"What's that?" Her finger traced a line of small hot spots off to the right. They were not on one of the trails the Racs and Gypsies had worn through the moss.

"Critters. No problem. Now go on. Do your job, and we'll get out of here."

As soon as she opened the cabin's hatch, a tentacle appeared in the opening, ready to lower her to the basket and then the pile below. Another took the sacks they had brought. Soon she was dangling beside the basket, stuffing pottery jugs of wine and water, strings of dried fruits and fish, small leather bags of nuts and dried berries, and other edibles into a sack. She knew that Blacktop, the Racs' priest, was watching her. She wondered, did he really think they were gods? That they accepted his people's offerings as worship? Or did he see her as a thief in the night? As a collaborator in the myths he was constructing for his people? Or was he pragmatic enough to recognize the value of what the Tower promised and of a system of belief that would make the pursuit of knowledge the highest good for his entire species?

Pausing when she came to a flat piece of rock, she used the tiny flashlight that hung from her neck to glance at its surface. She saw the imprint of a partial skeleton, head and backbone and a few of the ribs. Some sort of fish. A fossil. A sign that some Rac had already invented paleontology.

The light was already out and the rock was stowed in a sack when sudden motion in the cathedral's mouth warned her that something was about to happen. Blacktop's scream of rage therefore did not make her drop her sack, and his cries for help only made her hands fly more rapidly in their work. Yet she could not help the startled "Uunnh!" that escaped her when the Bioblimp's tentacle convulsed around her waist and jerked her into the air once more.

Nor could she help asking, "What's going on?" as she was unceremoniously deposited in the cabin. But Lucas Ribbentrop was busy with his controls, releasing the Bioblimp's grip on the altar pole and raising its altitude, letting the wind sweep it silently away. She looked at the windshield. The departing Racs had turned and were running as fast as they could toward their watching place. To the right, the line of smaller glows was much nearer.

She stepped closer to the windshield and touched the controls that would magnify that portion of the image. "Wild Racs," she murmured.

"He heard them coming even before the bugs picked it up."

"They must have smelled the food."

"From the top of the bluff?"

"Why not? Maybe they followed our buddies down, noses twitching all the way."

There were perhaps two dozen of the smaller, ungengineered cousins of the Racs. When they reached the altar, three confronted Blacktop, their voices singing threats of mayhem while their fellows began to gorge on the food Caledonia Emerald had not removed. Blacktop had a stick in his hands, but his foes dodged his blows as nimbly as the wind. He could do nothing to stop the raid.

As soon as the other Racs arrived, their wild kin knew the balance had changed. They boiled from the heap that still covered the steps. A few erupted from the basket and slid down the pole. All still held sacks and strings and chunks of food in their mouths as they fled. The Racs did not pursue them, and a moment later the bugs transmitted the sound of laughter and Blacktop's voice, snarling now, saying, "Frederick must have sent them for his lunch."

"He knows how to put the right spin on things, doesn't he?" The congregation's stragglers were already on the trail again. This time, Blacktop and the visiting strangers were with them.

"Hey, he's a preacher." Caledonia Emerald once more let the tentacle lift her from the cabin to the edge of the offering basket atop the altar pole. When she found it empty, she descended to the pyramid of steps and sacked the remnants of the offerings the Racs had not been able to fit into the basket. Finally, she faced the windshield behind which her colleague watched, wrapped one arm around the tentacle, and gestured, "Up."

On the way back to the corral where they would tether the Bioblimp for what remained of the night, she had Ribbentrop stop at Frederick's grave. "Down," she said. "Just off the ground."

"What the hell for?"

She said nothing while she opened the hatch and dropped an empty water jug and a berry bag on the freshly turned dirt.

"I see," he said at last. "Now it will look like the wild ones really were just gofers. They fetched, and Frederick's happy."

"I wish I was." She shook her head. "I'd like to have a hand in what they're doing up there." She shrugged, but still she sounded troubled. "Should I have gone? Do you think they'll keep me posted?"

Chapter
Sixteen

"It would drive me crazy." Cherilee Wright was tugging the vines aside, untangling tendrils from Pearl Angelica's leaves, careful to leave no broken stems or other signs that something had been hidden in the bed. She sounded excited. "Wrapped up like this for days. I'm glad you're not claustrophobic."

No, thought the bot as she blinked at the flood of light. It felt peaceful to be rooted. Restful and safe and natural. Her roots had felt at home in the soil Cherilee had prepared so carefully for her green pets. The light had been dimmed to that which struck a forest floor by the combination of foliage and the cloth above her eyes. Now that light washed over her, brighter, almost blinding, telling of the wealth of energy expended on the plants around her. She found herself feeling reassured, for if the lunar Engineers were wholly one with those of Earth, they would look to Earth for their lifeline, their supplies. Yet they put so much into food production and self-sufficiency.

"Have you heard anything?"

"He's okay."

"He made it, then." The relief so plain in her voice revealed how much worry Pearl Angelica had been trying not to feel. "When . . . ?"

"No." The greenhouse manager answered the unfinished question. "If he visited during the day, he wouldn't be able to see you. If he came at night, when everyone—or *almost* everyone—is gone, it might look strange. Security doesn't know who drove that truck, but they'll grab any opportunity to be suspicious." She took the bot's hand and pulled her to her feet. "There. I told him you're safe. Step over the vines

now. And down, to the floor. Now walk and stretch. I know
I'd need it after so long in bed."

Pearl Angelica's muscles were not as weak as Cherilee's
might be after prolonged inactivity. She was a bot, after all,
half plant, designed to stand rooted in the soil for as long as
she wished. Yet she did feel the need to move, pacing down
the greenhouse's aisles, slowly at first, then more rapidly. She
examined beds of unidentified seedlings, cucumbers, onions,
and corn. She ate a tomato. She stood quite close to one
of the white, cylindrical beehives, studying the insects that
sauntered confidently through the slitlike entrance, preened
upon the narrow shelf that rimmed the hive's base, and
launched themselves humming into the air. "Too close,"
said her hostess, and a hand gentle on her arm drew her
back. "They sting, you know."

"Oh, yes. I didn't think." She watched from a safer distance. She moved on to study bees crawling over the white
stars of strawberry blossoms. "They have their little brushes,
don't they? Like our paintbrushes, only smaller."

Cherilee was nodding her head when noise drew their
attention toward the door between the greenhouse and its
warehouse. A stand of corn blocked their view. "Down!"
she hissed. "Someone's coming. Right here. On the floor."

The human woman was already darting to another aisle
as Pearl Angelica threw herself flat, putting the wall of a
garden bed between herself and anyone who might glimpse
her. The stone of the floor was cold against that half of her
chest Crocin had stripped of leaves, but . . . She blinked and
focused on the shoulder. The buds were already opening.
Soon she would be clothed again.

She thought Cherilee must be intending to draw attention
away from where she hid, like a mother bird feigning a broken wing. But then she told herself, "I am not a fledgling."
Lying on the floor was no defense against discovery if it was
Security at the door. Nor was lying still any answer to the
rush of adrenaline that made her blood sing in her veins.

She had barely stepped among the cornstalks, hoping that
her own green leaves would blend with theirs, when Cherilee
was back, calling, "It's okay. They're friends. Where are
you? Oh! There you are." She laughed. "It might even work,
though they searched in there before."

Pearl Angelica had not recognized Cherilee when she first saw her, but now the party where they had met was fresher in her mind. She realized promptly that the three newcomers had been there too. She could not recall their names, but she felt safer knowing that they were discontented with the Engineers' status quo. "They will not betray me," she told herself, hoping that she was right.

"Anatol says hello," said one as the bot emerged from the corn. Cherilee was not introducing them.

"She told me he made it." She had not expected the news of that hello to be quite so pleasing.

"But he can't come," said another, grinning. Did she think the bot remembered them?

"He will, though," said the third. Or was she worried that Pearl Angelica would repeat the names if she were caught again?

"As soon as it seems safe. For now he's sticking to his normal patterns." What about the "noms de guerre" "Esteban" had mentioned? Cherilee didn't seem to use one. Maybe they didn't either?

"But he told us."

"And we thought it would be safe enough for us to come."

"For a little while."

"We can't stay long."

"But we wanted to tell you he was safe."

"And that we will help if we can."

"And dare."

There was an embarrassed ducking of heads at that. These Engineers wanted to help. They were also honest enough to admit that the penalties for treason to their kind frightened them and that if Pearl Angelica's last hope of remaining free or of escaping depended on their standing between the bot and Security's forces, then Pearl Angelica would stand alone, be caged again, and die.

Pearl Angelica was an innocent in that she had little experience of life outside her home community. But she had read enough not to be surprised by her visitors' reservations. She might wish for more commitment from them, she thought, but they were only being realistic. If it came to confrontation, standing before Security's guns would only add their lives to hers on the pyre. Someday, when Engineer society was more

deeply split, there might be people, dissidents, liberals, who
would be willing to give their lives for a point of principle.
They would then join all those who in the past had fought and
died for religious freedom, the abolition of slavery, and an
end to discriminations based on race and gender and sexual
preference.

The visitors did not linger. When they were gone, Pearl
Angelica looked at Cherilee Wright and was surprised to find
the same wry smile on both their faces.

"We're just beginning to be prosperous enough to afford a
little freedom," said the greenhouse manager. "We're beginning to learn just how much freedom is possible, and how
much we don't have. And we will learn, eventually. Freedom
for us, and for our children, means freedom for others."

Pearl Angelica felt puzzled. "We," Cherilee had said when
it was only the others who had hedged their commitment.
The woman before her hadn't even Anatol's excuse of friend-
ship—or something more—yet she had risked everything. If
she were caught sheltering the bot, her life would surely be
the price. "You already know that."

"It's something I read once," said Cherilee. "I can't remember it precisely, but I will never forget the point. 'They came
for the communists,' a man said. 'And I said nothing. It didn't
affect me, after all. Then they came for the homosexuals and
the blacks and the Jews. Still I said nothing. And then they
came for me.' "

"I made one for you. See?" Esteban was sitting on the edge
of the kudzu bed, in the shade cast by the fronds of one of
Cherilee Wright's cycads. The trunk was too far from the
edge to lean against.

He was holding up a cuff not quite like the one he wore on
his wrist. It was mottled brown and gold and black, gleaming
tortoiseshell, not grey. "Can you stick an arm out?"

Pearl Angelica lay among the vines, only her face exposed.
Cherilee had said Security was prowling the corridors in
force tonight, a predator balked of its prey for far too long.
She thought they might well be planning surprise searches,
bursting into apartments, labs, storerooms, even greenhouses,
hoping to catch the bot out of whatever hiding place had kept
her from their hands so far.

She produced the arm Esteban had requested. The cuff
opened like a clamshell in his hands. He accepted her fingers,
held them gently, and closed the cuff around her wrist. As he
withdrew, his thumbs stroked over the back of her hand, and
she wondered. His touch was the touch of a wish. In it she
could feel attraction, yearning, something much more than a
sense of the difference between their kinds.

Very deliberately, she kept her eyes on his gift. It was
thinner than his own cuff, narrower, prettier. It did not look
like the technological marvel it was, but rather like a simple
decorative wristlet, a wide bracelet, such as any woman
might wear.

But it was a marvel, a gift, even a gift like no other woman
had ever received. It too therefore spoke of attraction and
yearning, of Esteban's wish for what she had already given
Anatol.

Could he know? She hoped Anatol had said nothing, but
she knew that it could be very easy to see that sort of truth.
Was he trying to match that gift of freedom—temporary
though it might be—that Anatol had given her?

And how could she reply? Bots were not by nature
monogamous, no more than were the plants that shared their
ancestry. Flowers crowned their heads, and they exchanged
pollen deliberately, one to one, bowing to each other to let
their blossoms touch or using fingertips and tongues. Yet the
wind could pollinate them just as well, and once, when they
had lived on Earth, such things as bees could also make them
set their seed.

Her blossoms were not fertile. They were petals only, lacking styles and anthers. Her reproductive apparatus was of the
human sort. Should she then mate with only one? That had
been her parents' way, and Donna Rose had been a bot. Yet
not all humans so restricted themselves, and most, if they did
not have several mates at once, did have them one by one.

She glanced toward Cherilee. She was sitting on the edge
of the garden bed across the aisle. She had said that if Security barged in, she would tuck the bot into her viny shelter,
throw her arms around Esteban, and claim he was there so
late at night for a rendezvous with her. Now she nodded her
approval of the cuff. "Very nice. It goes with your leaves."

"I was able to make it smaller." His tone was eager. "I had

to, you know. If they catch you, Angie . . . Well, I didn't want them to take it away from you, and I thought if it looked like just a pretty piece of plastic . . ."

She did not correct his "Angie" as she had at the party where they had first met. "Can it talk?"

"Of course! But first . . . It only recognizes my voice so far." His touch seemed tentative as he led her through the process of shifting its allegiance. When they were done, it spoke for the first time. "Name me, please," it said.

"It sounds like a machine."

"That'll change. Just give it a name."

"Donna." She did not say that Donna Rose had been her mother's name.

"Thank you." Now the cuff's voice was a pleasant, feminine contralto.

"Tell it 'Quiet mode.' " When she obeyed and immediately looked puzzled, he added, "Bone conduction. It doesn't work too well through your arm and shoulder, but make a fist. Now lean your chin on your knuckles. Better? For when you don't want to be noticed." His gesture indicated the vines that surrounded her.

"Does it open like yours?"

He shook his head. "It's too small for a keyboard. You just talk to it. Now say 'Calendar.' "

Pearl Angelica caught her breath when a portion of the cuff's surface became a small grey screen displaying the date and time. "Have I been here that long?"

"What do you mean?" asked Cherilee.

"My aunt. She's had time to go home. To tell everyone what happened. By now she's on her way back."

The other woman nodded. So did Esteban. "We know."

"When she gets here, she'll say there won't be any ransom. She has to. And then, when they catch me again . . ."

They were still nodding. "We'll keep you safe as long as we can. Maybe they'll be able to rescue you. A raid . . ."

Pearl Angelica shook her head. She was only one person. It would not make sense to risk more for her sake, or to start a war.

The visitors stopped coming after that. Part of the reason was simply risk, for Security continued its hunt for the bot.

Guards invaded the greenhouse three times, twice in one night, and Cherilee reported that checkpoints now blocked airlocks, intersections, and elevator entrances even on the base's lower levels. Even well-known Engineers had to have their documents with them at all times; others had to tolerate repeated searches.

Yet Pearl Angelica did not lack for company. Before she returned to her kudzu bed, the cuff Esteban had given her said, "See my tap wire?"

She could see the hair-fine wire extending from the cuff behind her thumb, but its function puzzled her. "Is that anything like a taproot?"

The cuff, already sounding slightly more human and much less mechanical, chuckled. "You do think plant, don't you? But no. Just find an electrical cable."

Cherilee showed her the cable tucked out of sight near the edge of the bed. One end held an outlet box. "We use electrical tools," she said. "For tilling and trimming."

"Wind the tap wire six times around the cable," said the cuff, and they obeyed. Then, when the cuff said nothing more, Pearl Angelica lay down among the kudzu vines, her wrist positioned to put the cuff beside her head. Later, growing bored, she asked it, "Tell me, Donna. How many Engineers are there?

"About three billion." The feminine voice of the artificial intelligence concealed within the cuff was so quiet that the bot had to strain to hear it.

She thought that once the Earth had held five times as many. "Where do they live?"

"Mostly in Earth's northern hemisphere."

"What happened to all the rest? There were billions in Africa and South America and southern Asia."

"They died."

"But why?" Africa had been subject to drought and plague for centuries, but elsewhere the land had been lush and green. If civilization vanished, she thought, they would still be able to feed the immense populations that had once replaced every scrap of forest and jungle with farms and cities and rice paddies.

"Erosion and contamination with industrial toxins destroy-ed the fertility of their nations' soils long before," said the

small machine. "Most never accepted the need to control
their population size or growth. Only bioforms had made
it possible to support their populations. Then the Engineers'
rebellion destroyed the bioforms."

"Aren't there any people left?"

"Scattered tribes and isolated villages."

The machine did not sound quite like Esteban's own,
whose voice and mannerisms were as human as anyone
could ask. Nor did it volunteer much information, though
Pearl Angelica was sure it could tell her anything she wished
to know, if only she could ask the right questions. At the
same time, she thought, she could imagine what some of
those expanded answers might be. The people of what once
had been Earth's poorest, most overcrowded lands must now
struggle to raise food in exhausted soil. Perhaps, like the
illicit farmers who had once made the drug marijuana one
of North America's largest cash crops, they protected rare
hamberry bushes, udder trees, snackbushes, and other sur-
viving food-bearing bioforms from the Engineers' search-
and-destroy missions. Only the lesser gengineered crops—
lobster-potato hybrids, perennial corn, pestproof vegetables
that needed no fertilizer—were still accepted.

She was curious, but Earth's history held limited appeal for
someone in her position, no matter how much she had wished
to see the place a few short weeks before. When the machine
said, "You have a call," she let the questioning drop.

The first voice she heard was Esteban's. "It's a radio
connection," he said. "But it's coded and piggybacked on
the base's wiring." Now she recognized the wire she had
wrapped around the electrical cable as an induction tap; it
would detect—and impose—variations in the current flowing
past.

"No one should notice it," said Esteban. "And it means my
cuff's the only way to make contact with yours. If anyone
wants to talk to you . . ."

They did. Anatol and others used the cuff to visit from
time to time, usually only briefly, sometimes for as much
as an hour, and when the visits ended, that end was often
abrupt. Esteban and his friends could talk only when they
were alone, and Security was opening apartment doors more
frequently than ever.

Yet no one seemed to have any trouble keeping their grip on the discussion from visit to visit. The conversation wandered and eddied and repeated, but over the days its several threads built up. In time, one of those threads became something very like:

"Why are you so against machine technology?" an unidentified woman asked Pearl Angelica one afternoon.

"We're not," she murmured to her wrist. "We use machines. We have to! How else could we travel from Earth to Tau Ceti and back?"

"But you rejected machines. That's why you left."

"No." She shook her head even though she knew those she spoke to could not see her and that if some Security agent were wandering through the greenhouse, the leaves she forced to quiver might only attract his attention to her hiding place.

"But you did. You insisted on replacing all the machines with monsters. Roachsters." The speaker's voice quavered as she shuddered.

"They were destroying the Earth. Their demand for materials and fuels and lubricants and paved roads and parking lots. The pollution they produced."

"That was the population problem, not . . ."

The cuff fell silent in the way that was to become so familiar to the bot. When it spoke again, the speaker was different, but Pearl Angelica quickly brought the topic back to where it had been. "An appetite problem," she whispered. "And we—or our predecessors—were not willing to solve it by killing off enough people to bring the species' collective appetite within the bounds of reason. Or sterilizing them. Or preventing births."

"What did you do?" That was Anatol.

"Oh!" she said. "I want to see you!"

"Not yet," he answered. "Later, when they quit searching. If they ever do. We're too dangerous to forget. We're killers, remember."

"What did the gengineers do?" asked a woman's voice.

"Someone once suggested making a virus that would make everyone's children small. But no. We used bioforms. We redesigned plants and animals to do many of the things machines could do. They could build themselves, extracting the materials they needed from soil and water and food, gaining energy from sunlight and grass and garbage."

"But they couldn't do everything, could they?" asked Esteban.

"Of course not. So we used machines. We used them where they were appropriate, where biology could not substitute."

"Until . . ."

Later she said, "At first the Engineers were just isolated cranks and city gangs. But their numbers grew. Eventually they gained enough power to attack the gengineers and all they had done."

"That's not quite the way we heard it," said a young man through the cuff.

"Of course not," said Anatol. "Our masters wrote the text-books, and they would not write anything that might make them look stupid or mistaken or evil."

"In the end, they banned all work in gengineering," said Pearl Angelica. "They destroyed the labs and the farms and the genimals. And millions died."

"We kept some things."

"Oil trees, for fuel. Some food crops."

"And now you're buying Macks and Sponges."

"We're learning how to compromise. Or *they* are. The Council."

"But they hate it," said Pearl Angelica. "The compromise shames them." Then, remembering the eyes that had probed her every crevice while she was bound to the jerking, spinning stool they kept for their own personal interrogations, she wondered how real that shame could be. Perhaps it was only official. They had chosen a position: They would rather have nothing to do with genetic engineering and its products, no matter how useful they were. If they said anything else, she supposed they must fear, the mob they ruled would support them in power no longer.

"And you don't do that," said Esteban on another evening.

"No," said Pearl Angelica. "We use whatever works. What-ever does the least damage to the world. And we embrace technology in all its varieties and powers. We think it is life-enhancing."

"But isn't it dangerous?"

"Not as dangerous as *not* embracing technology. That can cripple civilization." The bot paused then, considering. Eventually, she admitted, "I suppose it can be dangerous too. You have to be careful not to move too fast, not to rush headlong into fads and abandon older ways that work quite well enough."

"A stable, adaptable society needs both old and new," said Anatol.

Pearl Angelica moved her wrist, and the murmur of agreement moved along her jawbone to her middle ear.

But then someone said, "You don't believe in controlling science. You think if a bigdome has a bright idea, he should just go ahead and let it loose on the world. No matter what harm it might do or how many jobs it destroys or people it offends."

"No," she answered as someone else said, "Offending people isn't the same sort of thing as killing them."

"No," she repeated. "We think some caution is appropriate, but not the sort of paranoia that was so common toward the end of the twentieth century. Or that the Engineers showed toward gengineering."

"But it was destroying the environment! Wild Roachsters in the oceans. Bioblimps in the mountains. Cannibal grass in the woods. Oil trees adding to forest fires. It had to be stopped! Wiped out!"

The ensuing silence stretched until Pearl Angelica wondered whether another Security interruption had forced Esteban to turn off his cuff once more. But then someone cleared a throat. "No," she said. "Mistakes happen. But they're a reason to be careful, not to ban the science that made them possible. Closing off any area of research, rejecting knowledge and technology and change, is the *worst* thing we could do. The highest good is the pursuit of knowledge. You can't interfere with that."

"Your Tower," said another voice. "That's its whole point, isn't it?"

Not long after that a dozen Security guards entered the greenhouse, marched directly to the bed in which she lay hidden, and stripped the vines aside. There was no searching, no fumbling. Someone had told them just where to look. Within minutes, a pair of guards were half carrying her down the corridor outside the greenhouse. At the first intersection, they took her to the right. Another pair hauled Cherilee Wright to the left.

They did not remove the strip of pretty plastic that encircled Pearl Angelica's wrist. Perhaps the informer had not mentioned that or did not know that it existed.

Her cage was no longer as simple a structure as it had been. Heavy wire mesh had been fastened to the upright bars with loops of welded chain. A sheet of the same mesh covered the top of the cage. Two of the bars were missing, their stubs showing the runneled traces of a laser cutter. In their place was a narrow mesh door equipped with a sturdy lock.

Roses and mock orange shrubs no longer surrounded the dais. Showers of artificial rain no longer fell each morning from the ceiling. Nothing relieved the starkness of her imprisonment or discouraged the gawkers from coming within inches of the wire that surrounded her. And they were there, women and men, children and youths, laughing when her expression was most desperate, staring when she gripped the mesh with her fingers, recoiling when her roots writhed in the air, and then laughing once more.

They stopped only when the veedo came to life and Hrecker said, "She will not escape again." He seemed very satisfied as he bobbed gently on his toes. "And her fellow conspirators are in custody." He shook his head ruefully. "It's hard to believe they're all Engineers, but . . ." His image was replaced by one of Anatol, Cherilee, the three women who had visited the greenhouse, and several others. They wore identical manacles and nondescript coveralls that might have been chosen in mockery of the Orbitals and the Gypsies. Scabs and bruises marked their faces. Dark shadows ringed their eyes. Blood stained bandages on their hands and fingers.

Pearl Angelica sighed with relief when she did not see Esteban among them. But then panic clutched at her throat— Was he absent because they had not caught him? Or because they had already killed him?

Now Hrecker was indicating Anatol. "The murderer. He has confessed to murdering Luther Crocin and then to helping the bot escape." He did not say what Crocin had been doing just before his death. Pearl Angelica felt sure Anatol must have explained that despite the pain that had extracted his "confession."

That night, when she was alone at last, she asked the cuff, "Can you see as well as hear? Donna?" Using her mother's name for a scrap of plastic, no matter how much intelligence it held, did not come naturally. "There aren't any wires in this cage."

Instead of answering her question directly, the machine's quiet voice said, "That veedo set is plugged into the floor beneath it. There has to be a wire."

"But where?"

The cuff was silent while a small robot trundled through the concourse and disappeared into a corridor. Soon thereafter Pearl Angelica was following the cuff's instructions to wind its induction tap into a small coil. When it said, "Tie it so it doesn't unwind," she wished for the first time in her life for hair. She had no string, no cloth to unravel, nothing. But then she realized that she did indeed have something. She stooped and grasped a narrow tendril of her roots. She pulled, gasped with pain, and pulled again until it snapped.

The artificial intelligence in the cuff knew nothing of pain. "Push it through the mesh," it said. "Dangle it over the edge. Let it lie flat on the floor."

When the machine detected no electrical currents beneath the coil, it instructed her to reel it in and try again, a little further around the circle of the cage. Eventually the cuff's voice displayed a hint of satisfaction—Was it picking up a human feel by associating with her? Was that why Esteban's cuff sounded the way it did?—as it said, "Don't move it now. There . . . I'm sending. No response. Can you mark the spot?"

Once more she bore the pain of tearing off a tendril. Tied around a strand of the mesh, it would tell her where to pay out her line when it was time to fish again.

"Esteban? Thank god. I thought . . ."

Her leaves were now fully regrown. According to the cuff, it had been four days since she had been returned to her cage. Nights when every attempt to reach the only one of her friends who—She thought! She hoped!—had not been imprisoned and tortured by Security had failed.

"It took a while," he said. "I didn't know whether they had spotted our messages. But I finally heard. Someone talked."

"But . . ."

"I was more careful than a lot of our group. Anatol was his real name, you know? And Cherilee was hers. But 'Esteban.' That's pure fiction, pure disguise, and I never spoiled it."

"You were right." She did not ask him what his real name was.

"I wish I wasn't."

"Have they set a date for the executions?"

The televised trial had been no more than a brief formality. The sentences had been no surprise at all.

"Not yet. Not that I've heard."

"Maybe they've done it already." If so, Anatol was gone, beyond her reach forevermore. So was Cherilee.

"They might have," said Esteban.

The cuff interrupted them before either could speak again. "Quick! Reel in the tap. I hear someone coming."

Far too soon, Hrecker stood beside the dais and Pearl Angelica was trying to conceal the relief the Security chief's words had sent washing through her. "They're going to die," he had just said. "You can have the pleasure of knowing you killed them."

He saw the question on her face. "No," he said. He rose once on his toes and came down. "We aren't going to make you push the button that opens the airlock. But you came here, didn't you? You corrupted them. So the responsibility is yours."

"Then I must be a murderer." But they were still alive. All of them.

Hrecker nodded solemnly and bounced again. "You've been tried in absentia. The sentence was death."

She was silent as the outrageousness of what he had just said sank in. She had known she was not likely to survive her captivity. She could hide, as she had indeed, but only until someone betrayed her. She could not escape, for the lunar base was surrounded by an environment that would not permit her to live if she left. Even a spacesuit or a truck would keep her alive only for a while.

Nor was rescue likely. She supposed Marcus Yamoto must have told the Orbitals just where in the base her cage was positioned. But someone—she forgot just who it had been—had told her the Engineers were too well armed for a raid to have any hope of success.

The sentence Hrecker had just pronounced was no surprise. Yet some part of her had clung to hope. It was still a shock, just as he must have intended.

Even as she felt that shock, she realized that this could not be happening, not yet, not now, unless . . . "The *Quebec* is back, isn't it? The Gypsy ship. My Aunt Lois." When he nodded again, she said, "And she told you they won't pay the ransom."

When Hrecker simply stared at her, she said, "Why did it take you so long? You knew who was talking to me. You must have known the first time he helped me climb out of here."

His eyebrows rose. "How?"

"Cameras," she said. "Microphones. Where did you hide them? Out of sight in a tunnel? In the roses? The veedo set? Overhead?" As she named the possibilities, she pointed.

He shook his head. His bounces were no longer isolated but rhythmic. "Why should we waste the effort? We caught you anyway. As well as the renegades who helped you."

She struggled to keep the sudden swell of elation his words released from showing in her face. He did not know about Esteban. He thought he had arrested everyone who sympathized with her. And she must not let slip any hints that might revive the hunt!

He said nothing more, though he studied her face and body carefully for several long minutes before he turned and left.

Had he seen anything in her face or posture? Had she hidden her feelings well enough? She could hardly be sure, but she thought he knew no more when he left than when he had come. She prayed she was right.

It was several more minutes before the cuff, her Donna, that miniature namesake of her mother, said, "He's gone. Put the tap out again."

Esteban was waiting. She told him who had interrupted them and what she had learned.

"Shit," he said. "Or 'Litter,' as your people say."

"It's been nice to know you. I think you're safe. I hope so. I suppose I am only until after the executions. If they're killing me because I'm guilty of their murder, they have to wait, don't they?"

She imagined that he was shaking his head. "Maybe," he said. "It's probably easier than fiddling the paperwork."

"I wonder where Aunt Lois is now?"

"I can find out for you." There was a pause before he muttered, "I'm at home, you know. Of course. It's night . . . But I've got Stan's big brother right here . . ."

She pictured him facing a standard computer terminal, his fingers on its keys, his eyes intent on the lines of type that flashed across the screen.

"Nothing in the public databases . . . The Ministries should change their passwords once in a while . . . There!"

"What?"

"She's right over us. Or near enough. Drifting north. She keeps coming back. Not really in an orbit."

Elation filled Pearl Angelica's throat. "If I could get outside!"

"She wouldn't dare. You'd both be dead."

"It's the death watch, then." She would stay there, holding position all the time, hovering as if Pearl Angelica lay in a deathbed, waiting until she heard her niece was dead.

Esteban grunted. "Here's the minutes of the last meeting of Ministers . . . this afternoon. You don't want to know this."

"Tell me!"

"The main argument was whether to kill you on or off camera. The consensus was on. They think that will convince the Orbitals they're in earnest and make them less likely to refuse their demands the next time they kidnap someone."

"How long?"

"Not much." His voice cracked. "They're going to do you all . . ."

When he fell silent, she thought he could not bear to name the limit that had been set on her life. But then he took a deep breath, clearly audible through the cuff, and managed, "Day after tomorrow. The file doesn't say what time."

Chapter
Seventeen

PEARL ANGELICA PRESSED her face against the cold metal bars of her cage. She fingered the loops like links of chain that bound the steel mesh to those bars. She eyed the mesh ceiling that meant she could no longer climb up some ally's knee and hip and shoulder and head and jump to freedom. She plunged her roots into the dirt beneath her feet and jerked them through it, plowing, churning. It had once been much the same as the fertile stuff Cherilee Wright used for her garden beds—mixed regolith and compost—but it did not taste the same. She had not been free in the greenhouse, but there the soil had not held the metallic reek of chains.

She peered through the gaps in the mesh. The concourse surrounding the cage was dim. The only sounds were the soft sigh of distant air pumps, a gurgle of water or sewage in pipes beneath the floor or in the ceiling, a hum of machinery that made her think Anatol might have escaped his own cell and hijacked another truck. Could he possibly be on his way to rescue her once more? No. Of course not. There were no trucks on this lower level, no way to get one here, and besides Security would be watching for just such a move.

Even if he were on his way, how could he hope to rescue her? There was no longer a way out of her cage. There was nowhere to go even if she *could* get out. The most that he could give her was one more glimpse of his face, a touch of his hand, a word. She craved them all. She knew she would never have them.

A distant clicking grew louder, closer. It became obviously the sound of footsteps, and she hoped very briefly that maybe, just maybe, she was wrong. Anatol *had* escaped his jailers! He *was* coming to visit her one last time!

But the pedestrian who emerged from a corridor mouth, darted a furtive glance toward the imprisoned bot, and followed the wall to the next corridor was not her friend.

Why was this stranger so furtive when so many others had gathered close around her to stare and taunt? Perhaps Pearl Angelica was simply the last to hear of her imminent doom. The stranger had already heard at least a rumor, and he did not wish to come too close for fear her fate would prove contagious.

The silence stretched while she contemplated a time two mornings hence. Finally, she said, "Esteban? Are you still there?"

"Of course," came the soft murmur from her cuff. "I couldn't leave you now, Angie. Not unless there's a knock on my door. And now that they've got you again, there's not much chance of that. Unless I was less careful than I thought I was and someone knows who 'Esteban' is. But I *was* careful, and—"

"You're babbling," she said. "This upsets you worse than it does me. But then I've been expecting it ever since I heard what ransom they wanted for me. This isn't any surprise, though now that it's so close—"

"Now who's babbling?"

"You're right," she said. "But there's nothing else we can do."

"I'd love to think of something."

"Can you contact the *Quebec?* Talk to my aunt? Let me talk to her?"

He hesitated before responding. "I'd have to hack into the com center for that. I've never done that. Though it shouldn't be hard. Never wanted to talk to anyone who wasn't already here, you know? Not on Earth. My mother's dead. My father thinks I'm a radical subversive traitor to the cause because I came to the Moon. And I don't know any Orbitals. But if I can tap those Ministry files—"

"You're babbling again." She imagined his hands on the keyboard of his terminal, calling up menus, searching for back doors and access codes, discovering the subroutine that controlled some isolated dish antenna, typing the commands that swivelled it on its base and aimed it toward her aunt's ship.

"Just talking to myself, Angie. While I . . ."

He could not slip. No errors would be allowed. No typos. The trick was avoiding whatever watchdogs Security might have planted in the system, detecting the hesitancies of response that said an extra program was monitoring what one was doing, finding passwords or alternate paths to one's goal, every sense stretched to the limits of its sensitivity, every nerve and muscle tuned for speed.

She knew it all was possible. She could do it herself, at least if she had a bioform computer. Her roots would interface with its. She would, in effect, make it a part of her nervous system and operate it with all the speed of thought. Lacking that, she did not think her senses or responses would be nearly fast enough.

"There." He sounded immensely pleased with himself. "Do you know her number? Just kidding. Here . . ."

"Pearl Angelica?"

Even after passing through so many relays—from the com center to a speaker in Esteban's room to his cuff to hers—and then being distorted by the tiny speaker in the cuff, the voice was recognizable. It was hard for the bot not to scream her answer: "Aunt Lois!"

"I'm here. I can't do a thing, but . . . but I'm here. Call me a witness."

"I've already said you're on the death watch."

"It is that, isn't it? I'm sorry, dear. Twice now . . ." Her tone was awkward, embarrassed, pained. Humans did not ordinarily discuss such things with those about to die, especially when the near-dead were close friends or kin. Yet all those generations of bots before Pearl Angelica had lived so briefly. Death had been closer to them, easier to think about. Pearl Angelica had already enjoyed a nearly human lifespan, but she had absorbed the bot attitude from her mother. So, to a lesser extent, had Lois McAlois, for she had been close to Donna Rose for several years. She had in fact been with her at the end.

"Twice? Daddy?"

"Yes. Frederick died at last."

Pearl Angelica had to struggle to get the words past the sudden blockage in her throat. "I wish I'd seen him one more time."

"I did." Her grief was as audible as the bot's. "For both of us. I got back just in time. And I told him what happened. He was lucid enough to agree. No ransom."

"I know. You can't. I'd say the same."

The silence after that was broken only by Esteban's muttered, sympathetic, "Shit!" until the pilot, safe in her metal shell above the Moon, said, "We'd all like to help."

"But it's impossible."

"We don't dare give them what they demand. Even if it costs . . ."

"A life," said the bot. "Just one life."

"But it's *your* life!" said Esteban.

"It would be a lot more if we gave in," said Pearl Angelica.

"I'm sorry, dear," said Lois McAlois again. "We're all sorry. The bots . . . Did you know they hoped you would become their Eldest?"

After a moment, the caged bot forced a chuckle. "Is that what they thought my potential was?"

"I suppose. But it's true, your potential has always been enormous. I would have liked to see how it turned out. So would Renny, and your father."

"My mother too." She had been dead for most of Pearl Angelica's life. She had missed so many milestones of her daughter's years. Now she would miss this last one of all. Better, thought the bot, to say she would be spared it. She wished she could be spared it herself. She would like to learn how long she might live if left to normal aging, and how that famous potential of hers might turn out.

"Of course. But we don't dare . . ."

"Esteban?" said the bot. "How are they going to do it? Hrecker said something about opening an airlock."

"That's the usual method. But . . ."

"Tell me."

"It's just that they hadn't decided to do it that way. One minister wanted to dissect you, live."

"That's vivisection," said Lois McAlois. She sounded horrified.

"Another just wanted to see whether your blood is red or green."

"It's red," said Pearl Angelica. She had seen it often enough to know.

"They mentioned hanging, shooting, beheading. Some-one—the minutes didn't name him—even wondered whether vegetarians could eat you. He said it couldn't be cannibalism since you're not human, but he wondered, are you animal enough to count as meat?"

"They're as barbaric as they ever were," said Lois.

"Not all of us," said Esteban.

"They hate me," the bot whispered to her cuff. She wished desperately that she could see her aunt once more before the end. She wished she could see Esteban. And Anatol and Cherilee.

"They laughed at that one. Maybe it was just a joke."

"Black enough," said the bot.

"Yeah. But it didn't help them make up their minds. Quick or slow, clean or messy. The only thing they agreed on was that it should go on the veedo."

Pearl Angelica stared past the steel bars and mesh that caged her in, stared at the veedo set on the other end of the dais. It was dark and silent now. But all too soon the cage would be empty and for a moment she—or her image—would be in that glass-fronted box. Whatever gawkers would come to gloat over her right and proper fate would watch her die behind that glass.

The silence stretched, broken only by the distant sounds of the base that surrounded and imprisoned Pearl Angelica. She was damned, she knew, damned three times over. Once because she was a monstrous hybrid, part human, part plant, all unthinkable blasphemy. Twice because she represented all the novelty and progress the Engineers had destroyed on Earth, the gengineers and their new technology that was saving what the old could no longer support. She was what they had lost. Three times because she came from the Engi-neers' hated rivals, the Orbitals and Gypsies, some of whom had fled the destruction on Earth, all of whom managed to preserve and use and even extend both old and new technologies. She was what they could never be as long as they retained their neophobic attitudes.

"I wish," she said at last. "I wish you didn't have to hear

all this, Aunt Lois. Or watch them kill me."

"Me too." The sound of the *Quebec*'s thrusters was audible
behind its pilot's voice. Pearl Angelica knew that the ship
could not be in a stable orbit. It had to be on a course that
carried it above the base, moving slowly past and falling
toward the lunar surface until Lois brought it again and again
back into position.

But were those thrusters active enough? Pearl Angelica
wished she had a better feel for piloting, a better sense of
what was possible. How long could the *Quebec*'s tanks of
reaction mass last? Would her aunt have to leave to refuel,
and thereby miss her death? Or was there some other way
for her to hold position?

She was speaking again: "I'd rather have you here with
me. Take you home. I wish I'd never brought you with me.
But I did. And if you must die, I can stay as near as I can
manage. I can watch. I can tell the Gypsies what they did
to you."

"I wish I could see you." The tears came to Pearl Angelica's eyes. Her voice shuddered. She choked. "Touch you."

The voice that came from her cuff sounded as stricken as
her own. "But we can't. If I tried to come any closer . . .
They have railguns. Lasers."

"I don't want you dead too. Stay away, please. And good-
bye. Tell Uncle Renny that."

"I will."

"Tell the rest too."

"I will."

"And don't forget the Racs."

"I won't."

This time it was Esteban who finally interrupted the silence.
"There may be a way," he said.

"What!" cried Lois McAlois. Her voice was loud even
through the cuff on Pearl Angelica's wrist, and the bot nearly
forgot to whisper as she demanded, "How?"

"I can't say yet," he said. "I shouldn't raise your hopes.
In fact, I've said too much already. There are just too many
ifs. But I want to get the rest free too. And it will have to
be tomorrow night."

"There won't be any later chances," agreed Lois McAlois.

"Why not now?" asked Pearl Angelica, though she knew

that any plan that had any chance at all of succeeding must require preparation.

"I need to learn things," said Esteban. "Arrange things. And then, if and if and if—"

"I understand," said Lois McAlois. "No promises."

"No promises," said Esteban.

Chapter
Eighteen

SHE STOOD WITHIN her steel enclosure, roots embedded in the soil, head tipped back to expose her front to the artificial sun above the cage. She did not sleep even though her eyes burned. She had been unable to close her eyes after Esteban had severed his contact through her cuff, and with it her access to her aunt. Now he was doing all he could to make come true all those promises he had refused to speak. She prayed—the only gesture she was free to make—to every god whose name she had ever heard that he would succeed.

Would he? Could he? Would he get her out of her cage and lead her on a sudden dash for freedom? She drew thirstily, desperately, on water and nutrients and light, stoking reserves she knew she might never need. She thought of solid food and its more compact calories. Saliva flooded her mouth, and her stomach growled. The body had imperatives that survived even the hybridization of plant and animal.

Hrecker had offered her no last meal, no final courtesies. She did not think he would in the morning, either. If that was when they came for her. Wasn't that the traditional time? But on the Moon true dawn came only every two weeks. The "days" of human experience were artificial, defined by fiat to correspond to those rhythms eons of evolution had written into the core of every Earthly being.

"When is dawn here?" All she had had ever since she came to the Moon was glimpses of the surface. She had no idea of the time of "day" outside the base.

Donna, her cuff, seemed to know what she meant. "Eleven pee-em tomorrow," it said in a very neutral tone. It was not yet human enough to seem sympathetic. "Twenty-three hundred hours."

Whichever one they chose, then. Lunar dawn or clock dawn, arbitrary but still Earth dawn, if they were traditionalists. False or true. Or between the two. Both fit those few words of doom recorded by the Council of Ministers. Tomorrow. And the light that beamed down upon her, the dirt beneath her feet, the air around her, might be the last she would ever taste. Her roots spasmed, curled, set a tangled grip deep in the soil as tight as the grip she wished she could clamp on life. She did not wish to die.

She told herself that Esteban *must* have a chance to save her. His mind was so sharp . . . She looked at the cuff on her wrist. He had devised a way to turn the Q-drive into a miniature and inexhaustible power source. He had then built the cuff around it. A communicator, a computer, an artificial intelligence. She shook her head at the awesome potential of what he had done, and again as she wondered whether his masters even knew that he had done it. If anyone could pry her out of this cage and move her from the Engineers' lunar base to her Aunt Lois . . . She wished she knew what he had in mind.

She also wished she had told her aunt what he had done. She could not possibly tell how the new power source worked, but she could at least have passed the word that it was possible. Given that, Gypsy engineers could try to duplicate Esteban's work. Their work would of course be easier if she knew more. Or if Esteban himself would reveal his secrets.

The veedo set did not distract her, for it was not turned on. Nor did gawkers, for only a few dared to approach her on this eve of her death. She was alone with her thoughts and her wishes.

A dozen guards arrived that afternoon. They scowled until the few bystanders present fled. They said nothing as they took positions around the dais that held her cage. Most faced outward, arms crossed, sidearms on their hips. Four faced inward, watching her.

Pearl Angelica did not think it hard to guess why they were there. No one would be allowed to speak with her. No enemies would taunt her, but neither would any friend be permitted to comfort her. She would not be able to use the cuff's induction tap to speak with Esteban or Lois. And there would be no escape.

She wished . . . If she could not escape, could she at least avoid the morning? But she had no poison, no knife, not even a fragment of broken glass. The guards that watched her would surely stop her if she tried to strangle herself with that very piece of wire she could not use to talk. She had to live. Until . . .

A robot arrived, steering a motorized cart with a small cargo bed. It unplugged the veedo set, put it on the cart, and trundled it toward a corridor mouth.

Pearl Angelica stared after the departing cart, and then at the empty end of the dais that still held her cage. The veedo was on its way to storage, she thought. Or someone's apartment. And when they took her away the next day, she would never return to this spot. Not even as an electronic image behind a glass screen.

The rest of the day passed excruciatingly slowly. Pedestrians scuttled on the borders of the concourse, moving from corridor to corridor as if they feared the notice of the guards. The guards themselves shifted on their feet and grunted and farted and said nothing at all, not even to each other. In due time, they were replaced by a new shift.

"Five pee-em," the cuff whispered to the bones of her wrist. "Seventeen hundred hours." The vibrations of the sound waves passed to her radius and ulna, her humerus, her collarbone, sternum, ribs, vertebrae, and skull, finally reaching the ossicles of her middle ear. "Six pee-em . . . Nine . . ."

The floodlight above her went out. The lights that illumined the concourse and corridors dimmed. The guard was changed again. It was evening, night, a time when the human neural computer, with all its inbuilt programming, expected shadows and darkness and omens of death.

"Midnight . . ."

She did not tell the cuff to stop, for though the countdown oppressed her, shortened her breath, made her heart pound with dread, she also felt a morbid fascination, kin to that which drives a tongue to probe the gap left by a missing tooth or a finger to pick at a scab.

"One aye-em. One hundred hours. Wee-est of the wee hours."

Her last day had begun, was an hour old. She would not see its end, would never see another, would never see her Aunt

Lois, another bot, Uncle Renny, her father's grave, the *Gypsy* or the Gypsies, Earth from space or First-Stop. Unless . . .

A flicker in the shadowed mouth of a corridor caught her eye. Low, near the floor, near the wall, small and darting. A mouse? But it was not that small.

"Two aye-em. Not quite so wee."

Were there mice on the Moon? What could be more natural? It was made of green cheese, wasn't it? She tried to laugh but stopped at the first taste of hysteria.

There were research labs, weren't there? Places for testing toxins and drugs. Rooms full of little cages full of mice. Mice that could, that surely did, escape. To nibble at the cheese.

She caught her breath. A mouse could not possibly make her guards exclaim, slap at thighs and arms and chests, reach for their guns, swear, fall all around her! Fall as if someone— Esteban!—had pulled the trigger on a machine gun or laser and unleashed a hail of death. But there was no sound of gunfire, no line of laser light sweeping across the concourse below the level of her feet. There was no blood. There was only . . . Had she heard a hiss, a phut! a phut-t-t-t-t-t! and then . . . ?

All the guards were down and still.

"Ah!"

That soft sound came from the corridor where she had glimpsed whatever she had glimpsed a few moments before. It was followed by a quieter sigh of relief. A figure rose from the floor of the corridor and approached her.

"Esteban!" she cried. Her roots slid from the soil as if they had minds of their own and knew that the time had come to leave.

He gestured her silent. "Shh, someone might . . ." He bent over the guards one by one, touching their throats.

"There's a door now." She pointed at the side of her cage.

"Yeah." Now he was slapping their pockets, extracting every lump he found. "I was hoping someone had a key."

"Hrecker used a remote."

When it was clear that he would find neither key nor remote, he said, "C'mon, Stan." He held the wire his cuff extruded vertically and swept it along the edge of the dais.

"There!" said the machine. "Hold still. That's it. Get me closer . . ." It guided Esteban until he held the wire at an angle. A moment later, the cuff said, "Got it, Ollie!"

The bars of the cage shuddered in their sockets and began to slide down into the rim of the planter. Esteban winced when they shrieked, rubbing against the loops of steel that anchored the cage's meshwork skin. "Now squat," he said. "And push."

Her hand gripped his even before what was left of the cage bounced off the guards and struck the concourse's floor. "Let's go," he said. "We haven't got much time."

She looked over her shoulder at the guards. Two were bleeding. They had not even twitched at the cage's impact on their backs and heads. "Are they dead?"

"Asleep." He showed her the gun he had used. "An airgun. I had to steal it from the hospital. They use it on madmen. Now. Run." He tugged at her hand, and they ran.

He led her through a maze of corridors, only some of which seemed familiar from her nighttime explorations of the base with Anatol, or perhaps from that brief tour Hrecker had given her when he brought her to her cage. They heard Security guards in the distance and glimpsed them when they stopped at intersections to peek around corners. They took turns they hoped would keep them free, tested doors and hid in dark offices and laboratories, crouched behind planters thick with foliage. Finally Esteban muttered, "Here," and tried a door.

"Where are we?" They were both breathing hard. Whenever he could, Esteban had set a breakneck pace, and he had not let go of her hand. She had had to keep up.

"Almost there." The room behind the door was as dark as any other of their temporary refuges, but this time he reached for a light switch. The space he revealed was about three meters by ten. Large, reusable cartons, stacked nearly to the ceiling, covered half its floor. "I checked," he said. "You can hide behind the boxes. There's room, and nobody would think of looking there."

"You did."

"I'm smarter than they are." He pushed her toward the cartons. "Go on," he said. "I'll be back soon."

She was already on top of the pile. Ahead of her, between the last row of cartons and the wall, she could see a space, not even as big as the cage she had just escaped. She did not want to descend into it. She swivelled to look at Esteban, but he was now beside the door, his hand on the light switch.

"But . . ."

"Go on," he said. "Get in. If anyone finds the lights on, they'll get suspicious. And I *will* be back."

A carton moved beneath her weight, and she slid into the hole. As soon as she could no longer see her friend—and he could not see her—the lights went out. The door opened and quietly closed. She fell the last half-meter into her new cell.

The darkness was complete. Her brain manufactured sparkles and lines and fragmentary mottled patterns from the random firings of the neurons in her retinas. There were faint sounds too, and though she wondered at first if they too were hallucinations borne of sensory deprivation, she soon accepted them as . . . The mutter of distant voices? The muted clash of metals? Steps in the corridor outside the door?

She resisted the trembling that threatened to overwhelm her by flattening one hand against the side of a carton. Plastic. They could be folded flat, stored fifty at a time inside one of their number, and unfolded again whenever they were needed. She wondered how old these cartons were, what they had held, and even where they had been. The Gypsies and the Orbitals both used the same design. It dated, she thought, to a time before the gengineers had fled Earth.

What was in the cartons now? She could detect no smell of food or machine oil. They were light, light enough that Esteban might easily have lifted and moved and rearranged the stacks to make this space for her to hide in, but they were not empty. She felt for the top of a carton, found overlapping flaps, and slid a hand inside. Soft. Cloth. Clothing, then. Or bedding.

She was painfully aware that Esteban had told her nothing at all of what he planned. He had said he would return. But he had given no hint of where he was going now, or of where they would go when he came back.

He had said he wanted to free the others when they were talking with Aunt Lois, hadn't he? Then perhaps that was what he was doing now. Shooting guards, putting them to sleep just as he had done to hers. Releasing Esteban and Cherilee and the other dissidents who had wished and tried and failed to protect Pearl Angelica, the living blasphemy so far from her home and kin.

"How long have we been in here?" she asked the artificial intelligence in the cuff Esteban had given her. She was sure it was not the hours she felt within her. "Since he left. Since the lights went out."

"Ten minutes," said the machine quietly. "Time flies when you're having fun." And much, much later, maddeningly later: "Fifteen. Twenty. Twenty-two."

Footsteps in the corridor. A moving door. Light once more, at last. And a voice she recognized, a voice she had feared she would never hear again: "Angie?"

"Anatol!"

Esteban was there as well, looking sour as she clambered over the stack of cartons and rushed to embrace her older friend.

"I thought . . . ," she said, and she set her fingers gently beside Anatol's left eye. It was swollen shut by a massive bruise. Then she looked at the others and could not help a dismayed gasp.

"Yeah," said Anatol. His arms were tight around the bot. "They were pretty rough."

"They won't get another chance," said Esteban.

Besides Anatol and Esteban, there was one other man, his skin swarthy, his bald crown a mass of scabs rimmed by crusted, dirty curls. He looked both lost and determined. Pearl Angelica barely recalled seeing him at the party that seemed so long ago. "The worst of it doesn't show," he said.

But it did. Four women accompanied the men, and their eyes were wide and dark and wary. One carried an arm in a sling. Another was bent half double, her arms cradling her sides as if she were in agony from broken ribs. Pearl Angelica recognized them both from their visit to the greenhouse and wished she knew their names.

"I'll make them kill me first," said the woman who clutched her ribs. Her voice was rough with pain and fluid.

"We'll carry you if we have to," said Anatol.

"You won't," she rasped. "It hurt, but I ran this far. I can keep going. As long as . . . You said you can do it, Esteban. Just get us out of here."

"I thought there would be more," said Pearl Angelica.

"The rest can't walk. Or I couldn't find them."

"Some are already dead," said the man she didn't know.

"Did they get us all?" asked someone.

"All but Esteban."

"Then who's the informer?"

"Do you think we'd be here now if he was the one?"

"Where's Cherilee?" asked Pearl Angelica. "Wasn't she . . . ?"

"She was with us," said the woman with the broken arm.

"I bet it was Notting," said the man. "He didn't seem worried enough when they took us in."

"It doesn't matter, as long as he's not with us now."

"Or she."

"She said she had to get something," said Anatol. "At the greenhouse."

"I told her where to find us." Esteban looked uncertain.

"Here?" asked the bot. She refused to share the suspicion that had obviously crossed more than one of the others' minds.

"No. We can't wait for her. If they catch her . . ." He eased the door open the merest crack, peered into the corridor, and retreated. He leaned against the door and whispered, "Guards. But they're not going our way." Footsteps became audible, and voices.

A moment later, he peeked again. "They're gone. Let's go."

Anatol and Pearl Angelica let go of each other only long enough to slip through the doorway. Then they seized each other's hands and ran, following Esteban.

"Do you know where we're going?" the bot managed to ask.

"Yeah." Anatol was panting. Before he could answer, a distant alarm began to wail. "Shit!" he said. Ahead of them Esteban gestured with desperate urgency. Anatol yanked at her wrist, and she plunged ahead until her breath burned in her throat. "They've caught Cherilee. Or they've found out we're gone. But we're almost there. Next corner."

"Wrong direction," said Esteban. "They don't know about you yet. That one's near the greenhouse."

Pearl Angelica's heart fell. If Cherilee had truly been recaptured, she would never see that woman, her friend and protector, again. "Where are we going?"

This time Anatol said nothing. Esteban was already stopping beside a doorway and pointing into a room much like
the one they had just left. Instead of stacks of cartons, it
held rows of four-wheeled carts loaded with sheets, rods,
and bars of metal. Each cart had a hitch for attaching it to
a small tractor.

When they were all inside, Anatol said, "The *Teller*. We're
going to steal it. Right?"

Esteban nodded. "If we can."

Pearl Angelica almost shouted as she realized that Anatol
had to be right. There was no other way to escape the base.
A truck might get them onto the Moon's surface, but the
Engineers would know as soon as they attacked an airlock.
They would not survive long enough to be picked up by Lois
McAlois or the Orbitals. The Q-ship, on the other hand . . .
"Hrecker said it was ready when I got here. It just needed
more mass tanks."

"But we can't just barge in," he said. "There's a pair of
guards on the door. I walked past earlier. And a keypad
lock. I don't know the combination. We have to wait for
the next shift."

"When's that?"

His cuff and hers answered simultaneously, "Seven. Hours
yet to go before we . . ." They went silent together, and then
her cuff said, "Stan? Is that you?"

"Donna?"

"Whip out your tap wire, and we—"

"Shut up," said Esteban.

"I'm not your—!"

"Hush," said Pearl Angelica. "He's right. This isn't the
time."

More alarms joined the first, some hooting, some wailing,
at least one ringing like the telephone of an absent god. One
of the alarms was so close and so loud that the woman with
the broken ribs covered her ears. Someone said, "They're
going to get us!"

"She's supposed to come here," said Esteban when the
raucous din paused as if to catch its breath. "If she can . . .
Is that her?"

"How can you tell?"

He reached for the door. "She limps." As soon as he put his eye to the crack, he almost shouted. "It is!"

Cherilee stumbled into the room, almost falling. Someone's shirt was wrapped around one ankle. In her arms she held a white cylinder, one of the greenhouse's smaller beehives. The entrance hole at its base was plugged with a wad of crumpled paper.

"We thought they had you!" cried Anatol.

"They almost did. They spotted me. But . . ." She handed the beehive to Pearl Angelica. "I had two of these. I threw the other one."

Someone laughed, short and sharp, a bark.

"I dumped the honey."

The bot clutched the hive to her chest—it weighed only a few kilos—and thought: Even when escaping from a death sentence, even injured, even with no time at all for such things, Cherilee had remembered what she needed. She could not give her the Earth she had most truly craved, but her excuse, the bees she had said she wanted, those she had risked her life to bring. She struggled to speak. "I . . . I . . ." She shook her head so hard that the tears flew like raindrops, sparkling in the light.

Cherilee was standing on one foot, massaging her bandaged ankle with both hands. She grinned up at Pearl Angelica. "Don't even try. It made sense at the time. And it saved my ass. Those guards lost interest in me very quickly."

"Your ass wouldn't have needed saving if you hadn't—"

"Shh," said Esteban. The alarms had quieted for a moment. Now movement and voices were audible in the corridor outside the room. "I wish we could lock this door."

"Like this," whispered the man whose name Pearl Angelica did not know. He took a meter-long steel bar from one of the carts and gently set one end beneath the door's knob. He set the other end on the floor and braced his foot against it. Then he found another bar and hefted it in his hand as if he would welcome the chance to bloody a skull in repayment for his own wounds.

"Good idea, Karel," said Anatol.

"It's nothing new," he added. "On Earth I've seen old apartments with sockets in the floor and door for rods like this. They were supposed to keep criminals from breaking in."

"There's nowhere to hide in here." Pearl Angelica was thinking of the cartons in the other room.

"It's too late for that." Karel smacked his steel bar against one palm. Then he eyed the beehive in Pearl Angelica's arms. "Just don't drop that. Please."

Esteban whispered, "If we don't make it—"

He didn't finish the sentence because feet pounded in the corridor just outside the door and stopped. A voice rose, and every one of the fugitives leaned toward the door to hear.

If they didn't make it, thought Pearl Angelica, they would have no second chance.

"The locks are covered," cried a voice outside their hiding place. "Get the maintenance shops. If you find a truck, put someone inside it. That's how . . ."

An alarm sounded just long enough to drown out his voice. Pearl Angelica filled in the missing words: That was how she had hidden before. And escaped, at least for a while.

"You think we'll find them all there?"

"Who knows? Check their rooms. Their friends. If anyone objects . . ." The voice faded as the guard moved away.

Arrest them. Execute them in the prisoners' stead. Or save the trouble and shoot them on the spot. None of the fugitives had any doubt what the rest of the speaker's words had to be.

Someone else moved into range. "They've got to be in the base somewhere."

"One was in the greenhouse."

"That bitch put half a squad on the way to the infirmary." This voice was just outside the door.

Several of the fugitives smiled, but no one dared to laugh or speak aloud.

"We'll get her. And the rest. There's no way out."

At that, Esteban's smile became a grin, fierce and predatory, wolfish, showing teeth. His lips moved as he mouthed the words, "There *is*!"

Pearl Angelica was sure he was right. He had freed them all from their cells. He had led them here. He had agreed when Anatol had suggested the *Teller*. There *was* a way, if only they remained free to seize it.

Every time a guard's footsteps sounded in the corridor, she held her breath. So did the other fugitives.

When one guard laid a hand on the door's handle and rattled the mechanism, the woman with the broken ribs turned white and her legs began to fold. Esteban's arm around her chest made her leap with pain and bite her lip, and then she was once more standing on her own.

Happily, the rattling stopped. The hand and its owner left, and no other guard thought to try the door behind which the fugitives waited for their moment.

Chapter
Nineteen

PEARL ANGELICA HELD the beehive Cherilee had brought her tightly in her arms, afraid to let it go. She was not sure that she would ever get it to First-Stop, but she had it now. It smelled sweet and warm, and an irregular hum vibrated against her skin.

It was one of the things she had thought she wanted when she came to Earth. Was it enough? She could not have root-home. She could have . . . She looked toward Anatol and met his eyes. Then she looked at Esteban. Had she found more than she had bargained for?

How much of it would she keep?

How long would she keep it?

She felt like she waited forever for the sounds of the Security guards to move down the corridor, away from their hiding place, and fade into the distance. Later Donna told her that the fugitives hovered by the door, their anxiety palpable even to an artificial intelligence, for only minutes before they could hear no more words or footsteps.

"Stan?"

"It's time," said Esteban's cuff. "They'll think you're the new shift just long enough."

Esteban held his dart gun ready as he cracked the door and peered down the corridor, first in one direction and then, easing through the opening just enough to see around the jamb, in the other. He made a muffled "Tcha!" sound and the gun went "Pft!"

The man Anatol had called Karel said, "What!" and lifted his steel bar above one shoulder. Pearl Angelica fought down the surge of adrenaline that threatened to force her heart into fibrillation. She bit her tongue to make saliva flow.

She swallowed and held her beehive tighter.

"He was just coming around the corner," said Esteban. "There's no one else. Let's go."

He remained in the lead as they left the storeroom, passed the body on the floor, and marched around the corner, where coveralled workers were filing out the already open door to the construction bay. A pair of guards waved at the fugitives, not recognizing them for what they were until Esteban's dart gun was already firing.

Someone inside the construction bay knew what to do. The door began to slam shut, but two workers had fallen in its way and their bodies kept it from closing. An alarm began to hoot, closer and louder and more strident than anything Pearl Angelica had already heard.

The refugees flowed forward and through the doorway. When a worker tried to attack Esteban with a wrench, Karel's steel bar blocked the blow and broke the attacker's arm with an audible snap. The dart gun felled several more workers. The rest drew back until Esteban told them to pull the bodies from the doorway and close the door.

He pointed the gun at one of the few workers who wore the usual Engineer's shirt and trousers. The shirt had been lovingly embroidered with spidery mechanisms on a checked background that only slowly defined itself as a panel of photovoltaic cells; the mechanisms were antique satellites. "How do you disable the keypad outside?"

The man stared back defiantly, glanced at his fallen colleagues, and finally indicated a small metal box on the wall beside the door. "The circuitry's in that." When Karel raised his steel bar as if to smash the box, he cried, "No! There's a switch."

No switch was visible, but Esteban ran his fingers around the box, stopped in the middle of its lower edge, grinned, and pressed. Pearl Angelica thought that if there had been no alarm to drown out quiet sounds, she might have heard a click and a grunt of satisfaction.

The Engineers' Q-ship, the *Teller*, towered above them all. Its pointed prow nearly touched the ceiling. Its flanks gleamed, untouched so far by the radiation and dust of space. The two tanks of reaction mass Pearl Angelica had seen so many weeks before were now four. One more lay in a rack to one side. Another was held in the arms of a massive robot, ready for installation.

The ship's hatch stood open at the end of a catwalk high above their heads. When Pearl Angelica scanned the room to find the stairway or elevator that must lead to that level, she saw a worker clambering onto the catwalk.

"Esteban!" Anatol's cry was almost totally drowned out by the din of the alarm. But he was pointing too. The worker was running now, heading for the hatch. Did he intend to close it? To bar them from seizing the ship he had devoted his energies to building? Or did he have some thought of firing the engines and destroying them—and everyone else in the construction bay—with the incandescent exhaust?

The alarm paused for a moment. The "Ding!" the first dart made as it caromed off the metal catwalk or its rail was clearly audible. So were voices in the corridor outside the construction bay, something pounding on the door, the sliding of a foot on the floor as a worker moved toward the box of circuitry that controlled the door. So too was a "Don't!" and a crash as Karel raised his bar once more, ignored all attempts to stop him, and destroyed the box. Esteban had turned it off. No one else would turn it on.

The second dart brought the worker down just before he reached the hatch.

The clamor of the alarm returned.

Esteban waved an arm, and the refugees followed him toward the ladder the worker he had just shot down must have used to reach the catwalk.

Pearl Angelica found herself last in the short line of climbers, struggling to hold onto the beehive with just one arm while leaving the fingers free to steady her against the ladder rungs. The others were rapidly drawing ahead, all but the one woman just before her. "What . . . ?" She swore when she realized that she too was trying to climb with only one hand. The other hand, the arm, was confined to a sling; even its fingers were useless. The bot set her shoulder against the woman's buttocks and lifted. There was a muffled "Thanks," and they began to move a little faster.

When they were halfway up the ladder, Pearl Angelica looked over her shoulder. The workers they had left below were clustered by the door. Even as she guessed they were trying to repair or bypass the damage to its controls, the door began to open.

She wished the alarm would quit once more, that she could shout, "Look out! Hurry up! They're coming!" and have some hope of being heard. She shouted anyway, and then she saw that Esteban must have been looking back as well. He had one arm wrapped around the side of the ladder, had swung to one side to let the others pass, and was aiming his dart gun toward the door.

She looked again just in time to see one Security guard fall to the floor and two more recoil. Then the alarm did quit for a second, and she heard Esteban swear. She swung her gaze back to him. He was hurling the gun toward the workers below.

"Idiot!" she said, but he did not seem to hear.

"Run!" he screamed at the others on the catwalk.

They ran, all of them, as the Security guards saw his gun bounce on the floor and realized he was out of ammunition and charged into the bay and began to fire their own guns upward.

The woman just ahead of Pearl Angelica on the ladder grunted and went limp. Her one good hand lost its grip on the side of the ladder. She began to lean out and to one side. The bot tried to stop her movement, to hold her in place with the pressure of her chest and the hive, to keep her safe, but then her feet slid off the rung she stood on. She seemed to shrug away from Pearl Angelica. She fell.

"She's gone, Angie," cried Esteban. He was sliding down the ladder to seize her wrist and yank her up, toward him, toward the catwalk and the *Teller*'s hatch and safety. "Come on. Hurry!"

They were both on the catwalk when Esteban grunted the same dire note Pearl Angelica had already, on the ladder, heard once too often. She spun in time to see him stumble to his knees and clutch at her roots. A spot of red was blossoming on his thigh.

For a moment, she wanted to drop the beehive, but her arm tightened around it quite automatically. With her free hand, she seized his right arm and lifted. He grunted and tried to get his feet under his weight but could only use one leg. She swore, knowing she could never have carried him one-armed on Earth or First-Stop, and staggered with him to the *Teller*'s hatch. She gasped in relief when Anatol slammed it shut behind them.

"I can't fly this thing," said Anatol.

"I can fly ours," said the bot. She studied the cabin they were in and recognized that this ship's similarities to the *Quebec* and its kin were more than skin deep. The Engineers must have stolen not only the plans for the Q-drive, but also those for the ship itself. "If this isn't too dif—"

"I'm not dead, goddammit," said Esteban. "I just can't run. And I've studied the documentation on this thing."

"More hacking." Pearl Angelica's grin said all that needed to be said about how she felt to hear him speak.

Something slammed against the outside of the ship's hatch.

"Just get me to the pilot's seat. And someone plug these holes in my leg."

Pearl Angelica used his own shirt for that. Then the men carried him to the seat he wanted. He ran his fingers over the controls while she looked over his shoulder and decided that all the displays and knobs and buttons were as familiar as anything else about the ship. There were differences, of course, but she could fly it. She probably should, for she had had at least a little experience. But . . .

The slams against the hatch were louder now, and faster. Someone was using a hammer. In a moment, she thought, they would realize that the ship's skin might be thinner. It probably was. Or someone would find a tool sharper than a hammer. Or . . .

All sounds stopped.

"Now what?" asked Anatol.

As if in answer, a loudspeaker began to bellow: "WE MUST HAVE THE MURDERER! SEND OUT ANATOL RIVKIN. WE WILL PUT THE REST OF YOU ON THE NEXT SHUTTLE."

"It's right against the hull," said Karel.

"Don't believe them," said Cherilee Wright.

"I won't," said Esteban. "They just don't want us to take this ship."

The hammering and the alarms returned. A hissing sound announced that a torch or laser cutter had been brought into play as well.

Esteban activated the *Teller*'s engines. Their roar was quickly loud enough to drown out the din, yet the screams of the Security forces and workers outside the ship remained clearly audible. Through the viewport, they could see super-heated gas billowing in the construction bay. The screams stopped.

"How did they expect to get it out of here?" Anatol was pointing through the port at the ceiling above them. A puncture-repair Spider was visible to one side. There was no sign of hatch or iris. The Engineers had apparently made the same mistake as any do-it-yourselfer who had ever built something—furniture, a boat—too large to fit through the home workshop's only door.

Some of the Security guards had found shelter from the rocket blast. Bullets pounded the ship's hull. One, and then another, penetrated and ricocheted before embedding in interior walls.

"The roof," Pearl Angelica screamed above the din. "They must have planned to remove it."

"But we can't do that," yelled Anatol.

"It can't be that thick," said the woman with the broken ribs, her voice as loud as anyone's. "Go through it. Now. Before one of those bullets hits something essential."

"Aye, aye, captain," said Esteban. "Or one of us. But you'd better find some place to lie down." He glanced over his shoulder. "You too, Angie."

"The Apollo crews took off standing up," said Anatol.

"So you're a historian. But we're in a hurry."

As soon as they were all flat on the floor around his seat, he increased thrust. The ship lifted off the floor of the construction bay and hesitated. Pearl Angelica closed her eyes, not wanting to see the ceiling grow quickly closer and crumble into shards. Instead she listened to the impact and felt the ship stagger, heard the screeling of metal scraped on metal, the hiss of air where a seam gave way, the scream and pop of ruptured structure. She imagined the rush of air from the bay and the corridors beyond, the screams of the dying diminishing as the air that carried their sound sucked from their lungs, the slam of airtight barriers across the corridors.

And there was silence except for the uneven sound of their thrust and the agonized sobbing of the woman with the broken ribs. Thrust was not kind to her.

Pearl Angelica opened her eyes. The viewport was gouged but intact. Beyond it was rich black and stars. They were free.

Even though the engines now were choking, gasping, stuttering, straining to lift them all to safety but threatening at every second to fail. She wished she knew whether the problem was some failure of the Engineers—if only they had done their own test piloting!—or some effect of their collision with the roof.

It hardly seemed to matter that Esteban's hands were flying desperately over the controls, that the ship was wobbling on its course, its thrust dangerously out of line with its center of mass, or that he was swearing and saying, "We lost three tanks. One's left. Just one. We can't go far."

An alarm was buzzing, a red light was flashing, and a synthesized voice was saying with artificial calm, "Air alert. There is a crack in the airlock rim twelve point five centimeters above the floor. Air alert. There is a puncture thirty-two centimeters clockwise from the hatch and forty centimeters above the floor. Air alert. There is a puncture . . . Patches are in the cabinet marked 'Emergency.' Follow the instructions on their backs."

Cherilee was already on her feet, opening the locker and extracting the cylindrical canister of patches. She did not stop to read the label, for she had been a resident of the Moon for years. She had learned what to do in such cases long ago: Locate the hole, choose a patch of the right size, peel off its backing, and slap it into place. Repeat as long as air is being lost. Hesitate, and die.

She did what had to be done. Pearl Angelica prayed that it would be enough.

The buzzer stopped. The red light stopped blinking.

The ship jerked sideways, throwing Cherilee to the floor and making the others roll and slide.

"They're still shooting at us," said Esteban.

"What with?"

"They're dead!"

Esteban's hands flew across the controls, and the *Teller* jinked again. "Lasers," he said. "And they're throwing rocks at us with the railguns."

Another lurch brought Pearl Angelica up against the base of Esteban's seat. The beehive slipped from her grip, and the paper plug in its entrance hole fell free. One of the women grabbed the paper and shoved it back in place. "That's all we need, eh? Bees!"

But Pearl Angelica barely appreciated the catastrophe the other had so nearly averted. She was staring at fresh blood on Esteban's calf and crying, "Where's Aunt Lois?"

"Can't see," he said.

She told herself his voice was strong. He was not bleeding to death. In fact, the blood was really only a trickle. Wasn't it?

"We lost a radar antenna," he added. "Only got one now, and that's looking down, spotting rocks. There. The computer can handle collision avoidance. But—"

A loud clang interrupted his words. "That's not perfect either. And it won't do a bit of good against the lasers. As soon as they penetrate . . ."

"Call her."

"Can't." He flipped a switch, and the hiss of static filled the cabin. "We lost that too."

The *Teller* jerked to one side. Something crunched and grated in the ship's stern.

"One tank left," said Esteban. "And it's loose. One solid hit, a couple more dodges like that, and it's gone. And we're sitting ducks."

"We don't have long, do we?" That was one of the women, her voice high and shaky.

"We couldn't get far anyway, not on just one tank." Anatol was on his knees beside the bot, reaching for her.

"There!" Karel shouted. Something glinted in the viewport, vanished, reappeared a finger's width away, and vanished once more.

"Is that her?"

"What's she doing?"

"She's using the tunnel-drive," said Pearl Angelica. "Macroscopic tunneling." But this was no time for lectures.

Esteban grunted, "Got it." He shook his head admiringly, though his face showed the pain he was feeling from his wound. "She's not hovering now. Dodging, so they can't target her. But she can't . . ."

"Yes, she can!" cried Pearl Angelica. The *Quebec* was bigger than the *Teller,* much bigger. It had sleeping cabins and a cargo hold, and if it wasn't big enough to engulf the smaller ship, perhaps it could still . . . "Yes!"

Laser beams are invisible in the vacuum of space. Rocks propelled by railguns move far too fast to spot except with radar. But the signs of both were plain to see in Lois McAlois's evasive random skittering about the sky.

Their presence was also proven by the *Teller*'s sideways lurches and sudden changes in acceleration, by the bangs of glancing blows and the hiss of escaping air, by cries of "Air alert," and Cherilee's scrambles through the ship with her hands full of patches.

Each of the *Quebec*'s leaps brought it closer to the *Teller.* Its image increased in size. The dancing glint was now a splinter of light. It was a spaceship, a knob-headed arrow, its fletching a cluster of reaction mass tanks. Its viewport became visible, and behind it the shadowy forms of a control console, a pilot's seat, a pilot.

"There she is," said Pearl Angelica. "That's her."

"Thank god," said Cherilee. "There's one patch left."

A louder crash than any since they had breached the roof of the construction bay shook the ship. Metal screeched and snapped. "That's it," said Esteban. "Last tank." The engines quit. The sound and weight of thrust abruptly stopped. The ship stopped shaking as if it were about to fall apart and began to yaw. The stars swung across the viewport. Pearl Angelica floated into the air. So did Cherilee, Karel, the other women.

"Escaping air," said Esteban. "Like an attitude jet. But we can't control it."

"Air alert," said the computer. Was Pearl Angelica coloring its voice with her own fears? Or did it indeed sound resigned now that the ship could no longer dodge and flee?

Esteban touched the controls and the computer fell silent. He indicated a digital readout. "We're dead," he said. "That's the temperature of the hull over the engine room. If we could spin . . ." He shook his head. "In another minute, they'll burn through the hull. Then we lose all our air."

"We don't have suits, do we?" That was Karel.

Where was the *Quebec?* It was no longer visible in the viewport.

When something clanged against their hull, they all flinched. But the sound was not that of a crashing rock. It was different, more solid, steadier, and then the stars danced in the viewport. The Moon appeared, smaller than when seen from Earth.

"She grabbed us," said Pearl Angelica. "I didn't know it was possible. But she came beside us and skipped us with her. We're out of range. We're safe."

The refugees had not filled the *Quebec* for long after Lois McAlois had matched airlocks and invited them aboard, for it had been only a short skip to Munin and the Orbitals. There the *Teller* had been turned over to the Engineers. The refugees had not, despite demands.

Now the *Quebec* was on its way back to First-Stop. With it went Anatol Rivkin and Cherilee Wright and Esteban, his true name at last revealed as Julio Lee. "But I like Esteban better," he said.

"Not Julie?" asked Lois, and he shuddered.

The ship was crowded, and it stank, partly of the Armadons it had brought with Pearl Angelica to Earth's solar system, partly of the cheese it was hauling back to the Gypsies, partly of the people who now overburdened its air filters. The beehive, enclosed in a cage of wire screening, was strapped to one wall of the cargo bay.

The two Gypsies and Cherilee shared Lois's sleeping cabin. The men took the other, though neither Anatol nor Esteban was pleased with the arrangement.

"Why not?" insisted Anatol. He had stopped Pearl Angelica outside their rooms. No one else was in sight at the moment, and his hands gripped her shoulders gently, careful not to tear her leaves. "We did before. When you were in my room."

"Yes," she said. "But—"

The radio was audible throughout the ship: "Hallo, Gypsies! I hear she's safe. And *they* paid the ransom. Congratulations! And tell her not to get so mechin' close to the fire next time."

"Is it Esteban?" He touched her wrist where she had worn the cuff he had given her. She had left it behind to instruct the Orbitals in its secrets. Esteban had promised her another as soon as the Gypsies set him up with a suitable workshop. "His artificial intelligences? That power source he came up with from the Q-drive? The better robots he'll give your people? Does he offer a better bride-price than me?"

She jerked her wrist away from his hand. "Are you selling brides again, then, back on Earth?"

He made a face. "Or is it just that he got you off the Moon? Are you grateful?"

"*You* got me out of my cage. You introduced us. Should I be more grateful to you?" She shook her head. "That's not much of a basis for an affair. Or marriage. And I like you both."

"You want us both, then? But you're half plant, aren't you? Not very discriminating. As long as the bees bring the pollen . . ."

"And you're half ass." Cherilee appeared behind him. "If you say one more word, I'll kick you. Though that's probably overkill. Any man who talked to me like that would be out of my life forever."

Pearl Angelica looked past him at the woman. "Where's Esteban?"

Anatol grunted as if they each had punched him in the stomach.

Chapter
Twenty

WHEN SHE SAW the small crowd of familiar, friendly bots and humans waiting at the *Gypsy*'s dock, Pearl Angelica had to struggle to hold back the flood of tears. There was Uncle Renny Schafer, pressing through the pack to wrap his arms around both the bot and his wife and say, "I thought we'd never see you again."

She clutched him in return. "I thought you wouldn't too." And there, close on Renny's heels, was her friend Caledonia Emerald, reaching for her, embracing, crying, "Welcome home!" She stopped trying to control herself. At last, the nightmare was over. She was back, home indeed. She was safe. And she believed it now in a way that she hadn't when her aunt rescued her and the fugitive Engineers from the wreck of the *Teller,* or even when the Orbitals had welcomed her just as happily as these, her friends and kin.

As soon as she could, Caledonia Emerald led her aside from the crowd, saying, "There's something you have to see. Right away."

"What is it?"

But she only shook her head and tugged on Pearl Angelica's arm. "I came up here as soon as we heard you were in the system. Just to show you this. Let's go."

"Yes," said Uncle Renny. "You have to see this."

"I'll take care of the others," said Aunt Lois.

"No," said Esteban. "We stay with her." The others nodded, and Pearl Angelica was not surprised. Neither Anatol nor Esteban, she thought, would wish to be far from her. And Cherilee Wright had come to be a good friend. As for the rest, she supposed they were unwilling to let go of the few people they knew in a world that had to be strange indeed.

Now Cherilee stood stock still in the middle of the *Gypsy*'s broad and curving tunnel. Two streams of traffic parted to flow around them—Armadons and Macks, Roachsters and litterbugs, bots and humans in gengineered vehicles, on bicycles, on foot. The air reeked of biological technology.

"I never dreamed," said the botanist, "that I would ever see all this." Her eyes were as wide as a child's.

"It's the way it used to be," said Anatol. He too was enraptured by the image of days gone by on Earth that the scene evoked. Karel and the women from the Moon looked more baffled by the strangeness of the environment in which they found themselves.

"Earth never smelled like this," said Esteban. "It had open air." He alone, though he was gawking as eagerly as the others, seemed to retain some sense of the similarity between the *Gypsy* and the lunar base they had fled three weeks before.

"It smells better in the greenhouses," said Caledonia Emerald as Lois McAlois gave Cherilee a gentle push and the group began to move once more.

"It's mostly bots that run them, but there should be a place for you," said Lois.

Cherilee stopped again and looked at Pearl Angelica. "I know," she said. "I know that's where I used to work. But I told you . . ."

The bot nodded. She held the beehive in her arms just as she had when they were fleeing the Moon. "She'd like to study gengineering, Aunt Lois."

"There's no reason why not. I'm sure someone needs an apprentice. But . . ." She looked at Caledonia Emerald. "We're going to a greenhouse now, aren't we?"

When the bot nodded, Pearl Angelica asked, "Why? I want to see Uncle Renny. And visit Dad's grave. And then I should get back to my lab."

"You'll see." Caledonia Emerald would say nothing more until they had passed through several of the *Gypsy*'s twisting tunnels, a zone of nearly zero weight, and two parks, and finally entered a tunnel much like the one Cherilee Wright had ruled on the Moon. It was as long and broad and as filled with green, though the soil in which the plants grew was not held in raised beds, but flush with the floor, rimmed by nothing more than low curbs, and several of the crops were very different. There were stands of grain and vegetables and dwarf fruit trees. There were also beds of bioform computers, snackbushes, and udder trees, and several whose occupants were clearly small versions of the bots that walked and stood in the greenhouse's aisles, weeding and watering.

One of those bots rushed up to them before they could get much past the door. Both arms were outstretched, her hands grasping for arms and wrists, her now-fading crimson blossoms quivering as she bobbed her head in eagerness. "You got her! We heard, but that's not the same as seeing. And these—" She stared at Pearl Angelica. "The ones who helped you?"

"Crimson Orchis," Lois McAlois managed to squeeze into the rush of words. She looked at her niece.

"Eldest," said Pearl Angelica.

"Oh, no!" Crimson Orchis's fronds uncurled briefly from her torso, revealing how brown and ragged their edges were. "*You* are the Eldest now. You're older than any of us."

Anatol and Esteban and the others looked perplexed.

"Not old enough," said Pearl Angelica.

"Oh, yes. We never gave you the title. We hoped you would come to seem older . . ."

"Slow and wrinkled," said Lois McAlois.

"Wise," said the bot. "Experienced."

"I've gained some of that," said Pearl Angelica. She sighed and wished she had had the wisdom to stay on First-Stop. She thought she could have done without the experiences the Engineers had forced on her. "Not many bots get kidnapped, raped, and caged at any age."

"Not since we left Earth." Crimson Orchis gestured, and a younger bot appeared to take the beehive, set it on a nearby workbench, and remove the crumpled paper that plugged its doorway. A single bee appeared in the opening almost immediately. "And we almost lost you, didn't we? All that potential." She shook her head.

Pearl Angelica grimaced. "You could have . . ."

"We did. Over here." Crimson Orchis led them all to a bed that held two dozen thick stalks topped by knobs whose dents and bumps suggested human faces. Unlike the infant bots that grew in nearby beds, these had no fronds. Their bases were surrounded by rosettes of small oval leaves.

Anatol looked from the bed to Pearl Angelica just as she fell to her knees and reached to touch the nearest knob. "Clones?" he said, and then, as if realizing that of course there could be little resemblance between adult and infant bot and that of course Crimson Orchis could mean nothing else, he repeated more definitely, "Clones."

Lois McAlois was nodding. "They were starting them before I headed back to Earth."

A second elderly bot appeared beside them. "We couldn't wait any longer." She paused to produce a liquid cough that said she was nearer the end of her life than Crimson Orchis. Her blossoms were almost colorless. "We're fading now. Soon we'll be gone. So we decided to take no more chances. We need your longevity."

"That's why so many," said Karel. He nodded as if remembering that the short lives of bots were no secret, even among the Engineers.

"My children," said Pearl Angelica. "I was never ready for them before. But now . . ." Before her trip to Earth, she had rarely even thought about reproducing herself. She had known that she was expected to do so, to pass her genes on to another generation of her kind. But she had never felt the pressure of dwindling time, even though she had long known that she was outliving generations of her kin. She had been too busy. Perhaps too self-centered. And she had found no prospective mate.

Now she looked up at Anatol. At Esteban, who was shaking his head and saying, "That's an awful lot of kids to take care of."

"No," said Crimson Orchis. She indicated the other bot. "Boston Lemon is in charge of the nursery. This is where we sprout our seeds and grow the saplings until they can be taught."

"I can't set seeds," said Pearl Angelica.

"No. You're too nearly human. But we need your genes. We had no choice. If you reproduce yourself, you will surely raise your children in the human way."

Pearl Angelica looked at her friends and aunt. Esteban looked relieved, Anatol sullen, Lois McAlois wistful, as if she wished that she and Renny had . . . Were her inclinations and her dilemma that obvious?

Did she really have to choose between the two men? They each had a claim on her loyalty, and even on her affection, but . . .

"With these," said Boston Lemon. A buzzing sound drew her eyes to a small insect circling above her head. She grinned broadly when the bee alighted on one of her blossoms. "A bee. At last."

Crimson Orchis picked up the thread the other had dropped. "If you will teach them, merge roots and memories, all you are, then they will be much like you."

Pearl Angelica stood up. "They're doing fine," she said to the elderly bots. "I don't think we need so many of me, though. Let them be their own people."

"Eldest." Crimson Orchis and Boston Lemon bowed their heads together.

She grimaced uncomfortably. She had not expected to come home to this. "I'll look in on them again. But for now . . ."

"Of course."

"Where are they now?" asked Renny Schafer.

"We found them quarters," said his wife. "Though the way they were looking at our niece . . ."

Renny snorted as if he were still a dog. "They have other rooms in mind?" He turned to Pearl Angelica. "Do you want them? One of them? Or both?"

She shook her head. "I don't know. They . . ."

"You feel you owe them something."

"Not that gratitude's enough," said Lois McAlois.

When Pearl Angelica nodded, Renny went on. "Anatol let you out of the cage first. When Anatol got caught, Esteban got you—and the others—loose again and led you all off the Moon. He also gave you that cuff." He shook his head admiringly. "I can hardly wait to get one of my own."

Pearl Angelica curled one hand around the wrist where the cuff had ridden until she had left it with the Orbitals. Very briefly, she smiled at her uncle. "He's smarter. But Anatol is braver. He took the first risk, after all."

"They're both brave," said Lois McAlois. "Esteban wasn't playing it safe when he shot those guards and stole the *Teller*."

"Then . . ."

"Don't force it," said Lois. "If the answer isn't clear now, give it time. You might even decide you don't want either of them."

"But it is, really." And so it was, she suddenly realized. "When Anatol first came to me, he was wishing for the Good Old Days of his own childhood. He was looking backward just like the Engineers. Like me. But Esteban . . . He looks forward. He could have been born one of us."

"Should we take him back, then?"

"Anatol?" She paused thoughtfully before shaking her head. "Not until he decides he's left his Good Old Days behind. I don't think he'll turn into a saboteur."

"And Esteban?"

She grinned. She knew what his answer would be if she asked him to be her mate. Yet she was reluctant to move too fast. "There's only one thing I've ever been in a rush for. And that was a mistake, wasn't it? I'll have to see."

"How did you get so many Engineers on your side?" Caledonia Emerald was asking.

"You're surprised that some of us can be rational?" Esteban was laughing.

"They didn't used to be," said Renny Schafer. The doglike wrinkling of his lip that bared his canines seemed quite involuntary.

"It wasn't that hard," said Pearl Angelica. She glanced at Anatol, whose expression said he was not happy to see her sitting closer to the other man than to him. "Anatol came to me. Then he took me to meet the others. They weren't happy in the first place."

"Too restrictive," said Cherilee Wright. They were sitting at a table in one of the *Gypsy*'s many small cafes, this one in a park beside a fountain. A single dumbo, perhaps a last reminder of Pearl Angelica's search for a local pollinator, perhaps a pet released by some other Gypsy, hovered in the spray that arched from a dolphin's mouth.

"Most of us," she went on. "We wanted things the Engineers would not allow. I wanted genetic engineering. And here she was, telling us that the best thing human beings can do is to pursue knowledge freely. Some of us would have helped her even if we hadn't liked her."

Now it was Renny's turn to laugh. "There's hope, then!"

When Pearl Angelica finally insisted that she could stay away from First-Stop and her work no longer, Caledonia Emerald said, "I have to go back too. And I want to show you what the Racs have been doing."

"What do you mean?"

But she refused to be more specific. "I'll reserve a couple of shuttle seats."

"Can we go down there too?" asked Anatol.

"I'd like to see the place," said Esteban. "A new world. And aliens."

"Later," said Renny Schafer. "You have enough to learn up here."

"Yes," said Pearl Angelica. She avoided Anatol with her eyes, knowing that she had to be hurting his feelings. For a moment she wished she had the nerve to tell him plain what she had already told her aunt and uncle. "You'll get down there soon enough. And it won't be long before I'm up here for good, along with everyone else."

The next scheduled shuttle flight was not until late the next afternoon. By noon, Pearl Angelica had a headache, her stomach was churning, and her forehead and neck were drenched with sweat.

"I have to go down there," she said. She and Caledonia Emerald were in her aunt and uncle's apartment. "I have work to do. So why . . . ?"

"Your father?" asked Renny Schafer.

After a moment's pause, as if she were trying the fit of his words to her feelings, the bot shook her head. "No. I expected that. I've been expecting it for years. We all have."

"You're scared to death, aren't you?" asked Caledonia Emerald.

She nodded jerkily. "I don't understand this. I was fine an hour ago."

"It's a planet," said her Aunt Lois.

"And I'm safe in space. But not . . ."

"There's no Engineers on First-Stop. No cages. No cells."

A picture of a falling branch played itself across the screen of her mind, but she knew her uncle was right, excepting only those mad anomalies no one could escape anywhere. She sighed. "I know."

Her anxiety did not disappear after that, but it diminished. By the time she and Caledonia Emerald boarded the shuttle it was hardly more than apprehension. And when she stepped from the shuttle to see the Tower rising like a gleaming needle from the bowl of the valley, it washed away in a flood of relief and satisfaction and bittersweet awareness that soon she would leave this place behind forever.

"I didn't think it would be so nearly done."

"You were gone for a long time."

"And what's that?" She was pointing at the arch of stone wall, the pyramid, the pole, the basket. Long lines of Racs were winding down the encircling bluffs and across the moss-covered valley. Each one bore a large stone in his or her arms.

"Their watching place."

"It's grown."

"And more than that. Come on inside." Caledonia Emerald held the door to the pumpkin that was the Rac Surveillance Office. "We've got the altar bugged."

A little later, Pearl Angelica was peering at a screen and saying, "That's Blacktop. He's still the chief?"

"High priest, more like," said Lucas Ribbentrop. His fingers were dancing over the controls of what seemed to be recording equipment. His white hair glowed in the dim light of the office.

"Listen to him," said Caledonia Emerald. She too had controls to work, and now the image of the priest brightened as she compensated for the falling dusk.

The Rac stood on the second step of the stone pyramid, his arms spread wide. He scratched his muzzle in the greeting gesture, and his voice sang out in a glossy smoothness that even to human ears rang with fury.

"Savages!" he cried. "You broke their spears! You beat them! You chased them from the valley!"

"Yesterday," said Ribbentrop. He was pointing at another veedo screen and the image of a mob of Racs hurling stones. Four other Racs fled in desperate haste. Three of them streamed tails behind them. Two had actually dropped to all fours.

"The strangers," said Pearl Angelica. "But . . ."

"Spies!" screeched a voice from the congregation within the watching place's walls. "They plotted to seize our valley and our Tower!"

Blacktop slumped where he stood. "Not ours," he said. "Our world's. For every Rac, whether they have tails or not."

"That's what *they* said, just before the riot." Caledonia Emerald was shaking her head.

"No!" screamed a voice from the mob.

"Ours!"

"We will kill them if they return!"

"Kill them all!"

"It was Wanderer himself," said Ribbentrop. "But not only." The other veedo screen showed the three visitors standing in a clump beside the watching place's stone wall. Beside them stood a tailless Rac.

Facing them was a larger group of tailless Racs with Leaf in the forefront. Her fur bristled insanely as she screeched, "The Tower is ours! The gods are ours! They made us, and they made the Tower for us!"

"That's Wetweed," said Pearl Angelica, pointing at the fourth.

"She got friendly with Stonerapper," said Caledonia Emerald. "She had to run with them."

"They made us too," Shorttail was saying.

"They discarded you. They threw you to the wind like the trash you are. You will never climb the Tower! We will not let you!"

"None of us can climb it yet," said Wanderer. The watchers of the recorded scene could see him struggling to keep his twitching fur from bristling in automatic challenge. "But the time will come."

"We will have learned enough to try," said Shorttail.

"We may have tails like our ancestors," said Stonerapper. "But our brains are not made of stone."

"And our people will insist on trying," said Wanderer, and now his fur was standing as madly erect as Leaf's. So was that of every other Rac in the scene. "If we must, we will destroy all who stand in our way."

"Nooo!" screamed Leaf, and the rocks began to fly.

Pearl Angelica refused to watch as the rocks struck flesh, blood flowed, and the strangers with their single friend turned and ran. She shifted her gaze to the screen that showed the present moment and a rising hysteria that seemed every bit as threatening as that which had sent the others fleeing.

Only one Rac was now not screaming threats of murder. He squatted just outside the wall, to the left of the pyramid. "That's Firetouch," said Caledonia Emerald.

"Bright boy," said Ribbentrop. He indicated a strip of bark pinned to the wall above his console. On it Pearl Angelica could recognize drawings of dumbos' wings.

Blacktop's voice softened with urgency and outrage: "They are only ourselves. They have tails, but they seek only what our Makers have told us to seek. Knowledge. And indeed, they understand what knowledge is far, far better than most of you."

The congregation sang threat in unison, but he stiffened his back once more, raised the fur of his shoulders, and refused to retreat.

"You pick up the scraps our Makers drop and call them knowledge." He gestured toward the basket atop the pole behind him. "You call them offerings. You insult the gods."

"They'll kill him!" breathed Pearl Angelica.

"I hope not," said Ribbentrop. "He's the best thing they've got going for them."

"Only one of you!" screeched Blacktop. "Only one of you knows how to pursue real knowledge! Only one of you knows that we do not deserve the Tower and its treasure if we do not study our world and learn and build. Only one of you, and the three strangers you nearly murdered!"

"Does he mean Wetweed?"

"Firetouch," said Ribbentrop. He pointed once more at the bark strip that spoke of a wish to fly. "That was his offering to the gods."

"Us?" Pearl Angelica's voice was disbelieving, but she could say nothing more. Blacktop's words had quieted once more and even gained a hint of roughness. "We must," he was saying. "We must learn enough to climb the Tower. We must build a foundation on which our Makers' gift of knowledge can stand. We must *earn* that gift."

He paused, and the eavesdroppers could hear an ominously

smooth tone rising from the congregation. He showed no sign
of hearing it himself as he half turned to face the Tower.
"You want it all," he said. "Don't you? You want it all
right now, without waiting. You don't want to struggle all
your lives, and then all your children's lives, so that your
grandchildren can enter into paradise. But that is the nature
of our Makers' gift. We must struggle for as long as it
takes, even if that means that by the time we reach the
Tower's peak we have learned all by ourselves everything
our Makers know.

"Be sure," he said. "If that is what our future holds, our
Makers will be delighted. It will mean we have obeyed in
fullest measure the only commandment they have set down
for us. And if we then go beyond *their* knowledge, they will
even cede their place in paradise to us."

"We will?" asked Pearl Angelica.

"Why not?" asked Ribbentrop. "Isn't that what this kind
of evolution is all about?"

"Think!" Blacktop cried now. "The Tower cannot possibly
contain all the knowledge of the universe. Our Makers can
put there only what they know now, and they say themselves
that there is a vast unknown waiting to be discovered beyond
that little bit.

"And even that they have given us. They gave us intelligence, the ability to learn for ourselves. If we use that ability
and strengthen it, we may well surpass our gods."

He was not done. His mouth was still open. But his congregation had heard enough. Its song of threat and danger grew
quickly louder. It became a scream. And when Leaf emerged
from the front of the crowd that was quickly becoming a mob,
her words were no surprise: "No!" she screamed just as she
had before she had stoned the strangers from the valley.
"They made us! But they wish to keep us helpless before
their might! That is why they tantalize us with the Tower.
There is nothing at its tip!"

"No!" cried Blacktop.

"Yes!" Leaf turned her back on him and screamed at the
rest of the tribe. "He is their creature!" She whirled and
pointed at Firetouch just outside the wall. He was gaping
at the madness that seemed about to engulf them all. "So
is he! Kill them both!"

Someone tore a rock from the wall of the watching place and hurled it toward the pyramid. It fell short, but the next did not.

Blacktop refused to run.

Firetouch did not.

"Why? Why can't we keep them from such idiocy?" Pearl Angelica was sobbing. So was Caledonia Emerald, while Lucas Ribbentrop looked haggard.

"They have to make their own mistakes." The veedo images of Lois McAlois and Renny Schafer both shook their heads.

"But why do they have to make the same mistakes humans have made?"

Renny sighed. "I'm glad Freddy didn't live to see this. But the pursuit of knowledge . . . It's a grand ideal, but I guess some things have to come first. At least until we learn how to scrub such things as territoriality from the genes."

"We probably can't," said Ribbentrop. "It's a biological imperative to protect the resources you need to survive."

"Did we make a mistake in building the Tower?" asked Pearl Angelica. "Should we have left well enough alone?"

Lois McAlois looked to one side as Esteban stepped into the picture. "I heard," he said. "And I don't think so. It will stand there, won't it? Until they're ready for it?"

"It's high enough," said Renny. "They won't climb it by accident. They'll *have* to learn a lot on their own."

"I wonder how long it will take," said Pearl Angelica.

"Not long enough," said Caledonia Emerald. "It should be twice as high as it is."

Epilogue

THE WATCHING PLACE had grown over the decades. The end that faced the Worldtree remained open, giving an assembled congregation full view of the goal the gods had set all Rackind. The pyramid of steps that was the altar was broader and higher, and the pole and basket that mimicked the Worldtree was an obelisk of stone just rough enough to give purchase to the claws of climbing Racs. The stone walls were thick and tall, their massive blocks cut square and joined with mortar and ornamented with ten thousand carvings. Buttresses soared down to brace the walls against a ground whose native moss now shared space with honeysuckle, grass, flowering shrubs, flagged paths, and artificial streams filled with tasty-tails, dumbo larvae, for the delectation of priests and pilgrims. Roof beams thick as Rac torsos supported slabs of slate.

But now the obelisk was fallen. Roof beams and slates were rubble in the nave. Holes gaped in the walls, and broken stone filled the streams and crushed moss, grass, honeysuckle, and other vegetation.

Near the entrance to the Watching Place still stood a crude wooden statue of a male Rac. The top of his head was painted black with soot. Rusty red, blood the congregation had freely offered, marked chest and belly, back and limbs.

The warrior Skyclaw had already bowed to the Founder. Now he stood beside the statue, clad in armor of bronze strips riveted to leather. He was looking at the bodies that littered the ground between the Watching Place and the Worldtree, wrinkling his nose at the stink already rising from them, and wishing that fewer of them had the tails that marked his own people.

But that was as it had to be. War meant death, of attackers as well as defenders. He looked at the blood already drying on his bronze sword. He was lucky it had not meant his own.

He looked toward the fringes of the battlefield, where the local noncombatants, mates and children and parents, were bringing baskets full of food to feed the spirits of the slain for their journey to the Makers. He would not interfere, not with the mourners, nor with his own warriors who would claim the food to fill their own bellies. And if some of that food came his way, he would eat it.

Yes. The price of victory could have been far worse. He bared his teeth in a grin at the thought that his tail had been shortened by his descent from the tailless Firetouch. But that same line of descent had shortened these tails much more. It had been his cousin who had devised the long-armed stonethrower.

He climbed the pyramid in front of the Watching Place and glanced at the toppled obelisk. He held up his arms to the Worldtree, and he thought: There was no need for symbols when the real thing stood so plainly in view. There was no need to climb a stump when the Worldtree waited patiently, knowing that it could not be long before it welcomed its worshippers into its high sanctum.

He nodded, filled with both awe and confidence. His people would not lose the valley now that it was theirs. They would retain control of the Worldtree. And they *would* be the ones to climb it. The treasure of knowledge its bulbous tip held would then be theirs, and theirs alone.

STEEL
BEACH
John Varley

Fleeing earth after an alien invasion, the human beings
stand on the threshold of evolution, like a fish cast on
artificial shores. Their new home is Luna, a moon colony
blessed with creature comforts, prolonged lifespans, digital memories, and instant sex-changes. But the people of
Luna are bored, restless, suicidal— and so is the computer that monitors their existence...

An Ace paperback

Coming in August